A GINSENG CURE

Lucy B. Hoopes

Abecedarian Books
Baldwin, Maryland

A GINSENG CURE

Disclaimer: Although inspired by an actual murder and its aftermath, this is a work of fiction. The characters and events portrayed herein are entirely products of the author's imagination.

Library of Congress
Cataloging-in-Publication Data
2012911266

ISBN 13: 978-0-9822985-8-9
ISBN 10: 0-9822985-8-7

Cover illustration by Molly O. Hoopes

Published by

Abecedarian Books, Inc.
2817 Forest Glen Drive
Baldwin, Maryland 21013-9574

*Dedicated to
the former Citizens for Cultural Enhancment
of Martinsville, Indiana.*

ACKNOWLEDGMENTS

Special thanks to

C.R. Schiefer for the idea for this novel, for his example of unflagging dedication to one's art, and for providing the author with what Virginia Woolf said is necessary for a woman writer—a room of one's own.

The Writers' Group of Bloomington, Indiana, for their encouragement and support, and especially Sara Frommer, whose kindness exceeds her enormous talent.

The Reverend Mr. Donald A. Tharp, a force for good wherever he is called.

CONTENTS

CHAPTER I

CHANGING SEASONS

At the moment the gas station attendant yelled, "Hey, nigger!" at the other customer, Maggie McGilvray, sitting behind the wheel of her car in Sardisvale, Indiana, was daydreaming herself at a Trappist monastery in Kentucky.

"Hey, nigger! Jus' get the fuck back in and keep on goin'. Niggers ain't welcome here!"

Maggie jumped. The sudden movement jammed her plump mid-section into the steering wheel. Not so much pain as a nauseating sensation of no air. She turned with a gasp to the half-open window.

While Maggie had been seeking imaginary refuge, a shiny white Cadillac had stopped in the self-service lane next to her dusty old blue Chevy. Her quick turn to the outside brought her face to face with the front seat passenger of the other car—also a middle-aged woman, but, unlike Maggie, elegantly coiffed and carefully made up. Maggie's pale blue eyes stared into the equally startled brown eyes of the black woman.

The brown eyes looked away first. The Cadillac rocked when a large black man threw himself into the driver's seat, jerked his door closed, gunned his motor, and screeched to the access road, then onto the four-lane state highway headed north, away from the "Sardisvale Full Stop" and toward Indianapolis.

Maggie rubbed the roll of fat at her midriff with both pudgy hands and breathed deeply.

The attendant replaced the gas nozzle and paused at Maggie's window. "Ten-fifty, ma'am, if you don't need no oil."

He grinned at Maggie, and she looked closely at him for the first time. Teeth stained yellow, probably from the wad of tobacco making his cheek bulge. Green-blue eyes barely discernible under the red and white Indiana University cap pulled low onto his forehead.

"Them niggers learn awful slow. Ever' two-three weeks one comin' up from Bloomin'ton tries to stop here. You'd think they'da heard 'bout Sardisvale by now. Jus' pull on that hood lever, ma'am."

After releasing the hood catch, Maggie took a couple of bills out of the worn leather French purse topping the pile of books and papers beside her.

The hood banged shut. "Oil's fine, water's fine, ever'thin's fine." The attendant took the bills and produced change from a grease-stained pocket of his coveralls. "Don't you worry none 'bout niggers takin' over Sardisvale. We keep an eye out. You have a good day, now." He headed back into the Full Stop.

Maggie continued to sit speechless. Idiots like him, like most of the town, weren't worth talking to. Listen to opinions not exactly their own? Fat chance! They were locked in their own ignorance, fortified against any onslaught of reason.

She expected the same narrow-mindedness from the church women for whom she was about to review Thomas Merton's account of becoming a Trappist monk. Would they listen to her? No, she was too different—didn't bustle around in a noisy family gossiping, meddling, acquiring ever more material possessions. And she wasn't concerned about appearances, especially her own.

She tilted the rear view mirror and patted down her wavy, gray-streaked brown hair. Some of her audience at Study Group would have spent the entire morning at the beauty parlor, but not Maggie! Smoothing a pale, hardly detectable eyebrow, she remembered the colorful face of the black woman. Now there was someone who cared what other people thought. Well, Maggie didn't care what people thought of her or of each other. Others' lives had nothing to do with hers. She snapped the mirror back to its original position, checked traffic, and reluctantly continued her solitary journey.

* * *

"They're a bunch of old biddies," Maggie said aloud to herself. She stood erect in the street beside her car and tried to unstick her blue chambray housedress from her back, already wet with perspiration. Rounding the car, she dabbed at her upper lip and broad, unlined forehead with a wad of linen handkerchief, even though Phyllis had repeatedly chided her for that "old lady gesture." Maggie opened the passenger door and leaned in to gather together the books and papers she needed to speak to the Sardisvale Indiana First United Methodist Church Thursday Study Group.

"It's about time!"

Startled, Maggie bumped her head on the car roof. "Phyllis! I didn't hear you."

Phyllis Stockton moved swiftly, gracefully, her splashy print skirt swirling around her bare, tanned legs. Her white blouse was impossibly crisp. Innocent of perspiration, Maggie thought wryly.

Phyllis smiled and took Maggie's load. "How could you hear me? You were too busy talking to yourself again. That dress is a good color with your eyes; the hem's a little long. And those loafers...really, Maggie, haven't you any summer sandals? Might as well enjoy the warm weather while it lasts. About talking to yourself...you need to be around people more. There's this interesting man I want you to meet after church Sunday..."

Maggie's lips twitched, but managed to retain their grim line. Phyllis's inveterate optimism was almost irresistible; Maggie relaxed, felt more benevolent. "I'm about to give my annual performance, Phyllis. Please let me stick to the subject at hand." Maggie reached for her books.

Phyllis read their covers before relinquishing them. "Thomas Merton. Oh, Maggie, not Catholic stuff! And Flannery O'Connor. Weren't her short stories your review last year? I might have known you'd start a racial discussion again. You do like to stir up controversy."

"I want to stimulate, that's all." She felt warmer than ever and shifted the books so she could mop her brow. Stimulate, yes, but she also wanted to make the church women understand something about peace and quiet and solitude, maybe appreciate her own need for privacy. Maybe then— Phyllis interrupted the fantasy by taking Maggie's arm and propelling her up the walk to the steep wooden steps of the parsonage porch. "Any change in your mother, Maggie?"

"Momma's weaker, and thinner. She eats so little it takes no effort at all anymore for me to lift her. She's just as interested as ever, though, in what everybody else is doing. She's lying there right now counting the minutes till I get back and tell her about the meeting."

"If only she could be leading the book discussion. She's so wise...so compassionate—" Phyllis stopped abruptly.

Maggie's turn to be gentle. "Never mind, Phyllis. I know I'm not like her and never will be."

"But I didn't mean—"

"Forget it. I don't want to change, you know." Maggie shook off Phyllis's hand and firmly climbed the rest of the stairs alone.

The front screen was opened by a favorite of Maggie's—Betsy Simms, the minister's wife, a very pretty young woman who was sensible, attentive, and, above all, cheerful.

A halo of soft brown curls bobbed when Betsy nodded with pleasure. "Oh, good, Maggie, you're here. The boys remembered your promise to let them pass out hymnals. They're in the dining room jumping up and down with excitement. Please speak to them before you go into the living room."

Matthew, four, and Mark, two, threw themselves in hugs around Maggie's legs as soon as they saw her. Why they were so fond of her was a mystery, since she had never even been touched by any other children, nor wanted to be. Betsy, however, assuming that everyone loved children, had trained the little boys to greet their father's parishioners with embraces. Maggie had learned not only to tolerate, but also to look forward to contact with the boys, though she continued to regard the minister as an insufferably pious ass.

"Miss Maggie, Miss Maggie, do you need our help?"

"Yes, indeed."

"Now, boys," said Betsy, "wait till you hear me play three chords on the piano. That's when you'll carry the books in and give one to each lady. You can sit beside me on the piano bench till the hymn is over, but then you must go right out to the kitchen. Remember Daddy'll be there to take you to the playground."

"We 'member, Mommy."

Maggie gave each boy a kiss.

Matthew touched the gray hair on her temples. "Silver," he said. Maggie's warm glow lasted till she faced the chattering circle of ladies in the parsonage living room. Barely suppressing her amusement at the irony of the scripture, she intoned solemnly, "Behold, thou shalt be silent." That did, indeed, shut them up—at least temporarily.

At a nod from Maggie, Betsy played three chords on the piano; the boys burst in.

When everyone had a hymnal, Maggie announced, "Number one hundred twenty-seven, both verses of 'Into the Woods.'" Someone murmured something about Easter. She might have known the group couldn't accept a traditionally Easter hymn in September. She quickly explained that Thomas Merton was first attracted to Franciscans because they made him think of woods.

The last notes of the second verse died away. The little boys scrambled down from the piano bench and out to the kitchen. Maggie heaved a loud sigh. Time to begin her plea for solitude and simplicity.

* * *

Forty-five minutes later, alone at last in her car, Maggie smiled with satisfaction and tucked her sodden hanky between her flabby upper arm and the blue chambray sleeve long since darkened by perspiration. Her ordeal of reviewing a book for the Thursday Study Group was over for another year. Definitely a relief. She'd even managed to slip out of the business meeting unnoticed while some young high school teacher was asking for clothing donations.

No, someone had noticed. Betsy appeared at the front door of the parsonage, balancing baby Mary on one hip and awkwardly miming applause, then waving good-bye. Maggie waved back and pulled her old Chevy away from the curb.

She always drove instead of walking—to church every Sunday, to the A & P, Hook's Drug Store, and the Sardisvale Full Stop once a month, and to the parsonage for Study Group one Thursday a month in the summer and every other Thursday during the school year except in December, when most of the women were busy with holiday preparations. Her most strenuous physical activity was minimal house- and yard-work, since nursing her mother required little strength as the chronically ill woman's health rapidly deteriorated.

Maggie expended most of her energy collecting data to report to her mother about almost everything and everyone she saw in stores or at church. Mumbling aloud on the drive home, she rehearsed the afternoon's events to be related to the invalid. No use mentioning the incident at the Full Stop. Such things had nothing to do with the McGilvray women.

Her mother, witnessing that incident, would probably have scolded the gas station attendant as if he were one of her former students. And she would have memorized the license plate, traced the insulted couple, and at least have written a letter of apology. Well, too bad the McGilvray daughter harbored no activist impulses and felt no guilt for the community. She could forget what happened at the Full Stop...definitely irrelevant to her life now.

Maggie turned onto her street slowly because the playground across from her house was crowded with children just released from their September prison. Some had already robbed the McGilvray driveway of handfuls of white gravel to draw hopscotch squares on sidewalks.

Maggie unlocked the kitchen door, then paused to strip half a dozen bronze chrysanthemums from a bud-laden bush. Snap...snap...snap...quick, efficient, eager movements. Good to be home, good to give her mother pleasure.

"Momma?" She went directly to the large, airy bedroom that stretched across the rear of the house.

The bed was pushed against a back wall of windows so low that the bed's occupant could have a clear view of the yard. Mrs. McGilvray responded immediately. "Oh, Maggie, what took you so long? How did it go? Did people pay attention?"

Maggie was awash with momentary sadness from the contrast between her mother's shriveled appearance and that of the vigorous elderly women in the Study Group. Once as tall as Maggie and almost as stout, Ann Mary Estes McGilvray had wasted to a tiny, stooped, fragile hundred pounds. Her face was delicate porcelain with a childlike openness and vulnerability that belied the bell-like tone of authority still present in her voice. Her feeble effort to raise herself on an elbow seemed hindered by the impossible weight of thick waves of silver hair. "What beautiful flowers! It's that time of year again...almost winter."

Maggie stuck the flowers into a jelly glass of water on the bedside table. She lifted her mother with one arm while plumping and propping up pillows with the other. "There. Let me get your medicine and some cocoa, and I'll tell you about it. I'll be right back."

When Maggie returned ten minutes later, Mrs. McGilvray lay sunk deep into the pillows, eyes closed. She roused quickly, however, at the clinking of medicine spoon on glass. "Now tell me," the old lady insisted as soon as she had swallowed a spoonful of yellowish liquid.

Maggie pulled a chair close to the bed and reached for a chocolate chip cookie from the bed tray. "It started out pretty formal, like always. I read the scripture but didn't tell them how Thomas Merton opened the Bible to that verse and thought it was God's message to him to become a Trappist. There was a long pause, surely the longest those women have been silent for a month."

"Maybe not, Maggie. You always think the worst of them." Mrs. McGilvray rolled onto her side and slowly massaged her neck with a papery, vein-ridged hand.

"And you always think the best. Next Betsy played the hymn."

"Did the boys help? They're so cute. Remember when they drank all the leftover communion grape juice while she was welcoming the District Superintendent's wife?"

Maggie nodded, smiling. "They're always lively. The second she played their signal, they came running out with the hymnals. Matthew distributed his stack, then Mark's. They sat fairly still on the piano bench during 'Into the Woods'— both verses, but I guess that was a mistake. The end about

Jesus' dying on a tree just distracted from my main point in choosing that hymn: Jesus went into the woods for solitude."

"Sidney Lanier's beautiful lyrics."

"You old English teachers never forget poetry. I do love that line 'The little gray leaves were kind to Him.'"

"Our black walnut leaves have begun to turn." Mrs. McGilvray looked out the back window. "Those trees have certainly grown; they're worth thousands of dollars now."

"Oh, Momma, surely not thousands."

"Yes, really, several thousand each; I'm positive. Bob Stockton commented on them when he and Phyllis visited me last spring. It's almost his birthday, by the way. Maybe they'll come over for cake. Anyway, old Ora Kemmer told me years ago that those trees were unusually fine, worth hundreds apiece back then. When I told Bob, he said they're worth thousands now. You shouldn't ever need to sell them, though, thanks to your father's trust fund. You're well provided for, Maggie."

"We are, Momma. Now let me tell you about the meeting."

The old lady refused cocoa and cookies with a weak gesture. Maggie herself drank the second cup and ate more cookies.

"After Betsy played and the boys left with Reverend Sims, she had to bring in Mary, who was crying for a bottle. From then on, the meeting was very informal...conversational, really...and aggravating. Nobody there ever agrees with me."

"Well, of course, it is a religious group, except for you. Usually their reviews make non-religious books sound religious. Yours probably did just the opposite."

"Certainly it did, Momma. I picked Merton's autobiography in spite of the fact that it's supposed to be religious. But that group refused to imagine why someone would want to enter a monastery. They think all the world should want to live in Sardisvale, where everything is sweetness and light. They want to keep it just the way it's always been—except, of course, for accumulating more and more worldly goods. I told them how Merton felt about simplifying, about getting rid of material things."

"With those young families struggling to buy their own homes! Oh, Maggie!"

"I was just emphasizing why I chose the book: Merton's longing for a simple life, for solitude and silence."

"And you talking to mostly mothers and grandmothers!"

"All mothers and grandmothers but me."

"And two little boys and a baby! Simplicity, solitude, and silence! Oh, Maggie, no wonder they think you're peculiar!"

Mrs. McGilvray sounded more amused than scolding, and Maggie had her frequent good feeling that her mother loved her as she was.

"Janice actually said I have awfully peculiar ideas... said that now I wanted them to become monks and that last year I tried to tell them Sardisvale had weird, evil people like Flannery O'Connor's characters. I told them Thomas Merton admired O'Connor for the way she recognized and described evil. Then the two new women wanted to know about O'Connor, so Miss Emma went into her literary critic act on 'Everything That Rises Must Converge.'"

"I warned you last year that that story would be too complicated."

"All Miss Emma could really remember was that the 'nigra' knocked the white woman down, and 'Thank God that can't ever happen in Sardisvale!' At last I got her to stop holding forth so I could tell them about Merton's Seven Storey Mountain. Fortunately, nobody ever asked what the title meant; I sure didn't want to talk about Purgatory or any other Catholic stuff."

Mrs. McGilvray shook her head, "Only you could avoid 'Catholic stuff' when reviewing that book!"

"You don't realize how informal the whole thing is. Oh, Momma, how I wish you could be there! You'd be patient and not irritate them the way I do. You'd have their respect. Still, I'll bet those very women who're so busy with so many people just long sometimes for peace and quiet."

Both women stared out the back window.

"I believe all of us could simplify and probably be much happier. I read them what Merton says about how a monk who hides from the world becomes more of a person...and how 'weird' it is to 'depend on someone else's applause.'"

"I suppose Ellen was sitting right there thinking about her husband running for Delegate!"

"And Phyllis frowning at me because I'm not sitting in a ladylike way. Sometimes she cares more about how I look than what I believe."

"She loves you, Maggie. She's tried to be your best friend for forty years."

"Also for forty years she's been trying to improve me. She is persistent. Some bachelor just retired and moved out on the old Shirrell farm, and she wants to introduce him to me after church Sunday. She wants me to be with somebody all the time."

"She wants you to be with people your own age instead of just with me."

"What difference should age make? I'm with the person I love."

"Phyllis loves more than one person; she wants you to know what that's like."

"I'll bet Thomas Merton would tell Phyllis to seek solitude, to look inside herself and figure out why she has to make everybody over so they're more to her liking."

"What do you think Thomas Merton would tell us, Maggie Dear?"

Maggie paused, recognizing suddenly the fatigue in her mother's voice. "Oh, Momma, Merton talks a lot about love's healing. Why can't my love heal you?"

"It has, Maggie. It has. I'm a happy person. Now go start dinner while I rest."

* * *

Sunday morning Maggie didn't go to church. Several hours before she ordinarily took two dozen donuts to the Bible Study Class, she drove behind the ambulance that was transporting her unconscious mother to the hospital. She kept a reasonable distance from the deafening siren and squealing tires and gave correct signals at the still-deserted intersections.

As usual, she scanned the yards for activities Mrs. McGilvray would enjoy hearing about. She remarked the fall foliage, the increased number of chrysanthemum blossoms. Unlike usual, however, a sob caught in her throat. In the gutter of Sardisvale's Main Street, Maggie had noticed some newly fallen little gray leaves that would never be so kind to her as her mother had been.

CHAPTER II

GLIMPSING THE WOODS

At six a.m. Maggie pushed open the screen door with her back and staggered down the steps. Unable to see over the three-foot stack of papers filling her arms, she waded slowly through deep leaves toward the alley behind the house. At the fence she shoved the shaky load over onto the spot from which Sardisvale garbage trucks made pick-ups Mondays and Thursdays.

She leaned hard on the fence for a few moments, then blew on her hands and flexed them a couple of times before re-tying her red flannel bathrobe. At the steps again, she picked off a handful of crisp leaves clinging to her gown, baggy gray athletic socks, and fuzzy pink bedroom slippers.

No one else on the block was up and about so early; of that she was sure. For three weeks she had taken out trash at six so that she wouldn't have to see or be seen by any neighbors. She had thus avoided not only greetings, but also questions about what she was discarding; and even Maggie would admit that the quantity of paper removed from her house during November appeared excessive.

The first trash morning of her Great Paper Throwaway, she had been naive enough to scoop up all the newspapers in her mother's room and run to the alley with them when she heard the roar and chomp of the garbage truck at the end of the block.

"Oh, Miss McGilvray," the young woman who had recently bought the house across the alley had called, "I'm so sorry about your mother. Let me come over and help you sort things. If you package those papers with string, the garbage man saves them for his son's Boy Scout troop. Watch out! I've got them. There! If they're not tied, they may blow all over the place before the truck even gets here."

Fortunately, the woman had to run back for her second garbage can. When the truck had moved on, Maggie was in her own house again—safe from sympathetic, and curious, neighbors.

After that first morning, on trash collection eve Maggie set the next morning's paper package by the door so she could surreptitiously deliver it to the alley before dawn. She carefully topped each pile with brown paper to conceal its contents from casual glances.

The contents themselves had been dragged from beneath beds and inside closets, basement, and attic. First to go were the stacks of *Sardisvale Journal*, Bloomington *Herald-Telephone*, and Indianapolis Sunday *Star* that had lain haphazardly around the first floor. Maggie didn't go through the stacks, but she did call each publication's circulation department to cancel what remained of her subscription.

Under Mrs. McGilvray's bed had been years of *Time* and *Reader's Digest*—quick reading the patient had been able to reach by herself until her last few weeks at home.

After those magazines were tied and letters written to cancel their subscriptions, Maggie emptied the closets and basement of decades of forgotten periodicals: *Better Homes and Gardens* accumulated in the days when Mrs. McGilvray supervised from her window while teenage boys weeded, mowed, and replenished the bird bath and feeders; *Family Circle* and *Woman's Day* saved during the years when the patient could still needlepoint, knit, and crochet for church bazaars.

Maggie had contributed her share: *Good Housekeeping* collected in her first years of preparing easy casseroles and soups good for a meal or two before being frozen to save kitchen time in the future. She had never liked cooking.

Breakfast now that she was alone necessitated no cooking at all. When she returned to the warm kitchen after her pre-dawn chore, she slathered three slices of bread with butter and orange marmalade while water for instant hot chocolate heated in the microwave. Having consumed every crumb and every drop, she made another cup of hot chocolate— extra energy for some unpleasant tasks.

She sighed and carried the cup into her mother's bedroom, where every inch of chair and bed space was occupied by her mother's personal correspondence lugged from the attic or extracted in bundles from the far recesses of dresser drawers.

She hesitated over half a dozen scrapbooks of picture postcards and get-well cards, then thrust them in piles against the far wall. Maybe some history buff would value them almost as much as Momma had.

Maggie frowned at the recent letters, some from pen pals in Europe, Asia, even Africa. Couldn't just throw them out. Ought to send a notice; maybe one message would do for all.

Five minutes later she had a rough draft: "My mother died peacefully in her sleep the end of October. She always enjoyed hearing from you and thought of you often. Sincerely, Margaret McGilvray." She'd just copy the note for each of Momma's current correspondents.

Four hours later, sealed, stamped missives had pro-liferated, and Maggie was pausing after every note to massage her cramped hand. On her way to the kitchen for a lunch break, she heard the phone.

For five rings Maggie debated with herself whether or not to answer. Finally, habit won.

"Maggie, at last! Are you OK?"

"I'm fine, Phyllis. What do you want?"

"Well, you don't need to sound so bad-tempered! I want to pick you up on my way to Sunday School this weekend—"

"No."

"—because you need to get out again. And you need to go to church again."

"No."

"What do you mean 'no?' Your mother, God rest her soul, has been gone a month now, and you're turning into a regular hermit. She wouldn't like you not going to church, and you know it. I think—"

"Phyllis, Momma's dead, and I'm not going to do anything I don't want to do, so please leave me alone."

"You're just upset about what Reverend Simms said to you about getting involved with the world. Anyway, the church does need you. Everybody admires the way you nursed your dear, sainted mother all those years, but it *is* time you got on with your own life, so I'll pick you up—"

"No, Phyllis. I'm busy now."

"Busy! Maggie, today's Thanksgiving."

"Thanksgiving? Today? Then there won't be a garbage pickup."

"Heavens, Maggie, you've got to get out of there. Bob'll be over in fifteen minutes to bring you here for dinner. It'll be quiet—just the three of us—and you and I can have a nice visit while Bob watches the ball games."

"No, Phyllis. I'm busy. Good-bye."

Maggie replaced the receiver firmly. Time, definitely, for food. She was eating only what was already on hand and had made hardly a dent in the supplies she had been laying in for years: hundreds of cans of soups and vegetables, dozens of packages of frozen rolls, pies, cakes, donuts, hams, chicken breasts, fried chicken, pizzas, breaded fish sticks, french fries, onion rings—enough food to last at least a year and a half, probably longer.

Maggie had spent little time at home during her mother's last month. For a change from the preceding five years, she had not had to feed or bathe her mother—the Sardisvale General Hospital nurses took care of all that—or talk to her, or listen to her. She had sat quietly by the bed all day and lain uncomfortably on the hospital recliner all night, coming home only every other day to change clothes and gorge herself.

She had started with the perishables, finishing off the milk, salad ingredients, and leftovers first. Sometimes she took cheeses and lunch meats to the hospital with her to supplement the inadequate meals intended for patients. Except for hunger, Maggie had felt numb, passive.

On Halloween morning, her mother had stopped breathing. Maggie's emotional numbness persisted. For the next month, Maggie remained alone in what had become her own house. When friends came to call, she spoke pleasantly through the closed door: "I'm not having company today."

Some callers had left covered dishes that supplemented the perishables, so even at Thanksgiving she was still using the cheeses and pancake mixes that had been in the refrigerator for some time. In another two weeks, she'd probably start on the refrigerator freezer—good for maybe two months of meals before she had to touch the deep-freeze or the pantry shelves. Such quantities of food hadn't seemed excessive in the days when she avoided leaving her mother alone or asking others for favors. The solitude such overstocking now allowed her was precious.

Phyllis's accusation was inaccurate, though; Maggie wasn't "upset about what Reverend Simms said." She hadn't really registered his words, only his phony tone of voice. Never again would she attend to that voice on Sunday mornings, since Momma wasn't waiting for a detailed report of the church service.

No more calling twenty busy women to remind them of the Thursday Study Group or washing the coffeepot after Fellowship Hour; all her church chores were in the past. Reverend Simms would never again try to work his sanctimonious pseudo-magic on her.

"Involved with the world, indeed!" she mumbled. "As the poem says, 'The world is too much with us;' but I'm going to be as free of it as possible."

By noon of the Saturday after Thanksgiving, Maggie had almost achieved her independence from paper. Before dawn she placed the scrapbooks on the porch of a librarian who lived nearby. She then refused to answer the phone's insistent jangling; surely her note taped to the top stack of scrapbooks was an adequate explanation.

She ate lunch in her mother's room overlooking the envelopes ready for mailing spread over the bed. Her gaze wandered to the window, to the empty birdfeeder in the bare apple tree, and finally to the magnificent stand of black walnut trees pronounced valuable by Bob Stockton and the old logger, Ora Kemmer. Those trees were worth nothing to her—might as well do some good elsewhere.

She could give them to Bob Stockton, but she really was not fond of him. He did a lot of harm while trying to help, he was boring, and he didn't need money. Maybe the logger needed money. He must be in his seventies or eighties. Momma had said many times that Ora Kemmer should be rewarded for his kind advice the time he had removed the ancient sycamore from their kitchen roof, then cut down three other trees threatening the safety of the widow and little Maggie.

Ora Kemmer had admired those trees. They would be an appropriate reward for a good man; Maggie would give him the black walnut trees to timber...right away.

Instead of reaching for her reading glasses and the yellow pages, she resolved to talk to Ora Kemmer in person. Surely she could find his place, even though she'd never been there; nobody else lived within five miles of the entrance to the state forest. Her only possible problem was starting the car, something she hadn't even tried to do for almost a month.

The weather had been dry and mild for November, and the little-used Chevy kicked over on the third try. Maggie nodded briefly and pulled her plaid cloth coat tighter before she backed out of the garage.

She never had enjoyed driving, had thought of it as an unpleasant necessity. Today, however, something was different. After she crossed the southern city limits, her breathing seemed easier. Stepping on the gas gave her a feeling of power—the closest to exhilaration she had come in her adult life.

The four-lane highway was relatively deserted Saturday afternoon, since most people were either downtown doing the week's shopping or at home watching college football. When Maggie passed the Full Stop, she determinedly looked away from the small gas station and attached repair shop slouching under the peeling red and white sign. Thank goodness she didn't need to stop there! She pushed the speedometer up to sixty-five and cracked the window an inch so that an icy wind stirred the hair waving over her dusty velvet collar.

Once past the scattering of gas stations and convenience stores, Maggie slowed to enjoy the scenery. She loved to be out in the country—rather, thought she would love it if she could ever be there. Ten years before, in the days when her mother was still well enough to go for Sunday outings, Maggie would drive the car around the back of the house onto the lawn and help her mother go down the single step and into the Chevy. Then they would cruise slowly along country roads that meandered through valley farms stretching to the breathtaking backdrop of rolling Indiana hills.

Both had enjoyed the change, though Momma was happier if they stopped at a farmhouse now and then to chat with one of her former high school students, grown and settled with children of their own. Since her mother had become completely bedridden, Maggie had taken no country drives.

That November afternoon she looked eagerly at the farm land along the highway, hoping to see soybean plants of the deep russet-and-gold shade they assumed before their final brown of harvest time. But no, too late; they were quite withered at last after an unusually dry autumn. The adjacent cornfields also awaited the picker, all ears pointing decisively toward earth to announce their readiness for change.

After the terrain became too hilly to farm, steep limestone banks lined the highway. Ten miles south of town was a sign indicating the entrance to the state forest that was supervised by the Division of Forestry, a landmark known locally as the "forestry" cut-off. Maggie braked for the next turn, an unmarked gravel road paralleling the highway for half a mile before changing to rutted dirt that wound sharply and steeply toward a heavily wooded ridge of Indiana foothills.

Where the dirt road began, Ora Kemmer's mailbox stood sentinel on a ramrod-straight oak post. November rains, though inadequate for the crops, had left troughs of water along the lower road. The higher Maggie drove, the drier and less distinct the car tracks grew. Finally, the road became a large clearing in which sat a small cabin surrounded by several trucks and pieces of heavy equipment. There were stacks of half-logs and stacks of lumber near a large roofed area housing the saws.

A couple of yapping tan mongrels scraped their paws along the driver's side of the car. While Maggie hesitated, a young woman stepped out onto the porch and whistled. The dogs abruptly quieted and ran to her. She shooed them into the house and with a strange, easy lope met Maggie half-way to the car.

"I'm Maggie McGilvray. Is Mr. Kemmer home?"

"I'm Grace Kemmer. Yes...that is, Daddy's up on the north ridge working, and I'm not expecting him back till sundown."

Grace stood tall and calm, her hands folded at the belt of a full, tan skirt that covered the tops of hiking boots. Her straight, taffy-colored hair was pulled back in a bun; and her smooth face, completely without makeup, wore an open expression more frequently seen on children than on adults. Maggie thought of the peasant women in Dutch paintings. Germanic, of course, but softer, gentler than the stereotype.

"I have a message for him from my mother. Can I go talk to him?"

"Of course."

"I don't have to drive to where he is, do I?"

"I guess not, but it's a pretty long way."

"It's a nice day, and I feel like walking. Which direction?"

"Just follow those tracks." Kemmer's daughter pointed to the far, wooded end of the clearing.

Maggie pulled some faded red wool gloves out of her coat pocket and put them on while she strode briskly across the yard. By the time she had reached the first trees, however, she was breathing heavily. Because she was sure the younger woman's eyes were on her back, she tried to keep up the pace until the trees hid her. Then she slowed almost to a stop and began to look around while she caught her breath.

Damp leaves, many layers deep, padded the faint wheel tracks she was following. On either side bare tree trunks were thicker and closer together than she had imagined. Dead-looking vines swooped down from almost every tree.

When her breathing had quieted, Maggie became aware of how noisy the woods were—chatters, squawks, rustles, rasps. She tried not to think about rattlesnakes or coyotes, both of which were occasionally reported by hunters. As for hunters, it was probably deer season; but she hadn't any bright clothing to protect herself, even if she'd thought in advance of dressing more sensibly for walking in the woods.

After twenty minutes' plodding, she rested on a rotten log and watched a couple of red-tailed hawks circle a stand of pine trees greening a rise to the east.

Another quarter-hour walk and Maggie saw a rusty flatbed truck parked heading down the path at her. She had by then slipped into a regular, though slow, rhythm. Her breathing was still uneven, and she stood for a few moments before she tried to shout.

"Mis-ter Kem-mer!" She was surprised at the faint, quavering sound she made.

"Or-a Kem-mer!" she called, much more loudly. She was sure the wind tossed the words away long before they could reach the old man's ears.

Scanning the uppermost ridge of deciduous trees, she finally discerned some movement and color and decided to head in that direction. The bareness of the trees at that time of year enabled her to see far through the upper forest and lured her to a steep, rough ascent that turned out to be deceptively far away.

Before she was even half-way to the ridge above which only evergreens grew, she heard a man's voice. "Wait there. I'll be down d'rec'ly."

Too winded to reply, Maggie waved weakly, then plopped down on a log. The sun warmed her, and she dozed for a few minutes. Snapping twigs woke her.

"Mr. Kemmer?"

"Yes, miss. You've had a long walk."

"Your daughter tried to talk me out of it, but the day was so nice..."

By then the old lumberman had reached the fallen tree. He rested a scuffed boot on the other end of the log and leaned an elbow on his knee. Maggie noticed two fingers were missing from his left hand.

His kinship with Grace was plain. Same high forehead, wide cheeks, open gaze. But where her complexion had an olive smoothness, his was dark and lined as a dried peach pit.

"Do I know you?" he asked, squinting while he looked her over carefully.

"Not really. You knew my mother and me when I was little. I'm Maggie McGilvray. You chopped—"

"Miz McGilvray! Sure I know her. Wonderful lady. How's she doin'? Need some trees cut down?"

"Well, sir, my mother died last month."

"Died? That's a shame. A fine lady! A wonderful lady!"

"She thought you were fine, too—really appreciated the work you did for us. That's why I'm here. She wanted you to have the stand of black walnut trees at the back of our property. I came to tell you they're yours any time you want to come for them."

"Mine? Miss McGilvray, you don't realize how valuable them trees is by now."

"I certainly do, and Momma and I both want you to have them. She always said there just weren't enough men like you around."

Kemmer's smile deepened a hundred creases in his suntanned face. "OK, young lady, I might's well collect my inheritance while the gettin's good. House all yours now, is it?"

"Yes, sir."

"You aim to keep it?"

"I'm not sure yet, but I want you to have your trees as soon as possible."

"I can start on 'em in about another week—soon's I finish haulin' what I left up on the ridge. Don't like to leave my belongin's up there—too strange for me."

"In what way?"

"I mean it looks strange, and strange things happen there...but I'm ready to go down home for today. Let's get in my truck so's you won't have to walk any more."

Maggie was relieved. Her legs were lead-heavy, and the breeze that had evaporated her sweatiness also chilled her.

The rattly old truck door had to be pulled open by Mr. Kemmer, who then shoved a pile of dead-looking plants with bulbous, forked roots to the floor to make room on the front seat of the cab for Maggie.

"Ginseng," he said.

When he had climbed into the driver's seat, Maggie asked, "Ginseng?"

"Yep." Ora had a definite twinkle in his eye. "Dealer from Hong Kong comes to Indy every year. Buys all I can find and begs for more. Supposed to restore youth and cure whatever ails you. I don't know if I believe in it, but I've been drinkin' sang tea myself for forty years now, and I still don't need any help. Who knows?"

Maggie didn't really care, but the old man was so amiable she wanted to seem interested. "Ginseng, you say?"

"Yep, and it's not the only powerful thing growin' up there, but it's the only one I've ever really fooled with. My daughter, Grace, she says the effects of sang's all in my mind. She knows about some other cures and stuff, but she keeps 'em to herself—keeps too much to herself."

The truck was bumping so loudly over the downhill path that normal conversation became impossible. At last they bounced into the clearing around Kemmer's house, and the dogs flung themselves at the truck. Grace Kemmer appeared at the back door.

"Fix Miss McGilvray some tea, Grace. She's plumb beat from all that climbin'."

Grace rushed out to help Maggie descend from the high cab and led her up the porch steps and inside.

The kitchen gleamed with bright, white, new-looking appliances. The windows were hung with blue and white checked curtains of the same fabric as the chair and dining alcove cushions. One glossy white wall of shelves held reddish crocks with tiny, neat, blue and white labels.

"Sit here, Ms. McGilvray. May I fix you some special herb tea?"

"I'd appreciate it. I didn't expect such a strenuous climb."

Maggie sank into the puffy cushions of a white rocking chair and closed her eyes—for only a minute, she thought, but the next thing she knew, Grace Kemmer was handing her a fired clay mug of steaming red liquid.

"What a wonderful smell! Some kind of berry, maybe?"

"The old woman who taught me how to make it called it soakberry, but that's not an accurate name."

"I think I've seen you in town."

"Yes, I teach at the high school—home ec."

"Of course! Now I know...you're the one who asked for the clothes left over from our church's yard sale. Why, yes, that's what I'll do with all those things of Momma's I can't use. Miss Kemmer, I have lots of clothes for you."

"Please call me Grace."

"And you call me Maggie." She sipped the hot brew. "This is such unusual tea; my sinuses and chest are all tingly...or maybe I'm having some kind of attack..."

"Oh, no, don't worry, Ms....Maggie, that's the way soakberry makes everybody feel. It'll relax you for a while; then you'll want to do marvelous things."

Maggie settled into her habitual role of inquisitor who would then take all the details she garnered home to entertain her mother. "Grace, what's in all those crocks? I can't read the labels from here, but I'm too comfortable to move."

"The labels probably wouldn't make much sense to you. I suppose you'd say I'm an herbalist, and those are things I use in my concoctions."

"Did you learn about them when you were studying home ec in college?"

"No, an old Sardisvale woman taught me about soakberry tea."

"Oh, Grace, you're right about this drink; I'm starting to feel very rested now. Who is the old woman?"

"She died last summer. I met her up in the woods, and we got to be friends."

"So she went up there to collect herbs?"

"Well, yes, at first; later she lived up there. The forestry people knew about her but just didn't tell any officials because she wasn't hurting anything. She was sort of a mother figure for me, since my mother died when I was little."

"My mother died a month ago."

"I'm very sorry, Maggie. I hope you aren't too lonely."

"Goodness, no! I haven't even thought about loneliness. This is the first time in my life I've been really alone; it's an interesting experience. Are you lonely?"

"Lonely? Not really. I miss old Willamae. And I don't run around much with my high school classmates; they stayed home and got married while I was away at college. Now they're all busy with bottles and diapers, and I seem different to them."

"But you're young. I went off to Bloomington, to I.U., then came home because Momma was sick. We were always so close that I couldn't bear to think of anybody else taking care of her. The years have just melted away, and I feel the same as always. In fact, right now I feel like doing something a little bit exciting. What's in this mysterious tea of yours?"

"The tea is one of the secrets Willamae passed on to me. Maybe learning about herbs would interest you; it's always fascinated me."

"I'm not much for cooking; I don't even like being in the kitchen. No, I think herbalism around here should stay in your competent hands. I would like to know, though, some more about the things your daddy hinted go on up in the forestry. Somebody at church once said there were witches—"

"Oh, Daddy didn't mean witches!" Grace blushed.

"Well, he definitely said something about strange happenings in the clearing."

"Strange? Sick is more like it. I'd rather not discuss it, if you don't mind. You can't fight City Hall, so the saying goes. Anyway, Daddy should know it's dangerous to even mention the meetings. He must trust you a lot."

"There's certainly no reason for him not to; I make it a point to mind my own business."

Ora Kemmer entered the house. "There's a feel in the air, ladies, and a look to the sky that smacks of the first snow."

"Why, Mr. Kemmer, it's a beautiful fall day. How can you even think of snow?"

"Daddy's always right about the weather, Maggie. He says his trees talk to him, and I'll never argue that point."

"Heavens," said Maggie, looking out the window, "how fast the afternoon has gone! I should be starting home."

"I'll be seein' you in two weeks, or maybe three, Miss McGilvray. Your momma's gift does me honor."

"What's that, Daddy?"

"Miz McGilvray's left us some mighty fine black walnut trees along the back of her property. Soon's I'm through with the forestry job, I'll take 'em down. Best if I finish at her house around the first week in January. After that, the weather's like to be below zero and the ground froze. Used to be my favorite time to timber, but not no more. I spend my winters now gettin' my equipment back in shape."

"I don't know yet how I spend my winters," Maggie said softly. She stood and pulled the plaid coat tight. "First, though, I'm getting together some things for your home ec classes. I really don't like to sew myself, and I know Momma saved all sorts of things you might use."

"Anything at all will be welcome. I have to keep reminding the town ladies just how much families of poor farmers have to do without these days."

"Good-bye, Grace. Good-bye, Mr. Kemmer."

"Here, Maggie, I've fixed a jar of soakberry tea." Grace gave Maggie a quart fruit jar of liquid and then, when the visitor's hands were full, embraced her quickly but warmly.

Ora Kemmer walked Maggie to the car in the gathering dusk. "Mark my words, them clouds are snow clouds."

Maggie agreed and took pleasure in watching them pile up above the highway while she drove back to town. Her chest still tingled; but she felt invigorated, ready to tackle a major cleaning up and throwing away. She imagined the privacy, the contentment, of being snowed in and smiled slightly when she glanced at the jar propped beside her on the front seat, its contents glowing redly.

CHAPTER III

APPRENTICING

Grace was sorry to see Maggie go and convinced that the visit had been something extra special, truly significant. The signs were abundant: Maggie was alone but not lonely; she was open to new things, curious about the woods, about witches; her gift of the trees and her promise of clothing showed her concern for others; and she had responded quickly and fearlessly to the brew. Yes, Grace had more than enough reasons to believe Maggie was the first of the "sisters" Willamae had predicted would come to Grace as apprentices.

"'Cause you love critters and folks," Willamae had told her, "you're gonna share our powers with our sisters after I'm gone."

Willamae's prediction had taken place during Kathryn Kemmer's final hospitalization, when Grace was eight and felt sorry for herself, crying with self-pity during one of her numerous afternoons up on the ridge with Willamae.

"I don't have any sisters, Willamae, and Mommy won't ever have anymore children now."

"Oh, Darlin', we both got lots of sisters. Some'll come to you on their own; some you'll find. They's a lot of diff'rent sisterhoods, but you'll have a special one. This'll all come clear when you gets to be a woman."

Perhaps the time wasn't far off. Grace wasn't anxious. She worked with herbs and potions, passed on the lore to interested students, meditated, and waited serenely.

Her apprenticeship had not ended the previous summer with Willamae's death, but continued while she prepared herself with diligence and receptivity for guidance from her inner powers. Their signs had begun.

Ora stamped into the kitchen, blowing on his hands. "Mighty chill wind 'companyin' the snow. How 'bout a mug o' tea for me?"

Grace quickly complied, then stood behind her father to stroke his temples. Such a good man. She was very fortunate. "The gift from the McGilvrays—I'll bet it's a pleasant surprise."

"Surprise, all right. And 'course I'm grateful. But now I'm thinkin' acceptin' may be a problem."

Grace sat down across the table from Ora with a frown on her usually smooth face. "What kind of problem?"

"You know how I allus take a wedge outta a tree right away, without loppin' off the top first? That's 'cause up in the woods a tree can fall just about anyplace without doin' damage. But in town, in Miss McGilvray's yard, those black walnuts got to have their upper branches and tops trimmed first so's they won't rip the whole neighborhood to pieces. The problem is I can't no more just shinny up trees like a crazy kid."

Ora stared into his cup; but Grace, in sudden elation, pushed back her chair and jumped up. "No problem at all! I mean, there's a wonderful, perfect solution: Maurice Saunders!"

* * *

After Willamae's death, Grace had needed to assert herself in an unusually active way. In addition to asking

30

women's groups—including Maggie's Thursday Study Group—for clothing donations for her second semester clothing classes, she had first persuaded grocery stores to donate items for her first semester foods classes.

A letter from the school administration and her own seriousness had even convinced a Bloomington appliance firm to present her home ec department with a floor model "deluxe" refrigerator, which had arrived very late on a Friday afternoon in September. Custodians as well as students left the building promptly on a weekend, so Grace had remained at school to receive the donation.

The delivery truck's sole occupant, a young black man, Maurice Saunders, unloaded and unpacked the shiny new appliance with proprietary pride.

"It's gorgeous! I can't believe it's ours."

"You sure must've pulled a con job to get them to give it to you. Wish they were as generous with their paychecks!"

"You mean they don't pay you enough, Mr. Saunders?"

"Hey, please, Ms. Kemmer, call me Maurice. I'm just a student myself, and I'm kind of tired of how university professors don't bother to know our first names."

"You're at I.U.?"

"Yes, ma'am, but I may not be for long. This is the only part-time job I've managed to get. Unless I can find something else soon, my first year in college will be my last, and it's back to Detroit for me."

"Here, Maurice, have a cup of tea before you hit the road for home."

"This tea—it's not ginseng, is it?"

"No, it's soakberry tea—much more effective, I promise."

"There's a guy in the I.U. chorus who makes a lot of money selling ginseng he collects in the woods somewhere around here. Maybe I should look into that as a way to make me some extra bread."

"Ginseng does grow around here, all right. My father sells it, even though I don't want him to."

"Why not?"

"Seems like in a way it's taking advantage of people's gullibility."

"You mean the tea doesn't really work?"

"Sure it works; people have been swearing by it for thousands of years—seven thousand in Asia. But I've studied everything I could find about it, even tried it myself, and there's no scientific reason for its effectiveness. Still, Daddy and a million others believe in its efficacy. They're getting what I call the 'ginseng cure.'"

"What's that?"

"One that happens because people believe it will, but they actually do other things to make the cure come about. Daddy, for example, has always taken really good care of himself."

"A placebo effect! We learned about it in science class; doctors get one sometimes when they test drugs."

"You're studying science?"

"Just a required introductory course. No, I'd like to be a 'throat,' a voice major; but I'm not really well-trained, and I can't spend much time practicing. I'm realistic enough to be an education major."

"Then you'll learn about the 'halo effect,' where what you already know about a student may influence your evaluation of him."

"Like stereotyping?"

"Yes."

"Like 'all blacks are lazy and shiftless?' That's probably why I'm having so much trouble finding part-time work around here."

"It's true there aren't many blacks in Bloomington, not nearly so many as in East Lansing, where I went to college. And there aren't *any* in Sardisvale. Well, anyway, if they

32

hired you and you did a bad job, it might be a negative halo effect. What I really mean is that even though something seems scientifically, or even sociologically, impossible, it might happen because some people really believed in it and acted on what they believed. So they'd produce a ginseng cure. You might actually convince some folks you're not lazy and shiftless. People usually have no idea just how powerful they can be. They... Well, you got me started! I sound like school's still in session. Usually I keep my definition to myself. What kind of job do you want?"

"Almost anything that'll pay, Ms. Kemmer. At the rate I'm going, I'll be out of savings by June. No way can I earn enough next summer to pay for another year."

"Write down your landlady's phone number for me, Maurice, and I'll keep an ear out for something for you. From time to time I hear about jobs at hours a high school student can't work. I'll keep you on my list."

"Much obliged, Ms. Kemmer, but I'll be glad to work for you for free. You sure can cheer somebody up! And thanks again for the soakberry tea!"

* * *

"Daddy, Maurice is the very person to help you. He's a student at the university who badly needs tuition money. He'll be on winter break starting week after next, and I'm sure he'll be a good worker. I'll call him tonight."

Maurice was not only willing, but experienced, having worked with his uncle timbering in the Michigan woods. He eagerly agreed to begin helping Ora in two weeks, when he could borrow a car from a friend who was going home from school for the holidays by bus.

Grace, exultant, reported the young man's acceptance to her father while she covered the phone's mouthpiece. Suddenly she had a thought that made her frown again. "Do you think Maurice will have any trouble in town because he's black?"

"I can't see as how he needs to be in town 'cept when we're workin'. Just tell him he's my apprentice, and he'll have to stay here with us. Anybody who don't approve can bring their complaints to me!"

Grace's brow cleared, and she relayed the message to Maurice. What a day! An apprentice for her daddy, and probably one for her. So much power to be developed! She couldn't wait to begin.

CHAPTER IV

TIMBERING

L eave me the hell alone!" Hiram Marshall shouted.

"Dad, you'll be late to work. I've got your breakfast all ready. If you don't eat it now, I'll be late to school."

"I said get the hell out of here!" Hiram roared. He sat up shaking his fist, then grabbed his head, moaned, and flopped back onto his dingy pillow.

Susan backed out of the room, gratefully closing the door on the sour odor. She ate quickly with her World Cultures notes propped against the toaster in front of her. Yes, she was definitely ready for a pop quiz. And she was a chapter ahead in biology, even though Hiram had been unusually difficult all weekend. She sighed and, remembering, fingered the swollen, blackened area at the outer edge of her left eye.

Now he would have to hurry so much he'd probably be in a bad mood tonight. Or worse, get drunk again because he wouldn't go to work at all...sleep all morning instead.

Sure enough, before she left for school, her father's snoring had resumed.

* * *

As soon as school was out at 2:25, Susan rushed home, hoping for time to air out Hiram's room and clean up the stinking bathroom before he returned. She slowed her progress up the front walk when she heard their TV's blast.

The front door was ajar in spite of the crisp December day. Andy Smythe lay asleep on the floor, his bald head glistening. Greg Haskins and Hiram sprawled on the couch, a fresh mustard stain between them. Packages of lunch meat and bread spilled their contents onto the coffee table amid lakes of mustard, mayonnaise, and pickle juice. An open fifth of whiskey stood safely on each end table.

"Susan, I wanna talk to you," Hiram slurred, lurching to his feet. From habit he attempted to tuck his plaid shirttail into his jeans, but coordination failed him.

Susan pulled the door shut behind her and stood with her back against it, arms hugging her notebook and textbooks to her chest.

Her father staggered toward her. His thin, pale face, so like her own, had the doughy look it got when he was drunk. Dark smudges lay under his large brown eyes. He often didn't sleep well...missed her mother, Susan knew.

"I don't like the way you left my breakfast cold. And we ain't got nothin' to feed my friends for dinner. I don't like your housekeepin', and I don't think school's doin' you any good. And I don't like the way you're lookin' at me in front of my friends."

Hiram slapped Susan. She shifted her books, covered her reddening cheek with one hand, and began to cry.

"Get out and leave us alone!" He turned away from his daughter.

Still clutching her books, Susan slammed the front door behind her and ran around the side of the house. She crumpled on the outside cellar steps and sobbed. Finally she quieted, stood, and began a slow walk—up the back alley, across the next street, on along the alley while it took her past houses larger and better cared for than her own—until she reached a truck blocking her passage: a rusty pickup filled with logging tools.

Her mouth dropped open with surprise when she saw a muscular young black man, bare arms and shaved head gleaming with perspiration, climb an enormous tree.

Entranced, Susan watched him lasso ever higher, smaller limbs, and scale toward the sky with catlike grace. She held her breath when he stopped at last, unstrapped a small chain saw from his back, and began to lop off the upper branches.

Susan looked around her, then moved across the alley. Against a garage door she kicked up a pile of leaves and settled into it so she wouldn't have to strain her neck to follow the logging operation.

Branches fell into the yard and along the alley beside the truck. After a while only a tapering spire with a bushy top remained. Then, under the shouted directions of an elderly white man, the young black man cut off the top of the main trunk, climbed lower, cut off another section, and at last returned to earth himself.

Susan then noticed a plump, gray-haired lady coming out of the house carrying a tray laden with mugs and a coffee pot. "Hey, you there," she motioned to Susan, "come have some hot chocolate."

Obediently, Susan trotted over to the fence. The lady handed the black man, who really wasn't much older than Susan, a steaming cup, which he promptly passed to Susan with a smile.

His red and white I.U. t-shirt was soaked with perspiration. The old man waved a quilted khaki jacket at him. "Put this on, son; you're hot only 'cause you've been workin'."

Susan shivered, suddenly aware that the sun had dropped behind the trees lining the alley and that her nose, fingers, and toes were icy.

While the lady poured hot chocolate for the men, the wrinkled old man turned to Susan. "How 'bout it, young lady, ever seen a tree chopped down before?"

"No, sir, I guess not," Susan replied softly.

"Mr. Kemmer's an expert," the lady said. Her round cheeks quivered, but she didn't quite smile.

"I've took down enough so's I ought to be, but I need a young fellow like Maurice here to do the town work."

Maurice spoke directly to Susan. "The Indiana Division of Forestry hires Mr. Kemmer to chop down hundreds of trees a year in the state forest all by himself. Up there, though, he doesn't have to saw branches off—he just does what we're going to do now."

"Hold on, son, not now. By the time we make the alley passable again, it'll be dark. Timberin' is maybe slower than you're expectin'. We'll be cleanin' up all this mess in Miss Maggie's yard most of tomorrow."

"Are you on your way home from school?" the plump woman asked Susan.

"No, ma'am...I mean, yes, ma'am," Susan stammered, putting a hand to her wounded cheek.

The woman stared at her for a moment. "Mr. Kemmer and Maurice'll be cutting down these black walnut trees for the next couple of weeks, so any time you want to watch, please feel free. What's your name?"

"Susan...Susan Marshall."

"I'm Maggie McGilvray, Susan. Next time you're by here, come on through the gate. You'll be warmer if you sit on the bench up by the house."

"Yes, ma'am. Thanks." Susan turned toward the men, but the young one, Maurice, seemed to be looking at her black eye. She ducked her head a little, gave Maggie her mug, and ran over to the neighboring garage to pick up her books. Walking back the way she had come, she turned to wave. The three adults were, indeed, watching her and waved, also.

* * *

Susan had forgotten her troubles while she was observing Maurice, and the hot chocolate had allayed her hunger. Out of sight of the adults, she caressed her throbbing face and shivered. Time to go to home.

Lights blazed in the living room, and the front door was closed. Susan peeked through a side window. Hiram and his two buddies sat on the sofa eating from a Colonel Sanders bucket. Someone had gone out for food; that meant Hiram would be angrier than ever at her. She rounded the house and huddled down on the cellar steps. Protected from the wind, she was relatively cozy and soon dozed off.

Shouts of a neighbor calling his dog woke Susan about eleven-thirty. A look into the living room revealed her father alone, asleep in front of the flickering Monday Night Football game. She quietly slipped into the kitchen, where she ate condensed soup straight from its can and a chunk of cheese washed down with a glass of milk. In her room she spent half an hour on homework before turning out the light.

Next morning she overslept and was relieved to find Hiram had already left for work. Skipping breakfast, she arrived in homeroom just before the bell for first period class.

* * *

The next afternoon and evening Susan shopped, cleaned house, and did homework in advance so she would have a clear conscience while again watching the logging operation at Maggie's.

It was a staggering exhibition of skill. Mr. Kemmer knew exactly which branch should be sawed next, and Maurice followed orders with fearlessness and dexterity. Each afternoon Miss McGilvray would sit a few minutes on the bench with Susan, then prepare hot chocolate for the crew. The two onlookers were companionably silent; but during the refreshment break, Maurice took Susan aside and told her so much about himself that she relaxed enough to comment briefly now and then.

One afternoon while Miss McGilvray was in the kitchen, a guest strolled around the side of the house, startling Susan.

"Well, hello there! Where's Miss McGilvray?"

Susan stared at the well-groomed lady about Maggie's age.

"Phyllis!" Miss McGilvray called from the door.

"Oh, Maggie, I just couldn't stand not seeing you at all."

The women embraced, beaming at each other.

"Here, let me get another cup."

The visitor followed Miss McGilvray into the kitchen. When they returned, the visitor was carrying a plate of still-warm, home-baked oatmeal cookies. Miss McGilvray introduced everyone.

"Of course, Mr. Kemmer," the stylish lady said, "I know Grace from helping drive the Meal Dealers around." She turned to Miss McGilvray. "Grace was just a high school student when she organized that group of kids to take meals to old people and shut-ins. She was so extraordinary that even her classmates were glad to take orders from her. A very unusual girl. Everyone we serve still sings her praises. And Susan, you're Hiram Marshall's girl, aren't you? My husband is your daddy's boss."

Susan nodded and edged away from the three adults. Maurice took the last two mugs and followed her after stepping back long enough to pick up a couple of cookies from the tray. He jerked his head and pointed an elbow. "We're going to look at the bulletin board for a minute," he called.

"OK, take your time," said Mr. Kemmer; and the young people strolled around the side of the house and crossed the street to the public park.

"I want to see if they've put up notices of my class's choral recital yet," Maurice explained.

A crowd of teenage boys played on the basketball courts at the opposite end of the block; but at the near end of the park, the rec building was deserted. The lights, as usual, had been broken, so the contents of the bulletin board were barely discernible in the dusk.

"Nope, nothing yet. I'll ask our director for a poster as soon as practice starts again. One of the chorus members designed it—red and pink hearts, professional lettering. It's even bigger than the graduate school posters."

Susan was wistfully eager to hear about college life and comfortable enough with Maurice to ask for further details to feed her fantasies. Her informer was equally enthusiastic, so their return trip to the McGilvray backyard was slow.

The loggers' quitting time was later than usual, and Phyllis Stockton was hastening away. "But I'll be back soon, Maggie. You can't escape me!" she insisted happily.

Susan, too, hurried home to fix her family's supper.

Hiram was already there. "Where the hell have you been?"

"Nowhere, Daddy. Supper in twenty minutes. The chicken pot pie and rolls just have to be heated. And dessert's your favorite—baked apples."

"You've probably been out with some faggot talking about all those books."

"No, Daddy—"

"Don't 'no' me! You be here when I get home from work from now on or you'll have to drop out of school!"

* * *

The following afternoon Susan went straight home, put on a hearty beef stew, and began cleaning house. The December daylight ended quickly, and she felt anxious because she had saved her father's room for last. She was smoothing the bedspread when Hiram rushed in.

"Get outta my way!" He pushed past her. Opening the nightstand's top drawer, he took out one of several handguns he kept there. "You never seen me do this, right?"

41

Susan cringed against the wall. He turned to glare at her. "Right?"

Susan's whispered "right" was lost in the blast of wintry air propelled through the house when Hiram slammed the front door.

CHAPTER V

HELPING

Bob Stockton almost always hummed on his way home to his wife. Large but agile, he sometimes did a little softshoe in time to his music. When Phyllis heard her husband knock their private code, he could count on her to— unless she was on the phone—throw open the door, eager to relate the latest project or scheme receiving her enthusiastic attention. That December afternoon was no exception.

"Oh, Bob, supper's a little late, but just wait till you hear why." Her hands were fluttering excitedly, but, as usual, even in bed—something that continued to amaze him—her hair, makeup, and clothing were in perfect order.

"I'm waiting. Let me open a beer first." One was all he'd drink; he wanted to stay as trim and young-looking as Phyllis.

Settled at the bar between the kitchen and the dining room, Bob listened with interest to the details of his wife's reunion with Maggie.

"...so my plan of laying low, not calling her for a few weeks, and noticing how she takes out snacks to Ora Kemmer finally paid off."

"Why do you suppose Maggie's having those walnut trees cut down? They definitely increase the value of her property."

"I don't know, Bob. I think Maggie said she'd explain later. We really didn't have time to talk with Ora Kemmer around, even though Hiram's daughter went off to the park with the black boy—."

"Whoa, there! What black boy? Hiram Marshall? That lush! He missed another Monday from work this week. What black boy?"

"Ora Kemmer—he's looking pretty old, you know—has some black boy from Bloomington helping him take down those trees. Susan Marshall was there watching; I guess she stopped off on her way home from school. She's pale as a ghost and so timid, like a scared animal, I thought she'd just scamper away in fright when Maggie introduced us and I mentioned you were her daddy's boss. Anyway, the boy realized what was going on and managed to get her to drink some hot chocolate and even eat some of the fresh oatmeal cookies I took over."

"Ah yes, fresh cookies—" Bob drawled his imitation of W.C. Fields while he lifted a cookie from the jar at his elbow.

"You're a lucky man. The Marshall girl looks as though she hasn't had anything decent to eat for months, and probably neither has Hiram. She ought not to have to cook for and pick up after her slobby drunk of a father, and she ought to have friends her own age and not be alone all the time, either. Poor child can't even look ordinary people in the eye. I think she'd have passed out if Kemmer's boy hadn't taken her for a little walk in the park. Not long ago the ladies at church discussed trying to help her—they suspect Hiram pushes her around some physically—but he's a tyrant, wanting her to work at home all the time just because his wife never did. I think the day has come—."

"Maybe I can wake up Hiram's conscience, though I doubt it. When it comes to women, he's still half-crazed from when his wife ran away. One of these days he'll snap out of it and start having fun again. Susan's mother was a pleasant person, as far as I could see. He's really bitter about her leaving him for another man. But tell me more about Maggie. Glad to hear she's coming back to normal."

"You can hardly call the way she's been living for her mother all these years normal. She doesn't look good, either. She's put on more weight...makes no effort at all to fix herself up. Actually, she's a mess."

Bob leaned back against the wall, smiling. "From the gleam in your eye, I can see you expect to change all that. Probably even have a man lined up for her."

"That's something we need a miracle for, but who knows? Maggie has absolutely nothing to keep her occupied now that her mother's gone, so surely I can get her to pay some attention to basic good grooming. Of course, I need to get her back to church, too. They miss her there."

"That's because of all the scutwork she's always done and not because they treasure her winning ways," Bob said. "Maybe she's wiser than you about Reverend Simms's brand of organized religion."

"There's more to our church than Reverend Simms. I admit he irritates people sometimes, but he doesn't much interfere with our really important projects."

"And Maggie is one of your really important projects."

"Amen! 'Liza Doolittle, here I come!"

* * *

Next day, Bob was glad to see Hiram Marshall was on the job as carpenter for the contracting firm Bob's family owned. Bob did no more than nod to Hiram until almost quitting time, which seemed optimal for broaching the subject of Susan. "Well, Hiram, how are things going for you and your daughter these days?"

"So-so, Mr. Stockton. Times are hard, and I do the best I can; but it's rough tryin' to raise up a teenage girl all alone, 'specially one sweet and pretty like Susan. It's worrisome makin' sure she can't get into trouble." Hiram, fidgeting with a screwdriver lying on the table, avoided looking Bob in the eye.

"I remember how much girltalk went on when my daughter was a teenager. As far as I was concerned, she might as well have been speaking another language. It must be hard for Susan to be alone so much. My wife saw her yesterday evening walking in the park with that black boy—"

"Black boy! Son of a bitch!" The screwdriver fell to the floor.

"Wait, Hiram, she'd just been—" Bob started after him too late. Hiram had already rushed out, not even taking his worn hunting jacket from the hook behind the supply room door.

Now how, Bob asked himself, had their conversation blown up so fast? One minute Hiram was a concerned parent, the next minute a raging maniac. Bob would have to weigh his words better, allow for what a powder keg Hiram was. Now the idiot would go chew out Susan, or worse—go looking for some kid who was probably the only friend she had, except for Maggie. Maybe Maggie ought to warn the boy... Bob locked up as soon as possible and went home to tell Phyllis what a fool he'd been.

As he expected, his wife made him feel better. "Honey, don't blame yourself. Hiram's always been stupid where women are concerned. Probably where blacks are concerned, too. I'll just give Maggie a call, though, to be sure Kemmer's boy is all right."

Phyllis dialed Maggie's number, then hung up with a surprised look. "No longer a working number! When did she do that? She's taken leave of her senses! First thing tomorrow I'm going over there and give her a piece of my mind!"

Bob felt a flash of sympathy for Maggie. Sometimes Phyllis's active concern was a mixed blessing.

* * *

Fortunately for Susan, Hiram projected onto males all possibile culpability in sexual issues: a wicked bastard had lured his wife to wanton freedom, and then a black scoundrel placed his innocent child in danger. He knew there were no blacks living in Sardisvale, hadn't been for thirty years. Now, suddenly, a sex maniac lurked in the park waiting for Susan or another female equally naive about the evil men could perpetrate.

So Hiram's first thought was not to punish Susan, but to scare away the stranger. He had not fired any of his guns, World War II souvenirs, for months; and, though the one he grabbed contained a clip of ammunition, he kept it uncocked. He was, for a change, sober.

Without really looking at Susan, he ran from the house and toward the park. While he ran, he cooled both physically and emotionally and realized he might not find his quarry. In fact, by the time breathlessness slowed him, it seemed crazy that the black boy of yesterday could possibly be in the park when his Susan was safe at home. If only he could have kept his wife safe at home instead of letting her out all the time with her friends... He especially thought of her when he was tired. She had never been tired, but always ready to party whether he was or not. Well, Susan was going to have to stay home more and keep away from boys, especially nigger boys!

By the time the park's rec building came into view, Hiram had given up all hope of success for his mission and was stunned to see a young black man sprawled contentedly on a bench facing the bulletin board.

Hiram retreated at once behind a clump of bushes. He crouched there, panting, until all was dark and the black man rose to saunter along the shrub-lined path toward the street.

Swiftly Hiram crept from his hiding place and held his gun to the back of the man's head. "Don't move, nigger!

Mind what I say! Get your parts out of this town. And if you ever show up here again, I'll personally see to it you never leave this place alive!"

To Hiram the words rang loud and brave. He shoved the black man to his knees, and then withdrew into the bushes beside the walkway.

* * *

Maurice lay, face down, absolutely still on the gravel path. At first he felt nothing. After a couple of minutes, though, he became aware of his stinging cheekbone, palms, and knees. He thought he heard fading footsteps, but he didn't move until a car passed at a moderate speed.

Then he scrabbled to his feet and stumbled blindly up the path, across the street, and into Miss McGilvray's yard. He felt as though his absence had lasted hours, but when he rounded the back corner of the house, Ora Kemmer was just setting an empty mug on the tray.

"Get those posters up?" Ora asked.

"Yes, but I...I've broken my mug. I'm sorry."

"Why, Maurice, don't give it a thought," Miss McGilvray said. "Accidents happen."

"I fell down."

"Are you OK? You've torn your jeans and your knees's bleeding. Let me see."

"No, please...I'm OK"

"Well, at least go in and wash your knee off. And your hands...you've scraped them, too."

"No, I'm all right. I'll do it later...really."

Ora was loading tools onto the back of the truck, and Maurice joined him, ignoring Miss McGilvray's uncertain frown.

* * *

Phyllis was good as her word. She pulled into Maggie's driveway before eight o'clock the next morning ready to normalize her friend's peculiar ways. She was hardly prepared, however, to see that Maggie's car had been backed out of the garage and stood with its trunk and back doors open. Maggie just then staggered up the cellar stairs carrying a huge cardboard box overflowing with clothes.

"Now I know you've lost your mind! Put that junk down and come in and talk to me. Maggie, you're just not yourself these days."

"Oh, Phyllis, good. Here, set this in the trunk. I'll be right back." Maggie thrust the box into Phyllis's arms and returned to the cellar.

Phyllis bristled. Maggie was not going to order her around and manage to evade the important issues. Phyllis put the box down on the driveway, and followed her friend.

In the dim cellar reeking of camphor, her eyes widened with horror. "Good Heavens!"

The basement ceiling was everywhere crisscrossed with sagging clotheslines hung with enough garments to stock a medium-sized secondhand store. Or perhaps a museum, for the garments were a panorama of the past thirty years' fashions in housewear. There were short, medium, and long lengths of skirts and pants in a mind-boggling array of fabrics: cottons, corduroys, wools, and doubleknits. One line dangled nothing but housecoats—flowered, plaid, nubby, silky, fuzzy—mute reminder of the decades Maggie's mother had been an invalid.

Ignoring Phyllis's response, Maggie stooped to pull clear another cardboard box from a four-foot stack of disassembled ones. She clumsily folded it into shape and began to stack in it dresses from the line nearest her.

"Maggie, this is incredible. Don't you ever throw anything away?"

"Throwing away is unnecessarily wasteful, especially when Grace Kemmer's clothing class is desperate for fabrics. Maybe you have some things you could donate, too."

"Some things! All the clothes I've had in my whole life wouldn't add up to this many. Can't you call Grace to send a truck? Oh, that's what I want to talk to you about—calling. What on earth possessed you to disconnect your phone?"

"I have other things to do these days besides talk on the phone."

"Like what?"

"Well, for one thing, like hanging up all these clothes to air so they won't smell quite so musty and mothbally. For another, like packing them all up to take to Grace, which I'm busy doing right now and which you could help me do instead of standing there trying to tell me how to run my life."

Phyllis stood gaping for another few seconds, then decided that the best way to fight Maggie might be to pretend to join her. She began to assemble one of the cardboard boxes. Appeasement was in her tone of voice when she spoke. "Now, Maggie, you know I have your well-being at heart. I just think you've cut yourself off from the rest of the world for quite long enough. Giving yours and your mother's stuff to the high school is a wonderful idea. Maybe I do have some out-of-style things I could add to your load. To tell the truth, I'd forgotten all about Grace's request. How did you ever remember, what with everything else you've had on your mind?"

"Miss Maggie...Miss Maggie!" a man's voice called from outside.

"There's Ora Kemmer and Maurice come to work on the trees."

"That reminds me," Phyllis said, "I need to tell you what Bob did that might cause some trouble, though it was a perfectly innocent attempt to help."

Ora Kemmer appeared in the doorway of the cellar. "'Mornin', ladies. Miss Maggie, I won't be able to work on your trees till Saturday. Somethin' odd's happened with Maurice." Ora dug a piece of paper out of his jacket pocket. "He's gone. Left a note on the kitchen table. Grace's goin' to try to call him later, but it's right peculiar. Well, I ain't got my glasses with me." He handed Maggie the note.

"And my glasses are upstairs." They both turned to Phyllis. "Would you mind?"

Phyllis took the note and fished her glasses, on a smart silver chain, from under her flannel-lined trenchcoat. She read the note aloud: "Dear Ms. Kemmer and Mr. Kemmer, Please don't misunderstand and think I'm not grateful. Nobody has ever been so good to me as you two. I can't work in Sardisvale anymore. It's better for everybody if I don't stay with you, either. I'm sorry for delaying Miss Maggie's job. Say good-bye to her for me. Thanks for everything, Maurice."

"Grace believes somethin' must've happened he don't want to tell us about. She thinks he's completely dependable, and so do I."

"I'll bet I know what happened. That's what I was going to tell you, Maggie."

Ora Kemmer and Maggie turned to Phyllis with surprise.

"What do you know about this?" Maggie asked with a trace of accusation.

"I mentioned to Bob, who was here the other day when I was, and he mentioned to Hiram Marshall at work last night that Susan went walking in the park with a black boy. As soon as Hiram heard 'black boy', before Bob could explain, he went running out of the office—"

"My God, Phyllis, what was Bob thinking of, telling that crazy drunk such a thing?"

"Hiram musta got to Maurice and threatened him somehow, but when?" Ora sounded puzzled.

"I know! Remember when Maurice came back from the park last night and said he'd fallen?"

"You got it, Miss Maggie! Hiram must've roughed him up and told him to leave town."

"What a shame!" Maggie exclaimed. "Such a nice young man. Now Susan hasn't any friends at all. This is just terrible."

"Bob was only trying to help Susan. He thought maybe he could make Hiram see that she needed less work at home and more of a social life after school. He was very upset when Hiram went running off half-cocked."

Ora Kemmer scratched his head. "Maurice is prob'ly too sensible to come back here to work. Grace says she can get me a high school boy to help for the next two weeks, 'cause school lets out for Christmas holidays tomorrow afternoon. We'll be here early Saturday mornin'."

"Holidays! That's it!" said Phyllis. "You've given me an idea for how to help Susan. All I have to do is call Betsy Simms. Oh, Maggie, if only you hadn't had your phone disconnected, I wouldn't have to go home to call. I'll definitely be back next week to speak to you about that foolishness. Right now, let me go fix Susan up."

Phyllis immediately rushed up the stairs, leaving a light trace of perfume, which quickly diffused among the mildew and camphor.

Maggie shook her head at Ora Kemmer. "It seems to me 'fixing up' sometimes causes more problems than it cures."

CHAPTER VI

HIRING A BABY-SITTER

When the phone rang, Betsy Simms was sitting in the middle of the kitchen floor nursing baby Mary while reading *The Cat in the Hat* to Matthew. Mark was pursuing the puppy along the hall toward the newly-carpeted living room, and Betsy knew she ought to stop the chase before it was too late. Jonathan had just left to make hospital calls, so she was going to have to answer the phone herself if it got answered at all.

"Reverend Simms's residence. Ms. Simms speaking." Her chin came up defiantly when she gave herself the "libber" title Jonathan believed to be belligerent and short-sighted.

"Betsy, dear, this is Phyllis Stockton. I know you're busy, but I'll keep you only a moment. Bob and I want to give you a little Christmas present—a baby-sitter for the next two weeks. The only thing we ask is that you first try to engage Hiram Marshall's daughter, Susan. She's getting out of school for Christmas vacation this afternoon."

"Phyllis, are you serious? I never heard of such a thing!"

"Oh, she's quite honest and capable, and if you think three children is too many for her, then maybe you can take one out with you."

"No, of course I don't mean Susan, I mean you getting us a baby-sitter. Why should you do that? Wait a minute, Phyllis, the puppy is on the new carpet."

The phone clattered, swinging, against the wall. Betsy ran into the living room, scooped up the puppy with her free hand, and deposited him, squirming, into the fenced-in backyard.

"Mark, wait with Matthew. I'll read to you both as soon as I'm off the phone.

"OK, Phyllis, please excuse the interruption. Now what's this about a baby-sitter?"

"Susan Marshall desperately needs to get away from that salt mine of a home, so Bob and I thought you might be able to persuade Hiram to let her work for you as our Christmas gift. Don't tell me you couldn't use some extra help right now. If you say no, I'm really at a loss about what anyone can do for Susan. Bob says Hiram's been missing work every Monday again, and I'll bet part of those drunken weekends are spent being mean to that pathetic little girl. You know the Circle of Help ladies have been trying to think up something—."

"Phyllis, you don't have to talk me into it. It's a marvelously generous gesture. Let me see, though...I probably better get in touch with Hiram first. It's really a wonderful idea! Maybe Susan will open up to me. I could have some high school kids over to spend time with her...I know: we'll have the 'Tween Group Christmas party here while Susan's working for me, and—."

"Well, dear, I have to go now. Tell Susan two dollars an hour for two weeks. 'Bye."

"Two dollars! That's too—Phyllis?"

But Phyllis Stockton had already hung up.

* * *

When Jonathan Simms said grace before dinner, he went on at more length than usual. His Lincolnesque body almost quivered with earnestness and vulnerability. Such was his response to happiness, and Betsy loved him for it. She smiled all during the prayer, for she knew her candlelight steak dinner had almost as much to do with his good mood as the proximity of Christmas.

"Do you write to Santy Claus, Daddy?" asked Matthew.

"Santa Claus has other ways of knowing what grown-ups want, sweetie," Betsy said. "For instance, Jonathan, Santa's commissioned the Stocktons to deliver a present to somebody you wish came to church more often. Want to guess who?"

"I haven't the foggiest notion what you're talking about."

"Guess, Daddy, guess!" Matthew chanted, anticipating a game.

Jonathan rarely played along with his wife's guessing games, but this time his good mood prevailed. "OK. A present from the Stocktons to someone with poor attendance...has to be to Maggie McGilvray."

"She is on our Christmas list. Getting her back to church is going to be my number one New Year's project."

"Well, good luck. She's such a crabby person. Seems determined to isolate herself from the world. Doesn't care about anyone else."

"Jonathan, that's not true. You should notice how her eyes light up when she sees the children. She pays attention to everyone and everything; she just doesn't want anyone to know how nice she is."

"Well, nobody knows but you. I take it she's not the recipient of the Stocktons' goodwill."

"What? No, it's not an adult. Phyllis and Bob want us to hire Susan Marshall to baby-sit while she's off from school for the next two weeks. They'll pay for it as a secret, anonymous Christmas present to Susan. Bob thinks Hiram's drinking more than ever and probably pushing Susan around."

"I don't like baby-sitters. Just you, Mommy."

"Matt, you'll like this one. She's young and pretty."

"Watch what you say, Jonathan, or your children are likely to enumerate the shortcomings in age and beauty of the Circle of Help ladies you're always bringing home," Betsy cautioned playfully.

"Many of those ladies need to see what a real Christian home is like. Susan, though, can probably profit even more from the experience."

"Actually, we shouldn't count our chickens out loud until I've talked to Hiram. I think I can put the proposition to him in a way he can't refuse."

"If I could get any proof that he abuses his daughter, I'd report him to the authorities! If only this county would outlaw the sale of alcohol... I know, you think that's an impossible dream; but we both know the world would be a better place if nobody drank. Seems to me that at least the members of our congregation could see the example you and I set."

"Oh, Jonathan, I'm not sure anybody really looks to us for a demonstration of right living. Most people around here are too busy trying to keep food on the table. Well, let me see what I can do for Susan when I call Hiram."

"Better call soon, or he'll already have started his weekend spree."

* * *

Hiram Marshall, however, sounded quite sober to Betsy. "We sure appreciate you thinkin' of Susan, Mrs. Simms. She needs to be makin' some spendin' money, 'stead of sittin' around readin' or gettin' into trouble with some no 'count kids for two whole weeks."

"Then it's settled, Mr. Marshall? I can expect Susan to come by here tomorrow morning about eleven to talk things over?"

"Yes, ma'am, and if she don't show, you let me hear about it!"

"Thanks very much, and happy holidays!"

* * *

Susan couldn't believe her good fortune, but she tried not to show how excited she was for fear her father would change his mind about letting her work for the preacher. Mrs. Simms was, to Susan's way of thinking, a perfect person: beautiful, happy, friendly, intelligent. Besides taking care of her handsome young husband and three adorable children, she cared about and was loved by everyone in the congregation. Working for her would surely be more fun than work.

Susan left home early for her appointment with Betsy. She hurried down the alley, hoping to have time to watch Mr. Kemmer and Maurice. Not since her mother had run away had Susan known anyone so cheerful as Maurice. Her mother had been always singing or humming or twirling around so her heavy chestnut hair had swung away from her shoulders. Actually, Susan was forgetting most other things her mother had done—how she had gone out with her friends before Hiram got home from work, how she had stayed out very late, and how Hiram had shut himself into their bedroom and cried for days after she finally left for good. Those bad parts were slipping away, and Susan liked it that Maurice reminded her of some good things when he hummed or sang or did a few dance steps.

He clearly enjoyed people, too, and especially admired Mr. Kemmer. Maurice had told her that a forest ranger was supposed to mark with a blaze the trees they hired Ora to cut down, but what the rangers had done for years was leave everything to the old man. He knew so much about forestry that experts came from other states to see Indiana's forest cared for by Ora Kemmer.

And Miss Maggie...Maurice treated her like a queen in spite of her plain looks, funny clothes, and general weirdness.

She didn't talk much at all...seemed to respect Susan's—and everybody's—privacy in a way that made Susan feel very comfortable.

Susan quickened her steps, hoping Miss Maggie would have hot chocolate, cookies, and quiet companionship ready again.

The lumbermen were indeed busy in Maggie's yard, and Susan had been sitting on the bench alone for five minutes before she realized Ora Kemmer's helper was not Maurice.

"Hey, Susan, what're you doin' here?"

Susan was speechless. Not only had she expected Maurice, but also she never knew what to say to Jerry Haskins. The police chief's son, he was considered by even her father to be "a nice boy." Right before Thanksgiving, while she had been working in the library on her history paper, Jerry had sat down beside her and started to talk. His voice was soft, gentle, like a caress; and his gaze was so direct she felt as if everything he thought would spill right out. It was scary, too scary. Susan had made some excuse and left the library. Besides, Jerry was also the nephew of Hiram's drinking buddy Greg Haskins, and Susan was embarrassed that Jerry must know how her father behaved.

"'Mornin', Susan," called Ora Kemmer. "Miss Maggie's not here today, but you're welcome to watch just the same. Jerry here's my new helper. Too bad he's not goin' to get some good hot choc'late like you and me allus do."

Susan smiled tremulously while examining her watch. Still half an hour before she was supposed to be at the Simmses'. Jerry kept looking her way, so she decided to leave, even though she'd have to walk very slowly.

Because Jerry said, "'Bye, Susan," she turned and waved, still without looking directly at him.

The shortest way to the parsonage was by cutting across the basketball end of the park. Since Susan had time to kill, and since she didn't want to have to be stared at by the

Saturday morning crowd at the courts, she continued down the alley for another two blocks, then walked along Chicago Street. That route took her past the side of Hoosier Hollow, her father's favorite bar.

While she approached the bar, Hiram, Greg Haskins, and Andy Smythe turned from the parking area behind it and proceeded ahead of her in the same direction she was going. Greg Haskins's big figure—bigger even than the police chief's, definitely bigger than Jerry's would ever be—bent down toward her daddy, while fat Andy Smythe bounced along behind. She knew Mr. Haskins was telling jokes again, always trying to get her daddy to "lighten up."

Not wanting to be seen, she ducked into the parking lot and sneaked forward on the other side of the long, narrow building. About ten feet from the street, however, was a locked metal gate she had never before noticed. It had a small central grating, almost like a jail cell, through which she could look unobserved. What she saw was merely a short passageway to a section of Foliage Street bounded by boarded-up houses long ago abandoned by people who disliked living across from the noise produced by Hoosier Hollow at its peak business hours.

Susan heard Greg's booming laugh, then the slam of the outer door of the bar, so she retraced her steps along the building's side and across the parking lot to Chicago Street and continued for another two blocks to the Simmses' enclosed side porch.

Betsy and the two little boys were playing some kind of clapping game while baby Mary sat cooing happily in a playpen nearby.

"Susan, great! I haven't seen you for much too long. Sorry we have to have our business meeting outside, but Reverend Simms always gets the house to himself on Saturday mornings to work on his sermons in peace and quiet. Did your daddy tell you what I need?"

"Yes, ma'am, I mean...I guess...a baby-sitter?"

"Well, you can imagine how many things need to be done before Santa Claus can come."

"Santy Claus, Santy Claus! Santy Claus is coming to town!" sang Matthew while Mark giggled and clapped.

Betsy laughed. "Santa's helpers need some private time. I'm also trying to plan the 'Tween Group Christmas get-together. Maybe you'll have some ideas for it."

"Daddy doesn't like for me to go out at night." Susan felt a rising panic.

"Oh, surely he'll approve of your coming to a party here. But we'll see about that next week. In the meantime, I'm offering you two dollars an hour for staying with one or two of the children every morning for the next two weeks you're off from school. How does nine to one sound? Of course, lunch is included. And of course I won't expect you on Fridays, 'cause that'll be Christmas and New Year's. OK?"

Betsy's breathless oration had overwhelmed Susan. She nodded but didn't quite smile until Mark patted her on the knee and said, "You're pitty!"

"There, you see, Mark knows a pretty girl when he sees one. Now if you'll just start reading this book to the boys, I'll tiptoe into the kitchen and bring out a surprise."

"Surprise! Surprise!" chanted Matthew.

Betsy thrust a child's picture book at Susan and, true to her word, tiptoed into the house, leaving Susan too occupied for the moment to worry about parties.

* * *

In the kitchen Betsy finished preparing a big tray with a plate of tuna fish sandwiches, Oreo cookies, and four glasses of milk. Before she asked Susan to open the screen door, however, she set the tray down on the floor and peeped out the living room window. She nodded happily to herself when she saw Mark cuddled into Susan's left arm and Matthew sitting straight and important on her right, intently turning a page for the equally intent reader. More people, Betsy thought, should look to Phyllis and Bob for an example of right living. She was certainly going to. This was, indeed, a fine place to live, and Betsy said a little prayer of thanksgiving because her children were growing up in Sardisvale.

CHAPTER VII

RITUALS IN THE WOODS

Because of Maurice's disappearance, Maggie changed her plans for delivering the clothing to Grace. She had expected Maurice to load the bags into her car and Ora's truck; but since she would have to do it all alone, there was no hurry. She might as well be more particular in sorting and packing. She took the already bulging bag and box back to the basement and began again. This time she labeled each container according to the kind of fabric it contained. The task took her all of Thursday and most of Friday morning; and by the time she had squeezed everything into the car's trunk and back and front seats, it was too late to go out to the Kemmers'. Maggie was tired, but satisfied that she was prepared to go early the next Saturday morning and thus enjoy another leisurely visit with Grace. At dawn Maggie dressed warmly in several layers of sweaters, anticipating a possible walk in the woods.

Although she hadn't driven since her other trip to the country, the car kicked over right away. At the turn onto the highway, she honked at Ora, who was on his way to her house. They stopped even with each other and rolled down their windows.

"I left some instant coffee on the drainboard. Please help yourself. I'm taking some things to Grace for her clothing classes."

"She'll be mighty pleased. Stay and set a spell; she spends way too much time alone. Ain't no need for you to hurry back for us today. Me and Jerry'll see you on Monday."

Grace came running out of the house as soon as Maggie bumped into the Kemmers' yard. "Maggie, what a nice surprise! But you're buried by all that stuff. What's going on?"

"It's a good thing I'm not claustrophobic, or I couldn't have backed out of my own driveway. These are the clothes I promised for your home ec classes."

"So many? I can't believe it!"

"There're more in the trunk."

"Wait, then, while I get my coat."

Grace and Maggie began unloading, but Grace soon persuaded Maggie to put on the tea kettle while the younger woman took all the bags and boxes down to the basement.

"And you've even labeled them so I'll know which to take to school the end of January, when the new semester begins, and which to save for spring. This will mean a lot to some poor farmers' families. The small operators just can't make it on their own anymore, but they won't admit it. Although they believe going on relief would be a disgrace, they can't face moving and training themselves for some other kind of work...probably think they're too old to start something new."

"I wonder how old is too old...," Maggie speculated.

"Of course they're not too old. I keep hoping their children can help them believe that. At least, that's how I try to reach them—through their kids."

"Is one of your kids helping your dad today?"

"Oh, you didn't see him? You did leave home early. Yes, Police Chief Timothy Haskins's son, Jerry. He has a special place in my heart."

"I'm beginning to think everybody does!"

"Hardly. Jerry's mother died of cancer three years ago, when he was a freshman. Chief Haskins was grieving so much that his brother Greg took them both in. Greg drinks way too much—everybody in town knows that—yet by some miracle he managed to stay sober and helpful till the chief and Jerry went through all their goods, sold their house, and settled into an apartment. Then, of course, Greg started drinking again. He sure was ready, willing, and able, though, when they needed him."

"He's probably bumming around with Hiram Marshall."

"Maggie, Daddy thinks Hiram must've threatened Maurice."

"It sure looks like it. Bob Stockton feels responsible. Still, he was only trying to help Susan, poor child. I guess Maurice wouldn't tell you what happened."

"He was gone. His landlady said he left for Detroit early Thursday morning, planning not to come back. He shouldn't have to abandon his education because of some stupid, drunken bigot. It's just not fair. I'm as responsible as Mr. Stockton, since I'm the one who invited Maurice here in the first place. I feel terrible about it!"

"You mustn't blame yourself. You were just trying to help."

"So were the Stocktons. And I guess Hiram thought—if he *can* think—that he was helping Susan and Sardisvale. Good intentions certainly can mess things up, and I don't know how to straighten this out. Maggie, I feel so confused. That's why I was getting ready to leave." Grace waved her hands toward the backpack and cooking utensils spread over the other half of the table.

"Leave for where?" Maggie was shocked. "You mean leave your dad, and school, and—?"

"No, no! I mean go up to Willamae's old place for the weekend. I go there whenever I need to sort things out. Daddy worries about me being up there alone, but it's perfectly safe. Probably nobody else knows about the place. Maybe a forest ranger or two, but they aren't around on weekends, anyway."

"You should have told me sooner. I don't want to keep you from going if you need to. I'll start back now—."

"Wait, Maggie. Please go with me."

"Into the woods? I'd probably give out halfway there. I was really pooped last time, till your tea revived me."

"You went too fast. We'll go slow this time. There's absolutely no reason to hurry. I have everything we need to spend the night; and we'll be back tomorrow, mid-afternoon. Please, Maggie. I've never taken anyone with me before, but I know you'll appreciate what it meant to Willamae...means to me. I think you're one of our sisters!"

Maggie scarcely hesitated. Perhaps Willamae's old home would be exactly what she needed: a place of real seclusion, a place Thomas Merton dreamed of, a place to be truly alone and become an individual. "All right, Grace, I'll go! I'm ready to learn the lore of your woods."

Grace laughed. "You never should have said that. It's bait any school teacher would rise to."

The two women worked quickly and well together bundling food, utensils, and bedding into two small backpacks. Grace outfitted Maggie with legwarmers and earmuffs. "No fashion experts looking on, so we'll wear whatever's necessary to be comfortable."

For an unprecedented moment Maggie saw herself as others must see her: ungainly, dowdy. She smiled at the ludicrous juxtaposition of herself and some fashion expert.

"I'll just leave Daddy a note so he'll know you're with me. Now don't worry for a minute about keeping up. We're going to walk slowly, rest often, and enjoy the scenery. I'll tell you some stories on the way."

The climb, however, was difficult for Maggie. Even with frequent stops, she found talking impossible and conserved breath by listening to Grace's account of her family's relationship with Willamae.

"I feel more at home in the woods than I do in the house. Before Momma got sick—when I was eight—she would take me right along with her and Daddy, pack a lunch, and spend the whole day while he was working. I don't know how often we went with him, but our trips in the summer are the ones I remember best. Even on hot days, it'd be cool in the deep forest. We'd wear long sleeves and long pants for protection from poison ivy and rattlesnakes. We all wore wide-brimmed straw hats to keep sticks out of our eyes and bird-droppings out of our hair."

"Maybe we're not dressed right for this trip," Maggie panted.

"Don't worry. We're staying on my beaten path this time, unless you want to go looking for wounded animals. That's how I first met Willamae. When we three would get to Daddy's work site, first thing we'd do was see if we could find any hurt animals—birds, squirrels, chipmunks. Mom was almost always successful curing the creatures we took home. Then she got cancer and was too sick herself to go with Daddy anymore. She missed it.

"That spring, about the time I understood how bad she was, Daddy took only me along when he went to mark some trees for timbering. Right away I found a rabbit with a broken leg writhing on the ground.

"Daddy caught it, but shook his head and said it couldn't live. I remember crying harder than I ever had before. It seemed like the end of the world." Grace paused in her narration, apparently lost in memories.

Maggie felt a quick catch in her own throat and wondered briefly, objectively—as though she were at a distance, watching her panting, teary-eyed self—if she wasn't going to sob as though the end of the world had come for Grace, for herself, for their mothers...

The moment passed when Grace's smooth, young voice began again. "Finally Daddy said he might know someone who could cure the rabbit. He let me help him make a stretcher out of a board, and we padded it with my sweater and tied the rabbit down with Daddy's bandana handkerchief.

"We took along our lunches because Daddy said the route was farther, higher, on the ridge than I'd ever been. It was more or less the one we're climbing now. My crying must have stopped completely while he was pointing out all the different kinds of trees to me: white oak, black oak, pinoak, sycamore, sassafras, shagbark hickory, beech. I learned some of my woods lore from Daddy before I ever met Willamae. At least, I learned to love this place."

Maggie stopped to shift the weight of her backpack. "Didn't your daddy ever have anyone work with him? I mean, to help with the heavy parts?"

"Never. Well, I think once or twice before I was born he tried hiring someone. He said he just couldn't stand the responsibility of watching out for somebody else all the time. I think mostly he loves being alone with his trees. He has the whole logging operation down to a science. The clearing right up ahead is where he drags the trees he cuts higher up. See, there's a road just above the clearing; that's the highest anyone can drive. In the clearing he strips the logs enough to load them onto his truck and haul them down to his sawmill."

The two women stared at the clearing. Maggie recognized it from her previous visit. Ora's truck had then been parked on the logging road separating the deciduous trees from the evergreens that continued thickly up the ridge.

"This is the site of some really sick meetings."

"You mentioned them before."

"The Ku Klux Klan. Daddy's seen preparations for and remnants of their cross-burning rituals, and they scare even him."

"Doesn't look as though there've been any meetings here lately," Maggie said, surveying the tangled underbrush.

"No, I think it's been quite awhile, but that doesn't mean those folks have come to their senses. Anyway, nobody ever goes above the road. Can you wait for lunch until we get up to Willamae's? This place gives me the creeps."

"Of course," Maggie answered; and the women entered the fragrant forest of the upper ridge.

A thick carpet of pine needles muffled their footsteps. Wild creatures no longer rustled and swished through dry leaves; twigs popped and snapped more loudly when they broke. The air was cooler, evergreen-scented. Grace had stopped talking, and Maggie was more aware of her surroundings. Suddenly they emerged into a much smaller clearing amid the scrub pines.

"What on earth...? It's beautiful!" Maggie exclaimed.

"The first time I saw this place, when we were taking the rabbit to Willamae, I asked who lived here. I was sure it was some fairies' 'Magic Circle,' and that's what I've always called it."

Sunlight streamed onto a perfect circle of deep pine needles. Edging the circle were smooth tree stumps. In the center was a large one on which was a clay pot of dried, richly colored autumn leaves. Bright yellow leaves had been arranged around the base of each peripheral stump so that the entire outdoor room seemed gilded by the midday sun streaming through the circular opening.

"Golden!" Maggie whispered.

"Those yellow ones are ginseng leaves. Daddy sells the roots, and I save and dry the leaves because they're such a gorgeous color."

"I've heard ginseng is good for everything that ails you."

"Only, I'm afraid, for those ailments that can be cured by positive thinking. That, of course, is quite a few. They do me the most good by making this place even more beautiful. I'm glad you like the looks of it, since this is where I do my most serious meditating."

"Yes, it must be a magical place to be alone."

"I'm hoping not to have to be alone here much more. I think you'll be the first person to join my group. We'll have our own rituals here, and we'll teach others—"

"Hold on, Grace. I'm not going to get into anything mystical."

"But I think—no, I feel—that you're the perfect person to help me start the sisterhood Willamae taught me about."

"I'm not, believe me. I want to do new things, but I want to do them alone. I'm through with groups—never really seemed a part of any and now don't have to pretend to be. Your plans suit you, and you'll find others with a mystical bent, but count me out. Solitude is what I want more of."

"But Maggie, I feel so close to you. I thought sure—"

"One thing I believe: that people shouldn't try to make other people over into something they don't want to be. I like and respect you the way you are, but I'm different and going to stay this way."

Grace smiled. "Maggie, I think you already have the wisdom I'm searching for. Maybe you're a Sister without even trying."

The women began to climb again while Grace talked, her voice now laced with excitement. "There isn't even a path from here to Willamae's house. I found out later that she took a different route every day to keep from wearing a visible track in the underbrush. She did value her privacy!

"Daddy knew the way, but he said to be extra quiet because she wasn't used to people. He kept calling to her before we got there so she wouldn't be frightened. He's very understanding of people who want to be alone.

"She scared me instead by suddenly cackling behind us, and I dropped my end of the rabbit's stretcher. When I turned and saw her, I was still scared. She looked so strange: tiny—about my size, and I was only eight—wrinkled, toothless; and she was dressed in a long, greenish-black robe with a hood like Biblical women wore." Grace chuckled.

"Daddy introduced us, and Willamae immediately took charge of the rabbit. She sent me off to the waterfall—you'll see it in a few minutes—to wash up. It looked like a magical place, too: rainbow-colored dragonflies, a purple martin. I must have stayed there for some time because by the time I got back, the leg was expertly splinted, and the rabbit was in a portable wire pen contentedly eating greens.

"Willamae took me into her house and gave me a jar of soakberry tea to take to Mom. I guess Daddy had explained about her while I was at the stream. Anyway, Willamae said I should visit again; Daddy had said I could."

"So you did?"

"I practically lived there weekends and summers after Mom died. I went by myself after the first couple of times."

"I'm surprised your daddy would let you go alone."

"He's not afraid of natural things, just human beings. The woods are his refuge—the way they were for Willamae and are for me, too, I guess.

"She tried, though, to help me relate to people, even though the Sardisvale community had been quite cruel to her because she was different."

"They don't go in much for diversity; that's for sure!" Maggie commented.

"It was her idea that I do something for the elderly and other shut-ins. I got the church to start the Meal Dealers."

"I know about them. They still deliver meals. My friend Phyllis Stockton is their advisor." As soon as the words were out, Maggie was smitten by guilt. She certainly hadn't been much of a friend to Phyllis, especially lately. Maybe Maggie should take her own advice and accept Phyllis the way she was, not try to change that sometimes intrusive but genuinely concerned personality.

Oblivious of Maggie's distress, Grace continued her personal history. "With Willamae directing the project through me, it was a big success. I honestly enjoyed guiding everybody as well as planning and preparing the food. In fact, that's when I decided to be a home ec major and then come back here to teach. At Michigan I learned a great deal about the outside world. I try to inspire my students to widen their career potential and to recognize their option to leave Sardisvale."

Grace's slip into educational jargon sounded familiar to Maggie. "My mother was a teacher before she became ill. She believed kids could stay right here and still have the broader view. She never quite convinced me, though."

"Did you ever plan to leave Sardisvale?"

"I had two years at I.U. before I quit to take care of Momma. I think I'd have kept to myself wherever I was. Now that Momma's gone... Oh, this is it!"

They had rounded a boulder that formed one side of a house built of irregularly shaped blocks of limestone. The structure was about ten feet by twenty feet, its roof thatched with pine boughs. It appeared to have no doors or windows.

"Over here's the stream." Grace led Maggie to a spot ten yards away where gray limestone boulders were almost hidden by brown vines. A waterfall formed a crystalline pool. "Wait till you see it when everything's green."

Maggie was even more intrigued by the waterfall and house than she was by the magic circle.

"The house is pretty dark inside at night, so we should use this daylight to get it ready for us."

The front door of Willamae's old dwelling was a natural hole in limestone, an entrance so low they barely missed scraping the tops of their heads. The thatched portion of the house was pitch black. The part within the boulder, however, was illuminated by another hole, a kind of skylight twenty feet over their heads.

Maggie could make out shelves of boards and rocks against all the stone walls. On the shelves were unlabelled reddish crocks interspersed with what looked like bunches of dried weeds.

The women swept out the thatched room and spread their bedrolls. Then they took their lunch out to the waterfall pool, where Maggie sank gratefully to the ground. "I think I could eat a horse and then sleep for a week!" she declared.

"After you eat and have a glass of soakberry tea, I bet you'll find you can stay awake till dark. After that, you can go right to sleep. Never will you have spent such a dark and quiet night, I promise!"

But the unaccustomed outdoor exertion hit Maggie too soon. She gave in quickly, saying, "I simply have to take a nap."

Grace recognized the older woman's fatigue. "That's OK. While you sleep, then, I'm going to the magic circle to meditate. If you wake up before I get back, wait here for me."

Maggie curled into her sleeping bag and closed her eyes. Peace, emptiness, but no messages from the Beyond, or Beneath, or Wherever. Just Maggie, alone. She slept.

When she awoke, Grace was standing in the darkening room holding a cup of steaming tea. "I've built a small fire around the corner of the boulders. Nobody can see the flames from the road, and they won't notice the smoke now that it's almost dark. It gets quite cold up here at night."

At the doorway Maggie could smell the soup Grace was simmering in a pot on an open campfire between the house and the waterfall. "Grace, this is wonderful! I had the most peaceful sleep, but I didn't expect it to last until dark."

"In the woods, twilight begins early, what with all the pine trees so thick. Notice how much colder it is, too. You're going to need another sweater now. By the time you wash up and put one on, dinner will be ready—an herb broth I think you'll like."

Cleaner and more warmly bundled, Maggie was indeed comfortable as she sipped the delicious, spicy soup from a clay mug. Conversing quietly with the young woman, Maggie was also aware of herself with a strangely objective perception. Her own voice had a clear, strong quality, as though she were a person fully in control of her own life. Invigorated!

Grace, ladling herself a second serving, jerked her mug, sloshing soup onto the hot coals. "Did you hear something?"

Maggie listened. She had just shaken her head when a shrill "whip-poor-will" pierced the hush. "Yes, I hear a whippoorwill."

"Shhh!" Grace commanded sharply.

The piercing whistle was repeated.

To Maggie's surprise, Grace gave a loud, accurate imitation.

"It's Daddy. That's our signal."

Maggie listened with wonder while the whistles echoed each other every minute or so until Ora Kemmer emerged from the woods into the circle of firelight.

"Daddy, what's the matter?"

Maggie, too, knew something was amiss as soon as she saw the urgent look on Ora's face.

Before answering, he took time to give Grace a kiss on the cheek and Maggie a nod.

"Mr. Kemmer, did the work go all right? The Haskins boy— did he show up to help?"

"Oh, sure he did. He's a good boy. Not strong or experienced like Maurice, but a good boy. No, it's nothin' about your job. The day went fine, but I didn't think you two oughta be alone up here, or even be up here at all tonight."

"Daddy, whyever not? I do this every few weeks, and Maggie—. Wait a minute. Something's really wrong, isn't it?"

"When I was comin' home from Miss Maggie's house, I seen a car in front of me turn into the forestry road. Then, in my rear view mirror, I seen the pickup behind me turn in, too; and I knowed somethin' was up. Walkin' up here, I had to skirt the clearin' to keep those Klan muckety-mucks from seein' me. They're settin' up a little gasoline generator for a PA system. There's bound to be a Klan meetin' there tonight."

"Really? The Ku Klux Klan? I can't believe it. I thought they disbanded years ago."

"It has been a long time since they've met up here, hasn't it, Daddy?"

"Yep, it sure has, Honey; but they ain't all dead yet. I wish we was back down home, but it's too late now."

"Well, Daddy, since you're here, have some soup with us."

"I'll definitely do that, but first I want to put out this fire and move this good-smellin' kettle inside."

"Inside?" Maggie asked.

"The last thing we want, Miss Maggie, is to be entertainin' those crazy Klanners for dinner."

With the fire out, the pine forest was pitch black, and Maggie was glad to be cozy in Willamae's boulder house finishing the soup by the light of a small hurricane lamp.

"Being here is amazing. I never would have guessed at all the interesting things going on privately in the public forestry," Maggie said.

"Well, o' course it ain't legal to be here. The Klan was warned years ago, but they's prob'ly a whole new bunch that's members now. Seems like they's mostly all bark and no bite, but you never know. It's been a long time."

"So you think they're planning some trouble again?"

"I allus used to let well enough alone—I was covered up with work and all—but now I'm so old I think I want to find out what they're up to. I brung a couple pocket flashlights here, and I'm goin' to check out that meetin'. I know a way to wind around and come in above and to the side of the clearin' so nobody down there can see my flashlight."

"I'm going with you!" exclaimed Grace. "Oh, Maggie, you don't mind being here alone, do you?"

"I most certainly do! I'm getting old and foolish, too. I want to see this Klan thing as much as you two do, so just give me the other flashlight and let me follow. Don't go slow on account of me."

Ora Kemmer and his daughter exchanged glances. Ora spoke. "All right, Miss Maggie, you come, too. Stay as close behind me as you're comfy doin'—but don't get all tuckered—and let Grace follow you with the other flashlight so's there's no way you can get lost.

"And let's agree now," he continued, "nobody's goin' to say anythin' that ain't necessary 'til we're safe back up here. I sure don't want to explain nothin' to no Klanner, so no noise! One reason we're goin' all 'round Robin Hood's barn to get there is so we'll be upwind in case they's got dogs."

"Dogs? You mean they have watchdogs?"

"Last time the Klan met up here, they had three or four police dogs with 'em. There'd be hell to pay if we had to mess with a German shepherd."

Maggie shivered—with eagerness, not fear. "I'm ready to go!" she declared in her new, stronger voice.

Grace produced warm scarves and mittens, though, and insisted they visit the woods "facilities" before she announced to Ora that the ladies really were ready.

Ora led them into the darkness, angling across the ridge instead of straight down. His pace gave Maggie, with her newly acquired energy, no problem. Even the terrain was inviting. She thought they must be following a deer path, as no major obstacles impeded them. She was able to follow Ora closely and to cause Grace few pauses.

Long before they saw the clearing, they could hear preparations for the meeting. Car tires spun and men shouted greetings to each other. Lanterns' glow filtered through the pines.

Then Ora turned off his flashlight and signaled extra caution, a message Maggie promptly passed back to Grace with a gesture to douse the other flashlight. Grace complied, moving closer to Maggie.

Ora dropped onto all fours and motioned for the women to do the same. Maggie's knees popped, but she followed Ora's example. After crawling only a few feet, the three stopped side by side against a gigantic old downed pine that formed a natural fortress twenty feet above the clearing.

Slowly Ora rose on his knees to peer over the log. He nodded to Maggie and Grace to do the same. Maggie's knees protested painfully as they assumed her full weight. She thought she would not be able to hold that position for a minute, much less for the duration of a meeting. She rested her forearms on the pine's rough bark, and they felt uncomfortable even through the several layers of clothing. Then the formal Ku Klux Klan meeting began, and Maggie lost consciousness of any body discomfort, of anything at all except the ritual convocation of some of her fellow citizens of the Sardisvale community.

CHAPTER VIII

THE MEETING

Dwight Mitchell was depressed because of the time of year. Not because it was coming up on Christmas, although he had learned the year before at the Law Enforcement Academy that more people kill themselves the week after Christmas than any other time. No, holidays weren't responsible for his life being a downer; basketball season was the cause. Sardisvale was hoop happy again, and Dwight didn't know if he could stand it.

Exactly three years before, he had been into his personal best season ever, his third year in the varsity starting lineup, his senior year at Sardisvale High. Every home game was a sellout, the Student Council printed buttons that said "Mitch Makes 'Em," and girls hung around wanting him to break training and prove how many of *them* he could make. Well, maybe he was kidding himself some about the girls, but he could have had his pick of dates if only he hadn't been so busy staying in shape. It had felt good.

Then—disaster. One teammate broke his leg in a car accident; another got arrested for shoplifting; and, in spite of Dwight's twenty-plus points a game, Sardisvale lost the conference championship. The college scholarship Dwight had counted on melted away.

He hadn't fooled himself that he was another Rick Mount or Larry Bird; but he was six feet three and growing, his grades were passing, his point average was good, and basketball was his life. If only his team had gone to the state finals...or that's what Dwight had thought at first.

For a while he'd blamed just about everything and everybody: the team, the driver of the car that broke Luke's leg, stupid Donnie who had no respect for the law or store property and got himself arrested, his teachers, CoachTracey. For years he'd longed for a place on Indiana University's team, so he hated to blame their scouts' judgment, but he did.

Finally, the father of a girl he took out a few times set Dwight straight. The guy was an I.U. graduate, a dyed-in-the-wool basketball fan who went to all the big college games, even had season tickets for the Pacers.

"Dwight," he said one night when they were waiting for Christie to get ready for a movie, "son, it's time somebody told you the facts of life. You'd never have made the pros. Why not is obvious to everybody who knows anything. You didn't get your scholarship for the same reason: since you're not a natural like Larry Bird, you're the wrong color. You want to be a basketball star in this decade, you got to go back where you came from and find a black momma and daddy." Christie's dad laughed while giving Dwight's knee a sympathetic pat. "Sorry, kid, but that's affirmative action for you."

Dwight never did find a written definition of affirmative action. He thought it meant that niggers were taking revenge for their imagined hurts. Whatever, Dwight tried to forget the big round ball and get on with his life.

He had worked as security guard at a shopping mall in Indy, where arresting a few kids got him friendly with some real policemen. He liked what he saw of law enforcement and decided to do things right by attending the state academy at Plainfield. The academy certificate wasn't required for a police job in Sardisvale, but it gained him a higher starting salary and more respect.

People still remembered his court stardom, reminisced with him, tried to make him feel good. But Dwight was definitely down, and he alone knew how much he missed playing basketball. Sure, he'd gone one-on-one at the park, messed around with a team of has-beens at the Y once in a while, but it would never be the same. Sometimes he'd sit and stare at his powerful, skilled hand...spread the fingers... white fingers...then turn them into an angry white fist. The guys at the Full Stop gas station heard him bitching about niggers one day and told him he ought to join the Ku Klux Klan. He hadn't known the Klan was still around—there weren't any niggers in town, even in the county—but he'd said he'd be interested. That's how he'd come to be initiated the previous summer in a dinky little ceremony with half a dozen fat old men in the back of Hackerman's barn.

Disappointing. His brother Klansmen had assured him they'd let him know when there was a meeting, but Dwight had long since stopped holding his breath.

He'd been surprised, though hardly excited, when told to be in the forestry Saturday night. He was just too down. Seemed silly to be putting on the white satin hood he'd had in his glove compartment ever since the initiation—silly because he was six-four and because nobody else had a shiny new black and red four-wheel drive like the one he'd put most of his first six months' salary on. So much for disguise.

Dwight went alone to the meeting. He wasn't really hanging out with anybody special, hadn't been tight with anyone since he'd become a cop. To most of his former buddies, obeying the law wasn't very important; when Dwight was around, everyone—including him—was a little uncomfortable.

So he arrived in the forestry alone, jolted into a parking place of his own creation, pulled on the stupid damn' satin hood, and tramped through some winter-dead brush to the clearing.

Half a dozen Coleman lanterns outlined a semi-circle, and another three burned in front of a rough wooden platform in its opening. A microphone-topped lectern on the platform bore a white drop cloth emblazoned with red block letters: KKK.

Hooded men unloaded folding chairs from the back of a pickup and placed them inside the circle, facing the platform. Dwight grabbed an armload of chairs, set them up as a back row, and sat down on one. Someone said, "Thanks, champ."

Every face was covered, though only two men wore knee-length white sheets in addition to their hoods. Those two talked together behind the platform.

Of the forty or so chairs, about a third remained unoccupied. The two men in robes swung chairs onto the platform and sat down on them.

Dwight jumped when a drumroll issued from the darkness opposite the platform. The men on the stage stood and motioned for the audience to stand, also. The roll changed to a steady march beat, and a small group approached the platform by a central aisle: two hooded children—one staggering under his burden of an American flag, the other more easily carrying a smaller white flag with a red KKK insignia—and a man in a full white robe that dragged the ground. Gold trimmed the cuffs of its flowing sleeves. On his chest was a gold cross outlined in black.

The children set the flags into bases at both ends of the platform, then stood among the audience.

The drum beat stopped suddenly, leaving a moment of unexpected, breathtaking silence.

One of the men on the stage advanced to the lectern. "Please bow your heads to be led in prayer by our revered Kludd."

Dwight hadn't much truck with religion, but he didn't mind, in fact, even liked public praying. The prayer that started the local basketball games had always made him feel good, accepted, an important member of the group.

The other robed figure on the platform came to the lectern, spread his arms aloft, and threw back his head. "Almighty God, Who punished Noah's son Ham by making him black and evermore a servant, bless tonight this gathering of Your children of the Greater Sardisvale Klavern of the Ku Klux Klan. Be with us as we seek to carry out Your will by ridding the world forever of those who would mongrelize the human race.

"We ask that You also be with our Province Titan as he represents our glorious state next month at the National Klonvocation.

"And we beseech You to be with our own Exalted Cyclops and with us as we daily carry out Your plans to destroy Bolshevik Demons and preserve the chosen Christian White Race, the Holy Institution of Segregation, and the Constitution of the United States of America. In the name of Your Son Jesus Christ we pray. Amen!

"You may be seated. I turn the meeting back over to our Province Titan."

The first robed figure returned to the microphone. "Thank you, Brother Kludd." He was less dramatic than the Kludd, his voice reminding Dwight of someone on television news—calm, educated-sounding. "Good evening, men, and welcome. Some of you are with us for the first time and have our special greetings. Many more found it too difficult to be here on such short notice, but are with us in spirit and will be promptly apprised of what transpires here tonight. We are many, and we will prevail!"

A scattering of tentative applause.

"I wish now to introduce to you the man chiefly responsible for our local success—our leader for twenty years, our master, the Grand Exalted Cyclops of the Greater Sardisvale Area Ku Klux Klan!"

Drum roll again. The audience on their feet, clapping, shouting "Yeah! All right!" as the man in full regalia mounted the platform. Dwight didn't recognize him.

The Cyclops permitted a prolonged standing ovation before he finally motioned for the audience to be seated.

"Thank you." He lacked the classy tone of the other man, but put Dwight in mind of Coach Tracey, someone who would enforce his own opinions, no matter what.

"This meeting tonight is a emergency. Somethin' happened this week that we shouldn't have allowed, and we won't never let it happen again! Here's the fella involved. He'll explain."

The Grand Cyclops stepped aside, but for a few moments no one came forward. The audience began to shift and murmur. Then a figure on the end of a back row rose hesitantly and shuffled forward. Dwight would have recognized that walk anywhere: Sardisvale's most frequent drunk—Hiram Marshall. Who would listen to him?

At the lectern Hiram adjusted his hood, clearing his throat several times. At first his speech was so soft that the Grand Cyclops grasped his arm and boomed, "Speak up, Brother Klansman!"

After that, Hiram was audible, barely. "Well, for a coupla weeks there's been a nigger in town."

Shocked murmurs swept the two dozen seated men, though some nodded knowingly.

"When I found out, I took my gun to where I thought he'd be and put it upside his head."

White satin hoods bobbed in approval. The Grand Cyclops, forestalling another awkward pause, said, "Go on."

"Well, I told him if he wasn't outta here fast he'd be dead."

He stopped, as though running out of energy, but the audience applauded. Except Dwight, who couldn't believe Hiram was being treated like a hero. All he'd done was mouth off—not so brave when your hand was full of a gun.

Hiram looked around nervously, then said, more shakily, "That's all."

The Grand Cyclops stepped immediately to the lectern, shoving the hooded Hiram aside. "No! That ain't all! Now that this here man's done done his part, it's up to us to make good his threat!"

Scattered applause, but the Grand Cyclops held up his hand. "Now just shut up and listen to 'im. We've been wearing out our asses sittin' while some old fool hires some shithead nigger to work for him right here in Sardisvale. Ain't no way that's gonna happen no more. We've gotta be more vilagent!

"This ain't no one-man job. It's gotta be all of us watchin' out all the time! You want black bastards to steal our jobs?"

"No," murmured the audience.

"I can't hear ya."

"No!"

"You want 'em to rape our wives?"

Shouts of "No!"

"You want 'em to marry our daughters?"

"No, by damn! No! No!" The woods rang with agitated cries.

"You want niggers to leave Sardisvale alive?"

"No! Never!" Shouts, applause, beating on the metal chairseats with feet for at least four minutes.

The Grand Cyclops at last raised both hands for silence. "Me and the other leaders of this Klavern been makin' some careful plans. We got the lines of contact all figured out, and your own contact'll be lettin' you know what you're supposed to do. We'll keep the same old signals of thumb in the belt with three fingers pointin' down and the Co-cola carton, but the lines of contact is gonna be tighter. Ever' one of you's important, so mind your duty. When you joined this Klavern, you pledged allegiance to us all. Now let's close our meetin' by pledgin' allegiance to the flag of this great country, God's chosen America!"

Dwight was agitated. In fact, angry. He could see that the group wasn't any important brotherhood, it was—except for him and that Titan from out of town—a bunch of wimps who couldn't wear their uniforms in public, who trespassed after dark, and who talked loud with no action. The worst of it was their idea of Hiram Marshall as a hero. A hero! A guy who draped himself on a barstool all weekend, then staggered onto the sidewalk, passed out, and wasted policemen's valuable time while they poured him home to his kid, who was so cowed she wouldn't even look in the eye of the policeman who rescued her drunken dad from spending the night on the ground. A hero! What kind of group thought anything permanent would come of Hiram's pitiful words?

Oh, they talked about action, but they didn't have a snowball's chance in hell of doing what a trained, powerful man could. Time somebody showed 'em!

Dwight whirled around and strode toward his Jeep, not bothering to salute or recite, separating himself from his brother Klansmen, ignoring their fervent promise of "liberty and justice for all."

CHAPTER IX

SUNDAY RITUALS

Jonathan Simms raised his head from saying grace, a mellow smile on his craggy features. Sunday was his favorite day of the week—the most structured, the most harmoniously balanced.

Not the least important part was breakfast, for he could count on Betsy to produce a special omelet and cinnamon toast. The boys were fresh and happy then, and Jonathan made an extra effort to include them in conversation.

"Matthew, want to go Christmas shopping with Daddy tomorrow?" he asked his older son on Sunday, December twentieth.

"Will we see Santy Claus?" asked Matthew.

"Sany Coz, Sany Coz!" Mark laughed, beating on his plate with his spoon.

"Yes, I expect so," Betsy said.

"Betsy, are you sure we should encourage—?"

"Not now, please, Dear. I'll show you the article that says there's nothing wrong with it. You know Santa Claus will be at the Christmas Eve party, anyway. That's been a tradition ever since this congregation began."

"Just because something is old, it doesn't have to be preserved—" The telephone's ring interrupted him.

"Get the phone, please, Jonathan. I'm sure it's for you. I'll have the boys ready to go by the time you hang up."

"Hello. Reverend Simms speaking."

"Jonathan, Tim. I won't be at church this morning, but I'll be over as usual this afternoon. Just didn't want you to make other plans. I need to talk to you."

"Tim, is everything OK?"

"Tell you later. Thanks."

Betsy had the boys coated and hatted, ready to be taken to Sunday School by the time Jonathan returned, puzzled—worried, actually—to the kitchen.

"A problem, Honey?"

"No...well, maybe. That was Tim. He won't be at church, but will be over this afternoon as usual. He sounded upset, though. I hope he's not back-tracking into depression again."

"He's been doing fine for so long; I'll bet it's something about work. Being chief of police has to be one crisis after another. I'm amazed he's in a good humor so much of the time."

"Jerry has certainly been a trouble-free son, even through his mother's illness and death and Tim's depression."

"Matthew, keep your hat on. 'Bye, Sweeties. I'll meet you in the hall after Sunday School. 'Bye, Jonathan. See you after the service."

Jonathan kissed his wife, leaving her to clear the breakfast dishes and listen for baby Mary.

He dropped the boys off in the Primary Department and hurried to his office, where he habitually spent a half hour in private prayer before Sunday School ended. That morning, however, his time alone was less satisfying than he expected.

Timothy's call had blown a cloud over Sunday for Jonathan, one that didn't even disperse later when the congregation sang "Joy to the World."

The first hymn was the time Jonathan scanned the sanctuary in a mental roll-check of his flock. The Stocktons were in their usual pew, but Maggie McGilvray was not beside Phyllis, hadn't been since Mrs. McGilvray's death.

Jonathan felt a twinge of guilt. He hadn't tried recently to woo Maggie back to the church. She had been witheringly cool to his last efforts—in fact, had always been cool, almost rude, to him. Maybe he should make a New Year's resolution to try again.

There on the next to last row was Susan Marshall, pale and scared-looking, but at least present, though her dad was, as always, absent. If he had been there, Jerry Haskins wouldn't be sitting behind Susan, trying to get her attention. Jerry also wouldn't be way on the back row if Tim hadn't been kept away.

Jonathan frowned. Maybe it was only some police business that was bothering the chief, since his son, Jerry, looked happy. But Jonathan's friend's voice had reverberated with the deeper, worried quality it had had in the days of his depression, when he and Jonathan had first become friends.

In those dark times following Lisa's death, Tim had been unable to function as police chief. Instead of removing him from office, the City Council ordered him to obtain counseling and imposed a mandatory leave of absence for three months.

The psychiatrist at the Community Mental Health Clinic was in town from Indy only once a week, so Tim had instead elected to see Pastoral Counselor Jonathan Simms, whom he knew in only a formal way on Sunday mornings.

Their sessions together were at first five days a week, then three, then two. By the end of Tim's leave of absence, Sardisvale had a police chief who was ready for full resumption of his duties.

After that Tim continued once-a-week sessions with Jonathan at the mutually satisfactory hour of three on Sunday afternoons.

When both men agreed therapy was no longer necessary, they continued to get together every Sunday afternoon to enjoy each other's company while they planned to bring righteousness, law, and order to Sardisvale.

Indeed, the Lord worked in mysterious ways, reflected Jonathan, for Lisa Haskins's death had resulted in a much-needed best friend for Timothy and for Jonathan, both of whose jobs were exceptionally lonely.

Tim had once remarked that preaching must be a lonely task, that he himself always worked better when there was dialogue.

Jonathan had replied that dialogue was fine for things like investigations and counseling. Instruction, however, required an instructor's monologue, and that was a part of his job the minister relished with never a trace of loneliness.

With "Joy to the World" ended and the congregation seated, he began the day's sermon with pleasure.

* * *

At the doorbell's ring that afternoon, Jonathan leaped to his feet. "I'll get it. It should be Tim."

"All right, Dear. Tell him I said hi," Betsy called from upstairs.

"Timothy!" Jonathan clasped both his more delicate hands around the police chief's large, burly one stretched out to him.

"Jonathan."

"Come in. Come in and tell me what's wrong. Something is, I know by your voice."

"It's not what you think, thank God. There's no problem with me, or even with Jerry. But this is confidential.Maybe dangerous."

"Nobody's here but us. That is, Betsy's upstairs with the kids. When they wake up, she's taking them over to Zion Baptist for a children's chorale and sing-a-long. She says to tell you hi."

"You're really lucky in your family, or have I said that before?" Timothy laughed.

"You have, but I don't mind hearing it again."

"And again and again. Listen, I'm feeling a little unlucky in mine right now."

"I thought you said Jerry was all right."

"Jerry's not my only family, remember. There's my brother, Greg."

"He wasn't at church this morning, and neither was his drinking buddy Hiram Marshall."

"No, of course not, and I'm here to tell you the reason why not and to pick your brain to stop them before they do some serious harm."

"Hold up long enough for me to get us a couple of sodas." Jonathan opened the door of his study, kept closed to exploring youngsters, and motioned Tim in.

When Jonathan returned, Police Chief Timothy Haskins had hung his coat on the doorknob and sunk into the big overstuffed chair. He had laid his head back and covered his eyes with the palms of his hands. He jumped to an upright position as Jonathan set two Pepsis on the desktop.

"Good Heavens, Tim, you are jumpy. Here, take a swig and let me in on the problem. What's this about Greg and Hiram?"

Tim took a long pull from the bottle, then rose and closed the study door. "Got to be sure what we say here is in strictest confidence. This town is crawling with spies."

Jonathan frowned. "Timothy, aren't you carrying this secret stuff a bit too far?"

"No, I don't think so. The Klan is activating again."

"The Klan! I thought that was long dead—and good riddance. Anyway, I can't believe there could be many of them, even if they are organized. They're a powerless minority, surely."

"That's wishful thinking. A couple of dozen men met last night, and Greg and Hiram were both there. Hiram, as a matter of fact, was guest speaker."

"I don't believe that! Hiram can't make a sensible sentence when he's sober, much less drunk, the way he always is after dark."

"He did, however, last night. He was actually a sort of hero. Seems he held a gun up to some black guy's head and ordered him out of Sardisvale forever."

"Whoa! What black guy in Sardisvale? There are none that I know about."

"This one was working at the McGilvrays', helping that old logger take down some trees. It must be the black guy's job Jerry took starting yesterday. Logger's daughter is one of Jerry's teachers."

"Maggie McGilvray's mixed up in this? She's even weirder than old Kemmer. But how did Hiram get involved?"

"That I don't know."

"Wait, are you telling me that Greg reported all this to his brother the police chief?"

"I wish! One of the reasons this discussion has to be confidential is that we've got to protect my informant."

"You have an informant who's a policeman?"

"I didn't say that."

"No, but that's how they finally broke the Klan in Mississippi and caught those civil rights workers' murderers. There was this policeman who'd always been a member of the Klan, and everybody trusted him...but you probably know all that."

"What am I going to do about Greg? If the Klan becomes active again, there'll be serious trouble; and he'll be right in the middle of it."

"I wish the Klan had been there to hear my text this morning—Isaiah:11—the prophecy of Jesus' coming: 'He shall not judge by what His eyes see, or decide by what His ears hear; but with righteousness He shall judge the poor, and decide with equity for the meek of the earth.'"

90

"Jonathan, think! Some of those Klan members *were* there listening to you this morning. Hearing a few words about equity isn't going to make them feel less threatened or make them suddenly love those neighbors they've been hating all their lives, were even taught by their own parents to hate. Preaching at them isn't the answer. No offense, Good Buddy, but talk isn't going to make them see blacks and Jews and 'preverts' and whatever else as being just as human as they are."

"Have you tried talking to Greg? Nobody could be more brotherly than he was to you after Lisa died."

"God, Jonathan, don't I know it! I owe him a debt I can never in a million years repay. That's part of my problem right now. I have to be very careful what I say to Greg. I don't dare jeopardize my informant. If I say the wrong thing, Greg's smart enough to figure out that I'm getting information from somebody on the inside. Then everybody will be in even bigger trouble."

"What do you think I should be doing besides 'preaching at them?'"

"I wish I knew. A few years ago, when the Klan reactivated down in southeast Indiana, I did do some reading up on prejudice."

"Gordon Allport, I'll bet! His is the classic work on the subject. We read him in seminary in my class on social problems."

Jonathan spun his chair around and quickly withdrew a large volume from a bottom shelf. He blew dust off its top. "I'll just do a little reading up on the subject. Maybe you're right: our churches should take more action than just preaching. I'll propose to the Ministerial Association that we form a committee to study prejudice."

"Everybody who needs some enlightenment isn't a member of a church. No, the action needs to be civic rather than only religious. Anyway, how're you going to explain your sudden interest in spreading tolerance without telling anybody I've confided in you about this?"

"Tim, I've been remiss, and I thank you for making me see it. I don't have a sudden interest in tolerance; the interest was always there, it's just been lying dormant. That's a disservice to my congregation and my community. We'll develop an ongoing program for raising this community's consciousness of diversity. That's it! A Diversity Awareness Program! I'm going to have to study this, think it through. I promise to start on it tomorrow. Soon enough for you?"

"I sure hope so." The older man smiled wearily. "I sure do, but I have a terrible feeling all of us should have been doing something about this long before tomorrow."

CHAPTER X

UNEXPECTED TERRITORY

The day Michelle Riddick was laid off by the Marco plant in Blue Grass, she left work so early she was home to her all-black neighborhood on the west side of Boonetown by three-thirty.

Her reflection in the front storm door looked smart as ever: just what John Molloy ordered—navy blue slacks, white shirt, wool blazer—a young woman dressing for success. Ha! A young woman without a job. She tried to keep her posture and walk as self-confident as ever; but her stepmother, Warine, immediately remarked, "I know by your face what happened. The strike's still on, isn't it?"

All Michelle could do was nod, sink to the sofa, and bury her face in her hands. What a bummer!

"I'll get you some iced tea." Warine lightly patted Michelle's stylish Gerri-curl.

Michelle roused herself a few minutes later to answer a knock at the front door.

There stood a beautifully dressed woman her stepmother's age, a fine image to emulate. "Why, Addie Pollard! Come right in. Warine's just in back. She'll be glad to see you."

"Whatever are you doing home from work at this hour?"

"The strike didn't get settled, so the plant's closing, probably for good. 'Most everybody but the foremen got laid off today."

93

"You poor thing. I can see you're upset. You've been there how long now?"

"Three years—ever since I graduated."

"I heard your voice, Addie. Here's iced tea for all of us. What can you say to cheer Michelle up?"

Warine was as tiny and bird-like as Addie Pollard was majestic, a ship under full sail; but Warine managed her family with the same calm practicality Addie used in her classroom. They had for many years depended on each other to give common-sense advice in times of crisis. Michelle turned to her stepmother's friend with hopeful expectancy.

"Warine, Honey, Michelle's got a right to feel bad for a few days. She'll be fine."

"I'm better off than JoAnne. She and Tyrone are supposed to get married right after New Year's, and they need every penny they thought she'd make."

"Time to get out the old want-ads."

The women drank for a few minutes in silence.

"Michelle, I think I know the perfect career for you; and maybe JoAnne would be interested in giving it a try, too."

"What's that, Addie?"

"You probably don't remember—Warine does, though— that when my Sam was changing jobs about ten years ago, I spent a couple of summer vacations from teaching by making us some good money selling encyclopedias door to door."

"I remember," Warine responded. "I was jealous of how nice you looked every day while I was flapping around in houseshoes among all these kids who were eating me out of house and home."

"Well, you know I envy you your lovely children and stepchildren. Michelle here is always so attractive and poised, I'd be real pleased to recommend her to my old district manager. He'll be lucky to get her."

Michelle mentally flashed to herself being received graciously in well-appointed living rooms, to herself lecturing knowledgeably to aspiring salespeople, to herself seated at the president's desk...a more refined, more exciting work than the factory could ever have provided. "I'd be much obliged if you'd talk to him about me. Let me go over to JoAnne's and see if she's interested. We make a good team, and she'd be really grateful to you, too."

"Good, Dear. You call me before school in the morning; and if you haven't changed your mind, I'll phone Mr. Hendrix tomorrow on my free period."

Michelle rushed out without even changing clothes and almost ran the few blocks to JoAnne's house. Her friend, however, had undressed already and was bundled into a chenille bathrobe, her face tear-streaked, make-up smeared, hair in disarray.

"Oh, Michelle, what am I going to do?" she wailed. "Tyrone made the security deposit, but I'm supposed to pay the January rent, and we have the furniture payments, and Tyrone's mother—"

"Just stop it, JoAnne; you're crying over spilt milk, wasting energy you're going to need. We've got to find different work now, and Addie Pollard has a great idea."

JoAnne was not enthusiastic about the proposed door-to-door selling. "Tyrone'll have a fit when he finds out I'm walking the streets. He's always thinking I have to be protected."

"Dummy! We're hardly going to be streetwalkers! You and me, we've taken care of ourselves through a lot of boys making moves on us. You haven't forgotten how just because you're in love. Here's a chance to dress up a little more than we could at the factory and talk to decent family people right in their own homes."

"But you're good at that—talking, persuading people. I'll forget what I'm supposed to say."

"It won't matter because all you'll have to do is tell people what a wonderful product we have." Michelle raised her voice authoritatively. "Those encyclopedias can help their kids do better in school, improve their own performance at work. Before you know it, we'll be top salespersons and get important desk jobs like we'd never in a million years have gotten at the factory."

"Hold on," JoAnne had covered her ears. "Don't make me listen to the sales pitch any more than I have to. You've convinced me; I'll buy three sets of encyclopedias just as soon as we make our fortune." She giggled and hugged Michelle. "You always make me feel better, and I love you. Tyrone's OK, but I wouldn't want to live without you."

Michelle went home happy, eager; today, JoAnne—tomorrow, refrigerators to Eskimos, or encyclopedias to Hoosiers. Yeah, she could do that!

* * *

By the week before Christmas, Michelle and JoAnne had completed their training: lectures, demonstration calls, and travel with and observation of experienced salespeople. Then began the real test: "working" a neighborhood on their own.

Their first assignment was to a "crew" of four—the rookies and two white men, experienced encyclopedia salesmen, but unfamiliar with the Central Indiana territory. Both were schoolteachers from the Chicago area who supplemented their salaries during vacations with door-to-door work.

The crew met at four-thirty Monday morning in the parking lot of Blue Grass's Pancake Parlor.

"How'd you manage to get here so early if you came all the way from Chicago?" Michelle asked through chattering teeth while she waited for a cup of steaming coffee.

Rick, the driver, offered donuts from a paper bag. "Jim and I drove down to Louisville yesterday, picked up all our samples cases, then came on here and checked into a motel so we could watch the ball game and be ready for an early start."

"Early is right!" JoAnne commented.

Jim climbed into the front seat with coffee for the group. "Let's get this show on the road. If we leave in the next five minutes, we should be in Fort Wayne ready to start ringing doorbells by nine-thirty."

"Hit it, Rick. We're ready."

"No coffee for me, folks. I'm going right back to sleep," announced JoAnne.

"Fish that blanket out of the wayback. Sweet dreams."

Michelle also curled up under the blanket as soon as she'd finished her decaf and donut. She, too, could make a few z's.

Rick hummed softly and steered them north through the December chill.

* * *

"What was that?"

"Hey, man, what's happening?"

"Sounds like there's an earthquake under the hood. And I was having the best dream."

Rick pulled onto the shoulder of the road. "I've no idea what's causing the bucking and missing, but it may be serious. Jim, get me a flashlight from the glove compartment and let's have a look."

The two men peered under the hood, then returned to the warmth of the car to report no enlightenment.

"I'm no good at stuff like this. Where are we, anyway?" Jim asked.

"I think we're five or so miles south of Sardisvale. I saw a sign not too long ago. Let's get as close to there as we can."

The passengers covered their ears with their hands while the ailing car again bucked noisily along the highway.

"I see a gas station, the 'Sardisvale Full Stop!'"

"Thank God! Another ten minutes of this and all my teeth will fall out."

"Don't get carried away; the station is closed and deserted."

"Wouldn't you know!"

"Look. That sign says they open in an hour. I'd rather not try to go on. This old heap may die on us. See if there's another blanket back there for Jim and me."

There was, and soon all four were settled with minimal discomfort.

* * *

An hour and a half later, a knocking on the driver's window woke them all. The gas station attendant seemed sympathetic to the problem, but could do nothing till the mechanic arrived in another forty-five minutes. By then everyone was wide awake enough to worry about work.

"Let's at least go inside and warm up."

Several young men in jeans were standing around the small office's space heater. Conversation stopped when the two white men and two black women entered and sat on the chairs along the wall.

"How long a drive is it from here to Fort Wayne, would you say?" Rick asked one of the men.

"It's a good two and a half hours, even if you have a heavy foot. That where you're headin'?"

"That's where we *were* heading," Jim said.

The local men exchanged glances and went outside, followed by the attendant.

Half an hour later, the mechanic entered the office and addressed Rick. "Just what I thought: bad carburetor. Got to be replaced."

"Can you do it?"

"Sure can—soon's I order one from in town."

"Uh oh! How far's town?"

"Only ten minutes, but they's busy and we's busy."

"How long before we can be on the road again?"

"Well, I can't be real exact, but I'd say four, maybe five, hours."

"Oh, God! Would you get on it right away, please? The sooner the better," Rick urged. He turned to Michelle, JoAnne, and Jim. "I hate to be the one to say it, gang, but no way are we going to make Fort Wayne in time to work today. Late afternoon is the worst possible doorbell-ringing—lots of kids around, parents rushing in from work to start supper."

"OK. We're convinced."

"Yeah, Rick, and we know it's not your fault. These things happen."

JoAnne sniffled and excused herself. Michelle rested her elbows on her knees and stared glumly at the floor, knowing full well her friend was in the restroom crying.

Everything was a catastrophe to JoAnne now that she had the pre-wedding nerves.

Jim rocked back on his chair's chrome legs and propped himself against the wall, hands behind his head, forehead creased with concentration, while Rick discussed costs of new versus rebuilt carburetors. Finally the attendant phoned an order for a rebuilt model and went outside again. A steady stream of cars and trucks passed through the gas pump lanes.

At the same moment JoAnne, red-eyed, re-entered the office, Jim leaped to his feet. "I've got it!" he almost shouted. "Look!" He pointed to the torn, grubby map of Sardisvale thumbtacked to the wall over the greasy old desk.

"So?"

"Yeah, so?"

"So we'll work Sardisvale today instead of Fort Wayne. Maybe we'll make our fortune. Maybe we'll bring knowledge to rural Middle America starting right here, where probably the only sets of encyclopedias are in the library and the schools."

"Let's don't get carried away, Jim. I have a feeling Michelle and I are a definite minority in this town and won't be very welcome here, to say the least. You saw that bunch of rednecks giving us the eye," said JoAnne. "My Tyrone'll be mad as hell if I work this town alone."

The group fell silent. The attendant came back from the pumps and sat at the desk.

"Hey, listen, crew," Rick began, "I think Jim's onto something. None of us can afford to waste the whole day. Since we don't have our own territory map, we'll just play it safe. JoAnne and I can work a street together—every other house or something, so we can stay in sight of each other. You two can work the same way if you want to."

"I'm not worried. In fact, I'm more than ready to work a street on my own for a change," Michelle insisted.

"Well, at least let's ask where the best neighborhood is and start you off there."

When the group turned to the attendant, he grinned and fidgeted with the credit card imprinter on the desktop, volunteering nothing, though he must have heard their conversation.

Rick asked, "Would you please show us the safest area for a young lady to go door-to-door by herself?"

"And also do you have any idea how we might get there? We do have a transportation problem!"

"Back in a sec," the attendant said, and he hurried out to pump gas.

"This map reminds me," Rick said, "I've been through here before. There's a courthouse square centrally located. Let's plan to meet there between twelve and one and see how things are going."

"And let's buy three of these city maps so nobody gets hopelessly lost. Maybe we can salvage this day yet."

The attendant at last returned and recommended a street for Michelle's first territory. In addition, he sold them maps and offered them a ride to their planned areas with one of the mechanics. "That there customized van's his. Got room for damn' near all of Sardisvale—leastways, all the girls." He leered and motioned them toward the door.

Michelle, who was the first out, noticed a bright red tow truck parked prominently, almost blocking the access road. Firmly anchored on the outside roof of its cab was an empty Coca Cola carton.

"Hey, folks, give me one minute." She hurried back into the office and bought four Cokes from the drink machine.

* * *

By the time she stepped down from the van with her shiny new samples case and tapped her navy-blue mid-heels along the sidewalk of Foliage Street, she was in good spirits again, rested, confident, energized by her morning shot of caffeine. Ready for anything.

CHAPTER XI

BESIDE HOOSIER HOLLOW

Monday morning Susan sprang out of bed the minute she opened her eyes. After a seemingly interminable weekend, the first day of her new job had arrived at last. Mrs. Simms had asked her to be at the parsonage by ten o'clock, prepared to stay later than usual, and Hiram had OK'd the plan. He seemed to trust the Simmses implicitly. That was enough to make Susan feel Christmas had arrived a few days early.

She was half-dressed before she noticed it was only seven o'clock. Hours to kill. If she made pancakes for Hiram's breakfast, cleaning up afterward would take more time, use up the long minutes till her job began.

Slow though she seemed to be, it was only eight-thirty when she burst into the gray, unseasonably warm day. She could walk through the park alone, beat on and put her ear to the bark of the giant oak housing squirrels, hear them scrambling up and down. She and Maurice had discovered that tree on one of their walks, but... No, she mustn't think about Maurice.

A park stroll was out, though, since the basketball courts were already full of vacationing boys; and little kids were roller skating around the rec building. She'd have to take the long way again, over to Chicago Street and past the side of the Hoosier Hollow Bar.

Normal opening time of the bar was not till eleven, so Susan was surprised when she reached Chicago Street and saw two high school seniors careen a rattly old car into the Hoosier Hollow parking lot, slam out of the car, and sprint to the bar's side door, on which they pounded. Susan watched, puzzled, from behind a myrtle bush. The door opened promptly to admit the boys. Were they working there? Having some sort of club meeting?

Brad Abel and Gary Scheider were barely known to Susan. Loud, swaggering, they always ignored her, nothing at all like Jerry Haskins. He was probably on his way to Miss Maggie's already. Susan had time enough to go back and watch the loggers, and she really wouldn't mind having Jerry talk to her a little if she were sitting beside Miss Maggie, the only grown-up Susan knew who wasn't always trying to make her tell everything that went through her head. Nobody else respected her privacy. But first she'd check out Foliage Street from the peep-hole she'd discovered on Saturday.

She crossed the Hoosier Hollow parking lot. Only two cars were there—the boys' and one that must belong to whoever let them in. Then she sidled along the narrow passageway between a high board fence and the building side opposite the one the boys had entered.

The gate was still locked, the grating peep-hole still obscured by knotted vines that left a small clearing just the right size and height for her eyes. Susan looked out.

No traffic. No voices. No signs of people. The house across the street, in full view, was not boarded the way she knew its neighbors were. In fact, it still had glass and curtains in the windows. While Susan was examining it, she saw a face peer out from one of the filthy windows—a face indistinct, but vaguely familiar.

Footsteps came tapping along the pavement. The face in the window disappeared. Susan shivered a little with anticipation. So much better to watch the world from a hiding place than to be exposed where others would watch her.

On the other side of Foliage Street, the source of the tapping came into view—navy blue mid-heels. Susan gasped at the unprecedented sight: a pretty young black woman, slim and stylish in a belted trench coat, her body listing a little to the side on which she carried an oversized briefcase.

The young woman slowed her brisk gait. Stopped. She set the case down for a few moments and seemed to be studying the house across the street. With the case again in hand, she walked to the front door and knocked loudly. Almost immediately a man opened the door and admitted the young woman.

Susan frowned. The man, she was now convinced, was Greg Haskins, her dad's drinking buddy, Jerry's uncle. How weird! Greg lived on the other side of town. Of course, he spent a lot of time at Hoosier Hollow, but all the houses in the block across from the bar had been vacant for at least two years. The owner was trying to find a developer from Indy, she'd heard Hiram say, so—.

The front door of the house flew open. Out ran the young woman, straight across Foliage Street, straight toward Susan.

"Bitch!" Greg Haskins shouted after her before he retreated and slammed the door.

The young woman was using both arms to clutch together the open briefcase. When she reached the curb, she stumbled, spilling pamphlets and several books onto the brown grass and rough sidewalk not fifteen feet from the gate through which Susan watched.

"Oh, damn!" the young woman muttered, kneeling. "And God damn that honky bastard who thinks he can have whatever he wants! I guess he'll think twice before he messes with me again. Smartass fool!" She dumped the remaining contents of the case onto the ground and began gathering, stacking, packing in a disorganized, almost violent way.

"Bad luck! Here, let me help."

Startled, Susan recognized Jerry Haskins bending down to hand the young woman a book.

The woman leaped to her feet and took a step backward. "Not another one! What the hell do *you* want?"

Shocking pink suffused Jerry's face to the roots of his red hair, but he continued to hold out the soiled volume.

"Oh." The woman snatched the book from his hand. "Thanks."

"Hey, your chin's bleeding." Jerry gestured toward her face.

"Don't touch me!"

Jerry jerked back his hand. "I was just going to—"

"Shit! I'm sorry, but it's better nobody messes with me right now. Nothing personal to you, you understand; it's because of the dirty old man in that house."

Jerry's color was normal again. He turned away from Susan to look across the street, but he was still close enough for her to hear every word. "That house? Nobody lives there."

"Well, somebody's there now, for sure! He tried to put a move on me, and when I tried to kick him where his brain is—almost got 'em, too—he slapped me. I got out of there plenty fast with my samples more or less OK."

"I don't know who could be in there. Listen, I think I better go call my dad. He's the police chief, and he ought to be told somebody's holing up over there. Are you sure you're all right?"

"Well, I'm having a Murphy's Law-type day so far. Oh, look—my stocking's torn, too. That figures. Not putting me on about your daddy the police chief, are you?"

Jerry shook his head. The dimple in his left cheek appeared along with his smile. Susan guessed he thought, like her, that the strange woman's talk was interesting and a little bit funny.

"Are you really going to call him?"

"Sure am. The bar's still closed, so I'm going to run on to this lady's where I'm working. I'll call from there, and

Dad'll come right over. You stay here by the bar—near the street, near traffic." Jerry peered in both directions. "Though it's mighty quiet here till Hoosier Hollow opens."

"I'll be in this little alley." The black woman gestured toward Susan's passageway. "Anybody else tries to get on my case, I'll tell 'im to wait for the big chief."

Jerry left running, and the young woman finished repacking her samples case. She set it down next to the old gray plank fence and sat on it, staring for a few moments at the brick wall of Hoosier Hollow with its single first floor window tightly shut. She glanced across the street, tossed her head, turned away, and fished for and opened a small make-up case extracted from her trench coat pocket.

Susan could see the young woman's face clearly: warm brown eyes, so much more definitive than her own pale hazel ones; full, pleasant mouth, even with the bloody cut beginning to puff. Susan touched her own thin lips, fingered a tiny scar under her nose, wished she felt like smiling. Jerry had such a friendly smile.

"That's the best I can do out here," the young woman spoke, apparently to her reflection in a mirror. "Damn' sicko!" she said more loudly, snapping shut the gold compact. She pushed up the coatsleeve covering her watch. "I'll give the cops ten minutes, then get on with this crazy job and hope there aren't anymore stupid—." She stopped suddenly when someone raised the opaque window opening from Hoosier Hollow onto the passageway.

"Who the hell's out there disturbin' my pissin'?" Brad Abel peered out from the bar's men's room.

"Hey, Gary, here she is, waitin' for us."

The young woman sprang to her feet, but Brad was quick. He vaulted the window ledge and grabbed her arms. The compact clattered to the pavement barely a foot from the gate hiding Susan.

"Let go of me!" The young woman's loud scream was cut short when Brad clapped a hand over her mouth. He barely managed to avoid her wild kicks while he attempted to keep one of her thrashing arms at her side. Gary had jumped out of the window and restrained the other arm.

Brad ordered, "Give me your handkerchief!"

The two boys wrestled the young woman to the ground, and Brad stuffed the handkerchief into her mouth.

Susan moaned, but the scuffle on the other side of the gate masked her soft expression of horror.

Gary jumped up and moved over the five feet of broken concrete to the sidewalk.

Brad was sitting astride the struggling woman. "You keep a lookout and tell me if anyone's comin'," he panted. "I'm gonna give this nigra bitch somethin' to remember Sardisvale by." He moved forward on his knees, pinning the young woman's arms with his thighs, and used his freed hands to unzip his already unbuckled jeans.

"A cop!"

"What?"

"A cop car. Quick! Let's get out of here."

Brad stared down at the young woman, whose head tossed violently back and forth, banging her cheeks against the pavement.

Susan's hands flew to her own cheeks, pressing and distorting her face.

"Here comes the car, Brad!"

The young woman's muffled moans grew louder.

While Susan stared, frozen in horror, at the figures on the ground, Brad lifted the young black woman up by the shoulders and banged the back of her head down onto the cement. He lifted her shoulders again, but when he saw her head loll insensibly sideways, he dropped her and leaped back through the window already entered by Gary. The sound of the window's closing echoed in the suddenly silent passageway.

Susan gasped in relief. Thank God! She took a step backward, then quickly positioned herself at her peephole again. Yes, the satiny white blouse, exposed where the trench coat had been dragged sideways, rose and fell in a regular rhythm. Susan sighed. Her gaze crept gingerly to the smooth brown face, now framed by irregular trickles of blood. The white handkerchief protruded from the lipstick-reddened mouth, now still. The silence lasted only a few seconds—until the police car stopped at the curb.

Susan clasped her trembling hands together in thanksgiving. Jerry's daddy! But no, it was someone much younger, vaguely familiar, but not anyone she knew personally.He looked immediately into the passageway. To the left. To the right. Behind him. He ran to the woman on the ground, kneeled over her with his back to the street. His fingers felt along the side of her neck, removed the handkerchief, shoved it into his pants pocket.

A gurgling sigh escaped the young woman. She turned her head, but did not open her eyes. He picked up one of her arms, his fingers clasping her wrist. Of course, taking her pulse. After an interval, he let go her wrist, spread and stared at her palm...spread one of his own hands, stared at it, frowned, then dropped her arm...no, pushed it hard toward the ground, so that the brown hand actually bounced from the pavement. Susan winced when the young woman's hand formed a fist for a moment before half-opening again. There was a moan—the young woman's, or hers?

The policeman stood up, his anger apparent when his head swiveled to survey the passageway, the fence, the brick wall, the window, the gate. Susan ducked her head below the grating.

When she raised it again, the policeman had returned to the patrol car. He'd have to call for help, an ambulance. Instead, he took something from the car, looked up and down the street, and came right back, bent swiftly down. In one hand he held what looked to Susan like a hunting knife. The other hand spread open the young woman's trench coat, farther exposing her white blouse, the white sweater over it—both gently rising and falling.

Susan could hear his intake of breath when he plunged the knife deep into the region of the young woman's stomach, thrust it toward her chest. Hard. He gave a deep grunt.

Spurts of blood followed the knife's passage. Great gushes of blood soaked the white sweater and blouse, reddened the trench coat, the sidewalk, the policeman's uniform.

The man wiped off the knife on the woman's coat, pushed it inside his jacket, into the waist of his pants, and returned to his car.

Susan didn't move. She scarcely breathed. The ensuing sounds reached her consciousness as though they were traveling through layers and layers of cotton...the policeman's voice, the static and response from his car radio...the horrified hubbub of the gathering crowd. She stayed exactly as she had been standing for half an hour.

Her vision had shut down. No longer significant who came within her range of sight. All she could do was stand there.

Jerry Haskins was first, with Maggie and Phyllis close behind; and Maggie knew something was wrong by the way Jerry stooped, then sprang upright again.

"Oh, no! She's all bloody!" Jerry shouted.

The policeman hurried around his car. "Don't touch a thing!"

Phyllis gave a little scream and stepped away. Maggie stopped abruptly in the entrance to the passageway, looked down for a moment, then raised her eyes to the grating in the gate. Her mouth dropped open when she recognized Susan's unblinking hazel eyes.

Sirens pierced the air—the ambulance and two other police cars, one of them driven by Timothy Haskins.

Maggie motioned Phyllis back the way they had come. "Go home, Phyllis. I'll see you later. There's something I have to do."

"But, Maggie—"

"No, wait...go to Betsy's house and tell her to put on a pot of tea. I'll join you there in a few minutes."

Maggie hurried past the front door of Hoosier Hollow, in the opposite direction from the crowd of people rushing toward the little passageway where the young black woman lay dead.

Maggie moved quickly around the side and back of the building, across the parking lot, and along the other side of Hoosier Hollow until she reached the girl leaning forward against the vine-tangled gate.

"Susan," she whispered.

No response.

She touched Susan's shoulder. The girl whirled to face Maggie, then sank to the ground in a huddled, almost fetal position.

Maggie stooped painfully, muscles protesting still from her vigil in the woods on Saturday night. "Susan, I want you to stand up and walk with me, all right? We're going to the Simmses', all right? Don't try to talk till we get there, all right?"

Susan at last raised her head and nodded. She rose and began walking slowly back toward the parking lot.

Maggie delayed following in order to look through the grating. Yes, an excellent view of the entire passageway. Paramedics and policemen milled around on the sidewalk just behind Perry Findlay, the newspaper and police photographer. A blinding flash from his camera made Maggie aware of the sun's absence. The day seemed suddenly colder and grayer. She shivered and forced herself to look at the photographer's subject.

No one stood near the young woman. Isolated, she sprawled on the pavement amid blood-darkened, much-longer-dead leaves.

CHAPTER XII

AT THE PARSONAGE

Maggie had intended only a glance through the gate's grating, but instead had felt wonder, satisfaction, and a numbing, magnetic pull to watch the world unseen. She stayed at Susan's peephole so long that when she turned around, Susan had disappeared.

Across the parking lot, around the building, along Chicago Street, Maggie hurried, still not catching sight of Susan. Had the police found her? Were they already questioning her? Could she even hear them, she seemed so out of it? No, there she was, standing, dazed, on the corner of Chicago and Foliage, staring away from the crowd in front of Hoosier Hollow. Maggie moved quickly toward her.

"Miss Maggie! Miss Maggie, wait up!" It was Jerry Haskins.

"Jerry, I'm going to the Simmses' for a while."

"My dad wants to talk to me about the girl," he said shakily, "about what she told me. He'll take me on over to your house first so I can tell Mr. Kemmer what happened. He must be wondering what's taking us so long."

"Oh, my goodness, I'd forgotten Mr. Kemmer's daughter was supposed to be at my house, too, this morning. Would you please tell her to come on over to the parsonage?"

"Sure...OK. Hi, Susan!" Jerry looked hard at the girl, who was still staring in the opposite direction.

She didn't turn or answer.

"She's upset. We all are." Maggie noticed Jerry's unnatural pallor and gave his arm a pat. "I'll see you later, maybe tomorrow."

"OK, thanks." Jerry turned slowly toward the large group of people surrounding the police cars and ambulance.

Maggie grasped Susan's arm and guided her across Foliage Street, on down Chicago Street toward the parsonage. Neither spoke. Before they reached the steep steps of the Simmses' porch, a siren shrieked—the ambulance beginning its trip to the hospital, no, the funeral home. Susan started, began to tremble. Maggie steadied the girl with a firm hug and accelerated their pace.

Betsy met them at the front door. "Susan, Maggie, what a horrible thing! Do you know what happened? Who was she? Phyllis said Jerry Haskins called for help from her phone, had actually talked to the girl. Susan, did you—?"

Maggie, who had dropped behind when they entered the parsonage, pressed a finger to her lips, shaking her head at Betsy. At the same time, Susan's strange demeanor registered with Betsy, who broke off mid-sentence.

"We could definitely use something hot to drink," Maggie said, unbuttoning her coat.

"Of course, just let me hang up your coats."

"Never mind, Betsy. I'll get them." Maggie waved the minister's wife toward the kitchen. Food and drink were needed; something, anyway, to join the watchers to the real world again. Maggie hung her coat up and handed Susan a wire hanger. "Give me your coat, then wash up in the powder room before we have our tea."

Susan very slowly followed Maggie's directions. As soon as the girl had closed the powder room door, Maggie joined Phyllis and Susan in the kitchen and spoke in a low voice.

"Susan appears to be frightened out of her mind. She was probably a witness to the murder."

"What makes you think so?" Betsy asked.

"She'll have to tell the police—" Phyllis began.

Maggie raised her hand. "Shhh! I'll explain later. Let's see what shape she's in first."

Betsy said, "I'm not sure I have this straight, so correct me if I'm wrong. Jerry Haskins saw some black girl who'd been hit by somebody who'd broken into the old Andersen place."

"And he ran to my house—" Maggie continued.

"But Maggie has no phone," Phyllis interrupted, raising her eyebrows at Maggie, "so they both came to my house. Jerry called his daddy from there and told him about the break-in at the Andersens', but said he thought the girl was all right."

"The trouble was, though," Maggie added, "Chief Haskins wasn't quite ready to leave home and said he'd try to send someone else. Phyllis thought we ought to go to Hoosier Hollow just to be sure the man hadn't followed her."

"And she was dead!" Phyllis's voice quavered on the last word.

"I still don't understand where Susan comes into all this," Betsy whispered.

"Neither do I, Maggie. I didn't see her in the crowd."

"She wasn't supposed to be here until ten o'clock because Jonathan's taken the boys to the mall to see Santa Claus. I wasn't going anywhere till after lunch. How could Susan have seen the girl being murdered?"

"Well," Maggie began, "it was really most peculiar. I was just—"

The bathroom door opened and the women waited in silence till Susan entered the kitchen from the hall, her gait stiff, her face pale and expressionless.

Maggie spoke in a louder voice, "—and I knew, Betsy, that you'd probably have the teapot on."

"Of course I do. Here's a cup for you and, Susan, one for you, too."

Susan hesitantly sat down at the kitchen table while Betsy brought a plate of bread from the counter. "Miss Ona's secret persimmon bread recipe."

"The secret," Maggie commented dryly, "is that she picks up the persimmons under the tree on the courthouse lawn."

The three women and the girl sipped their tea for a few moments. Maggie kept her eyes on Susan, who trembled, gulped loudly, giving the impression she might break into a thousand pieces if touched.

"Have some bread, Susan," Phyllis urged.

Susan ate a slice of bread without speaking, took another piece, and ate half of it with a second cup of tea. Suddenly she covered her mouth with her hand and rushed back to the powder room. Her retching could be heard through the closed door.

"Poor child. She'll have to tell what she saw, though," Phyllis insisted.

"Not right this minute she won't." Maggie glared at Phyllis. Such a difficult friend.

Phyllis straightened, looking hurt, and set her mouth tightly.

"I'll see if I can help," Betsy knocked on the powder room door, entering when Susan answered.

The doorbell rang.

"I'll get it," Maggie said, greatly relieved by the excuse to get away from Phyllis. "It's probably Grace Kemmer. She's supposed to meet me here."

It was, indeed, Grace. Maggie hung up her coat and escorted her to the kitchen.

"Oh, Grace," Phyllis said, "how good to see you, but under what terrible circumstances! Betsy just took Susan upstairs to lie down. Have you heard what's happened?"

"No, Mrs. Stockton. All Daddy said was that Maggie wanted me to meet her here."

"Where was Jerry?" Maggie interrupted.

"He'd just left when I got there. Chief Haskins had brought him by in a patrol car just so he could tell Daddy to have me come over here. He said something about having to go to the police station and not being sure how soon he would be ready to work. Daddy wanted to ask him some questions, but Chief Haskins said there wasn't time right then."

"We don't know much more than you about what happened," Maggie said. "Your daddy and I were beginning to wonder why Jerry was so late when he came running up all out of breath, apologizing for oversleeping. He also said he'd stopped to pick up some books a black woman had dropped next to Hoosier Hollow.

"She told him she'd been assaulted by some man in the old Andersen house. Jerry told her to wait by Hoosier Hollow, which wasn't open yet, till he called his daddy."

"But Maggie's had her phone taken out, so she can't even call the police in an emergency."

"That's enough, Phyllis."

"Enough! Too much for that poor girl! Too late for her!" Phyllis sobbed.

Maggie and Grace stared at Phyllis for a few moments, then glanced at each other with embarrassment. No one spoke until Betsy returned.

"Grace, it's been a long time!" Betsy exclaimed. "But what a sad way to get together." She turned to the older women. "Susan went right to sleep, out like a light."

"I still don't know what's going on. Susan who? Has there been an accident?"

"Worse, worse!" Phyllis wailed. "Maggie and the Haskins boy came to my house to use the phone to call Chief Haskins. He suggested his son go back to Hoosier Hollow to stay with the black girl till a patrol car could get there.

Maggie and I were afraid she might be hurt, so we ran back with Jerry, but it was too late." Phyllis stopped to blow her nose.

Maggie said softly, "She was dead."

Grace gasped. "Did you say she was black?"

Maggie nodded, then abruptly snapped her head erect. Of course, the Klan meeting! The threats, the vows to let no blacks leave Sardisvale alive. Grace had remembered sooner than Maggie the reason for coming to Maggie's house that morning: so they and Mr. Kemmer could talk over what they had seen Saturday night. They had agreed to think it over before deciding whether or not to take action. Seeing Susan's eyes through the grating in the gate had driven all thoughts of the Klan meeting right out of her mind. Now, though, she had to think clearly; maybe Susan, if she really had been a witness, was in danger. Caution was needed, even among well-meaning friends.

Phyllis stared at Maggie, then at Grace. "Hold on! Do you think this has anything to do with the business about Maurice? Is that why Susan's here?"

"Yes, how is Susan involved, Maggie?" asked Betsy. "I missed hearing why she's mixed up is this."

"I'm sure I did not see her at the scene of the crime," Phyllis announced, putting away her tissue.

"Phyllis," Maggie replied, "you sound like someone on a television detective series. We don't really know how the woman died. Maybe it was an accident."

"With all that blood? Hardly! She had to've been stabbed or shot. You know you think so yourself."

"I still don't understand, though," Betsy said. "Was Susan with this girl?"

"Susan? Susan who?" Grace persisted.

"Susan Marshall. Hiram Marshall's daughter. Do you teach her?"

"No, but I—"

Phyllis interrupted. "All right, Maggie, now tell us how you ended up bringing Susan here."

Maggie remained silent a few moments longer, then spoke reluctantly, carefully. "I don't really know why Susan was there beside Hoosier Hollow this morning, but she seemed so completely shattered by what she'd seen I was afraid for her sanity. The closest haven I could think of was here, Betsy."

"Of course, Maggie, you did right to bring her here. She wasn't supposed to babysit for me today till ten o'clock, though."

"When you told me to meet you here," Phyllis said to Maggie, "you were by yourself. I didn't see Susan anywhere."

Frigid air clouded into the kitchen through the open back door.

"Mommy, Mommy!"

"Mommy, Mommy!"

Matthew and Mark raced to Betsy's side.

"We saw Santy Claus! We did!"

"Well, hello, ladies!" Jonathan entered the kitchen. "To what do we owe this honor?"

"Jonathan," said Betsy, "please help me with the boys in the powder room." She guided him down the hall, and the boys stumbled excitedly with them.

"Betsy was supposed to take the boys out for lunch when Susan got here to mind the baby," Phyllis said.

"Susan is in no condition to babysit."

"Maggie, I'm quite aware of that. I'll babysit, and Reverend Simms can counsel Susan."

"Reverend Simms!"

"Yes, he's just the one to do it. He's a pastoral counselor, and—"

"But, Phyllis—"

Jonathan re-entered the kitchen. "Betsy tells me Susan Marshall—"

Phyllis cut in quickly. "Oh, Reverend Simms, you're just the one to help Susan at a time like this. Maggie thinks Susan saw—"

Maggie spoke firmly, "We're all upset by what we saw, but Susan is so fragile I really believe she needs some professional help with this."

"I'll be glad—"

"I meant a psychiatrist."

"Hiram would have to agree to it, but I can talk with her right now, as her pastor."

"I hadn't thought about Hiram."

"Maggie," Phyllis said, "you don't know Hiram Marshall. He, himself, is disturbed. He'd consider it personally threatening to have his daughter in therapy. If Reverend Simms counsels her, Hiram won't even have to know. People go to their ministers all the time in perfect confidentiality. Right, Reverend Simms?"

"Yes...well, adults do, but not actually many minors."

"I'm convinced," Maggie insisted, "that because Susan is so very upset, our amateurish efforts to play professional could be very dangerous for her."

"Maggie, what an insult to Reverend Simms! He *is* a professional. What are you thinking of, belittling him this way?"

Jonathan had reddened, but—Maggie gave him credit for some sense—when he spoke he sounded in control. "Please, Mrs. Stockton, let's not get off the subject of Susan. We're all concerned about her. If she's as emotionally labile as Miss McGilvray seems to think, all the more reason for me to evaluate her and make a decision about how best to help her. I'm going to my study now. Ask Betsy to bring me lunch there." He left the room abruptly.

Phyllis whirled on Maggie. "How could you, Maggie? How could you treat him this way? What do you know about professional counselors, or even about young people and whether or not they are 'on the edge'? You don't know the first thing about human emotions, even though your mother—God rest her soul—was one of the most loving and humane creatures who ever lived. You've never even—"

Grace's plea for peace interrupted Phyllis's tirade, but not before she had put into words Maggie's worst suspicions about herself. The contrast between Momma's life and hers. Her selfishness, her ignorance, her dearth of *real* living. Oh, Momma hadn't believed those bad things about her daughter, but probably that was further evidence of the woman's generosity of spirit. Other people believed them: the church women; her minister, *former* minister; her lifelong friend—some friend!

"Mrs. Stockton," Grace rose and held up a restraining hand, "we need to work together. Mrs. Simms was planning to go out. Didn't you say something about babysitting?"

"I did. I almost forgot. The boys know me best. I'll just go give her Reverend Simms's message," she shot a reprimanding look at Maggie, "and see what I can do to help." She sailed sedately out of the room toward the children's voices issuing from the family room.

Maggie turned to Grace with a tight smile. "Sorry to have brought you into this mess."

"Please don't apologize, Maggie. Seems like this murder—I guess it's murder—is affecting everybody, whether we want it to or not. I'm still not clear on how Susan Marshall got involved."

"I don't intend to be involved anymore. Let's get out of here, go back to my house, and see if you and I and your daddy can make some sense out of the Klan meeting. I was so shocked and exhausted yesterday I couldn't have discussed it rationally even if I'd wanted to."

"Good idea."

The two women moved to the hall closet, where they began donning their coats.

"I suppose before we go we ought to—" Maggie was saying when Betsy rushed down the hall to them.

"Maggie, please do me a big favor. Phyllis is going to feed and play with the boys till they're ready for their naps. I'm going to take Mary with me as soon as I carry in Jonathan's lunch tray. If you could possibly sit upstairs till Susan wakes up... I know she's been at your house some lately, and I think she'd feel better if you're there instead of nobody or just Jonathan. Will you, please?" Breathless at last, Betsy paused with a serious, winning look.

"I guess I could stay."

"Oh, wonderful! I knew you would. All you have to do is be there when she wakes up and take her down to Jonathan's study. I'm leaving sandwiches for her there. That way, if she wants to talk to him, she can; and if she doesn't...well, you can see whether she'll be OK to go on home by herself then. If not, Grace, maybe you'd be kind enough to give her a ride?" Betsy again paused for breath.

"Of course," Grace responded.

"Good-by, then." Betsy returned to the kitchen, leaving Grace and Maggie staring at each other in the hall.

Maggie shrugged and grinned sheepishly. "Betsy is very persuasive."

Grace smiled in reply and began removing her coat. "So is Mrs. Stockton. Looks like Reverend Simms will be having a talk with Susan after all."

The women drank more tea with more persimmon cake.

"Listen, Maggie, about the meeting Saturday night, Daddy thinks—"

"Grace, in the light of what happened beside Hoosier Hollow this morning, our talk about Saturday night had better be in absolute privacy in our own homes."

"So you, too, think there's a connection?"

"It seems probable to me; let's postpone our talk." Maggie bent her head and determinedly buttered the last piece of bread.

"By the way, Maggie, I called Maurice's landlady in Bloomington yesterday. She still hasn't heard from him and wouldn't give me his Detroit address. Doesn't trust me, I guess; but I talked her into giving me her address so I could send a letter there for her to forward. I mailed it this morning. It's a tricky business distinguishing individuals from groups. I mean, what really makes a community if the action of one person, or only a few, can change things for everybody?"

"Maybe, if you keep asking those hard questions, you'll understand why people like you, and your daddy, and Willamae, and me—and Thomas Merton—decide to separate ourselves from 'the community.' Merton, though—"

"Wait, Maggie, I'm pretty sure I heard... Yes, that's the bedroom door upstairs. It must be Susan. I guess you'd better go. She hardly knows me."

Before Maggie could put down her teacup, Susan Marshall walked, zombie-like, into the dining room.

"Susan, you're awake."

Susan stopped just inside the doorway.

Jonathan Simms entered from the kitchen through the other door. "Susan. Good. I thought I heard footsteps on those creaky old stairs. Mrs. Simms has prepared some lunch for you. It's in my study, so just come on in there." He motioned, and she preceded him. He stepped back into the dining room. "Please wait here, ladies, until we see whether Susan needs transportation. You do have your car available, Miss Kemmer?"

"Of course."

"Thank you." The door closed behind Susan and Jonathan.

* * *

The study walls were floor-to-ceiling books except for a long, narrow window at a back of the big, neat desk. The books registered in Susan's perception. How she loved books! They could take her far away, like magic carpets. If only she could read all of those, right then. In front of the desk were two arm chairs pulled close to each other. Susan moved to the larger, softer one.

"Yes, that's good." Susan jumped when the minister spoke. "I'm sorry. I didn't mean to startle you." He walked around the desk to sit in the swivel chair behind it.

He pushed a plastic tray toward her. "Mrs. Simms made these for us. I've already eaten mine, since I wasn't sure how long you would sleep."

Susan took a bite of a pimiento-cheese sandwich. She was so hungry. But hadn't she eaten the persimmon bread? Oh, God, that must have been hours ago. Her job! She almost choked trying to speak with her mouth full. Reverend Simms handed her the glass of milk.

"Matthew and Mark...I'm supposed to be babysitting! I forgot."

"Everything's taken care of. Mrs. Stockton is with the boys, and my wife took Mary with her. There's nothing for you to worry about. I know you had a bad experience, and we thought you'd probably just want some peace and quiet to get it straight in your head. Then maybe you'll want to talk to me about it."

Susan was conscious of being hungry, ravenously hungry. She ate the three half- sandwiches, drank all the milk, ate the candy bar Reverend Simms handed her from a desk drawer.

"Now, Susan, I want you to think back to what happened this morning. Take your time. We're in no hurry here. You can tell me anything you want in private. I'm your minister, you know, and I'm also a trained counselor. Anything you say to me is confidential. That means I won't tell anybody, not even your father."

Mention of her father got her mind going at last. Her father—drinking, shouting, breaking things, pushing her into the wall, slapping her, punching her in the eye, the mouth...

122

And then she remembered the black girl, sleek, beautiful, her make-up soft, colorful...the girl looking into the mirror of a bright golden compact, gently probing a cut on her upper lip, wiping away the blood, re-applying lipstick over the place where her lip was puffy.

Susan ran her right index finger over the scar above her own lip. The black girl, too, must have felt pain around the cut, empty numbness over it. How unfair, how cruel, for a man to punch a girl in the face. Susan's head jerked sideways, as though Hiram were again punching her. It wasn't fair! It really wasn't fair! No one should punch them that way, no matter what they did. The black girl had done nothing bad. And she, Susan, got punched for nothing, too. It was true— for nothing.

The revelation hit her as painfully as Hiram's punch. "For nothing! Over and over for nothing! It's not fair!" Susan moaned the words out loud. Her shoulders shuddered with sobs.

Reverend Simms leaped to his feet, ran around the desk. "Susan, what is it? What's wrong?" He sank into the chair beside her. "What's the matter? Tell me!"

Her voice became louder. "Daddy punches me for nothing, and it's not fair! It's not fair! He hurts me, and it's not fair! It's not fair! It's not fair!"

* * *

Sugar sprayed over the tablecloth from the teaspoon Maggie had been holding. Never in her life had she heard such a desperate sound as Susan's wail. The words were unclear, but their tone drew Maggie immediately. Ignoring the spilled sugar, the sloshing tea, she rushed down the hall, burst without knocking into Jonathan's study, and kneeled beside the girl.

Susan stopped shouting and spoke directly to Maggie, "Daddy punches me for nothing, and it's not fair. I'm sure

123

of that now. Please make him stop! Please, Miss Maggie, please!"

Maggie's hands were clutched by Susan in a death grip. Maggie's face was only a few inches from the girl's desperately pleading one. "I'll stop him, Susan. I will. I promise. I'll stop him." Maggie was dimly aware of the irony of her positive words. What, after all, could she do? Something, though, surely something.

Susan finally released Maggie's hands and hugged her clumsily, mumbling, "Thank you. Thanks. Thank you."

Grace, surprised at Maggie's quick response to Susan's shouts, lagged behind in reaching the study. Jonathan met her in the hall and explained the revelation accompanying the girl's distressed shouts and sobs.

Grace spoke to him quickly, softly, so that Susan, who was quietly embracing Maggie, couldn't hear. "I guess it's all right to tell you now that about a year ago a policewoman and a case worker with the Department of Social Services investigated the Marshall household because of suspected child abuse, but to no avail. Susan refused to admit anything.

"Just this fall—in fact, right before Thanksgiving, Amy Norris, the high school Guidance counselor, called a conference with Susan because a teacher reported suspicious bruises and a black eye. But again Susan insisted everything was fine. Now, at last, we can help her!"

"I'm glad you told me. Maybe the school should be contacted first. Do you know this Miss Norris?"

"Yes, of course. She lives near the school, and I heard her say she'd be in town during the holidays. She'll know whom to contact."

"What is going on?" Phyllis turned into the hall from the stairs. "I'd have come down sooner, but I wanted to be sure Matthew and Mark were asleep to stay for a while."

Maggie and Susan came out of the study. "We'll be in the kitchen, making a fresh pot of tea."

Phyllis stared after them.

"Miss Kemmer, now would be a good time for you to use my desk phone to call the Guidance person and find out what steps we take next."

Over her telephone conversation with Amy Norris, Grace heard Mrs. Stockton ask Jonathan, "What did Susan see this morning?"

Grace lost the thread of her report to Amy when she waited to hear whether or not Susan had told of witnessing a murder.

"See? It's not really what she *saw*, but what she's been experiencing, probably for years. She's finally admitted that Hiram Marshall physically abuses her, 'punches,' she calls it. So Miss Kemmer is contacting the school Guidance counselor, who actually has had a conference with Susan within the past month to try to establish the physical abuse."

Grace sighed and tried again to concentrate on her phone conversation.

"Well," said Phyllis, "I guess that's what we've always suspected. Maggie was certainly wrong about this morning, though."

Grace was hanging up the phone when Maggie returned to the study alone.

"Where's Susan?" Jonathan and Phyllis asked in unison.

"She's in the powder room. She seems much more in control, but I think some strong tea will help."

"I was able to talk to Amy Norris, the school Guidance Counselor," Grace reported. "She's going to stop by school on her way over here and pick up some papers to be filled out and signed. It seems the first step is to get a court order preventing Susan's father from seeing her. Later, if he'll get some therapy, visitation will be possible."

Phyllis exclaimed, "She'll be taken away from him! I should have known that would happen."

"Yes, she'll be in the state's custody until they believe she can return home safely."

"But where will she live?"

"A foster home is the next step," the minister said.

"Amy, Ms. Norris, says that's a much bigger problem than it ought to be. Little children are easy to place; but with a teenager, education and social life are really crucial.

She asked that we try to come up with some possibilities for a temporary foster home for Susan."

"Betsy and I want to do everything we can for Susan. Maybe we—"

"Reverend Simms," said Phyllis, "I've read enough to know that taking Susan in might undermine your counselor-client relationship. That wouldn't do. She should be able to come to you from outside."

"I suppose you're right. I haven't had such a strange situation come up before."

"That's somewhat the reason Bob and I can't take her in, either: Hiram works for Bob, and it would be awkward if she were staying with us."

"According to Amy, ideally Susan should be in town so she could get to school, church, friends, and a job on her own. That seems to let Daddy and me out," Grace said.

Jonathan, Phyllis, and Grace all turned to Maggie.

Phyllis spoke first. "Of course! Maggie! Perfect. Susan can walk everywhere from your house. You have absolutely no other responsibilities and plenty of money. Perfect!"

"But—" Maggie began.

"Nonsense, no buts," Phyllis overrode her.

"Actually, Miss McGilvray," said Jonathan with his usual patronizing voice, which, Grace realized, had been absent for the last hour, "this seems to be the Lord's way of involving you in His work again. We should all thank Him for it."

Maggie flushed and sputtered in a, for her, loud voice, "Reverend Simms, you have no business—"

Here we go again, Grace thought, admiring Maggie's

126

spunk; but Susan appeared at the door. Maggie broke off mid-sentence. Everyone looked at the teenager.

Her face was scrubbed, hair freshly combed. She looked only at Maggie and moved toward her with a timorous smile. "I'm ready to help you with the tea, Miss Maggie."

Grace had her familiar experience of rightness, of contingencies, of inevitability. Surely the older woman would understand what was meant to happen.

Yes, Grace was not disappointed. The high color drained from Maggie's face, leaving it unnaturally pale. She swallowed noisily, spoke hoarsely, "All right, Susan, we'll give it a try."

CHAPTER XIII

SANCTUARY

Susan's lips tipped in a tremulous smile, and Maggie congratulated herself for reacting favorably to her first taste of the spaghetti sauce Susan had simmered all Tuesday afternoon.

"Susan, this is, without doubt, the most delicious spaghetti ever prepared in my house."

"The garlic bread is sorta different, too; it's spread with mayonnaise mixed with parmesan cheese and garlic salt."

"Never mind giving me the recipe. Just take some yourself and pass me the rest. Well, really, I can reach it myself; this table's so small.

"My mother had to eat her meals in bed, so I'd just fix a tray and eat with her in the room you're using. After she died, I started getting rid of furniture, and the dining room suite was first to go."

"I like eating here in the kitchen," said Susan. "There's plenty of room for just two people."

"I hope your room has everything you need."

"Oh, Miss Maggie, that desk is wonderful. Daddy never...I mean...studying for school is my favorite thing to do, and—"

At an insistent knock at the back door, Maggie pushed back her chair quickly. It crossed her mind—and probably Susan's—that it might be Hiram.

Susan suspended her next bite half way to her mouth until she heard the response to Maggie's "Who's there?"

"It's Phyllis, Maggie. Let me in."

Maggie opened the door. "Phyllis, what are you doing out at night?"

"This is the night of the 'Tween Group Christmas party. You know, Susan, when the young people always decorate the big tree in the sanctuary and wrap presents made by the Circle of Help ladies for the Primary Department children. Thursday night's Christmas Eve, and Santa Claus always gives the Primary kids presents from under the sanctuary Christmas tree."

"You're all out of breath. Sit down here while I fix us some hot chocolate." Maggie realized that she harbored no grudges for Phyllis's insults and anger the day before. Life was just too short.

"Ummm! That tomato sauce smells great!"

"Susan made it."

"Susan? My goodness! I didn't know...but of course you can cook. I suppose—" At a warning glance from Maggie, Phyllis blundered to a halt.

"Do you want some spaghetti, Mrs. Stockton?"

"Oh, no, thank you, Dear. I ate dinner, but I did rush after Betsy called. Seems several of the 'Tween parents didn't want the young people out alone when the police haven't caught... well, anyway, she's called off the party; but she still needs help with the decorations and wrapping. I stopped by—since I can't phone—" Phyllis looked accusingly at Maggie, "to ask you two to go with me and give Betsy a hand."

"Susan and I have had a very busy day moving furniture around, washing and hanging curtains, and beating rugs for her room. I think I need to go to bed early."

"Susan, won't *you* come with me? Betsy has so many things on her mind."

"Miss Maggie, is it all right?"

She was being asked for permission. Unprecedented. "Yes, I guess so. Go ahead. Wait, let me give you my key to the front door. I may be asleep by the time you get back. Remind me to have a key made for you tomorrow."

* * *

Maggie was greatly relieved when the front door shut behind Phyllis and Susan. She couldn't remember when she had been so weary, mentally even more than physically.

She hadn't even had time to consider how and why she had become a foster parent by default; things had moved too swiftly. The Guidance counselor had come prepared with papers for everyone—for Susan, Jonathan, and Maggie— papers of testimony, a court order to prevent Hiram from seeing Susan, and papers to make Maggie a foster parent.

Then there had been a hectic trip to the Marshall house in Grace's car to get Susan's clothes and school things before Hiram could get home from work, even though Phyllis had called Bob to try to delay Hiram, and even though Susan insisted her father would stop at Hoosier Hollow before coming home.

Finally, Maggie had had to decide which room would be Susan's—her mother's was the choice—and they had done some cleaning and arranging Monday night, enough for Susan to be reasonably comfortable. The real work had begun in the morning, and Maggie had to admit that Susan had pitched in, worked with surprising enthusiasm and energy to make herself a nest in her new foster home.

Foster parent! *In loco parentis*—that's how her mother used to say teachers had to be. Incredible that even by default Maggie could be acting *in loco parentis*, could be even a teeny bit responsible for Hiram Marshall's daughter. Susan, that pathetic little rabbit, had worked extremely hard and thanked

Maggie effusively. More than just grateful, Susan seemed to feel comfortable—settled—in the McGilvray home. Most strange, considering that Maggie felt uncomfortable about having Susan under her care, had slept fitfully, and been too weary to think productively. Her strange experiences the last few days jumbled together in an impossible heap: Willamae's place, the Klan meeting, Hiram's threat to Maurice, that poor girl's death. No, she didn't want to think about all that until later. First things first. Maggie put away the dinner things and laid out breakfast dishes for two. Odd to be doing that again.

Then she took a long, hot bath and bundled up in her red flannel robe and fuzzy pink bedroom slippers. Her ankles were cold, so she added the pair of athletic socks. Susan would probably, if she were a typical teen, be disgraced by what her foster parent was wearing. Adolescents were reputed to concentrate on superficialities.

Actually, Susan didn't seem obsessed with clothes, though she had wanted to pull out and pack her summer wardrobe yesterday. Grace had diplomatically suggested that it was a long time till spring, and Susan would need some new things then, anyway.

Grace, as a teacher and a young person, understood adolescents. Maggie, on the other hand, couldn't remember that she herself had ever exhibited the adolescent confusion now proclaimed to be normal. She didn't empathize with today's teenagers, didn't understand them, and, furthermore, didn't care to. All she could provide Susan with were physical safety and material necessities.

Maggie sprawled in the overstuffed chair she and Susan had dragged from her mother's bedside to the rarely-used living room. Determined to divert her thoughts from her new responsibilities, she nibbled the end of her pen and adjusted the notepad on her knee. Time to be organized, to make some lists.

She thought of planning meals for the rest of the week. No, that was something Susan could do, probably better than Maggie. The girl did seem to have good cooking skills.

A Christmas list. She had only Wednesday and half a day Thursday to shop, since stores in Sardisvale always closed at two o'clock the day before Christmas. No, shopping was ridiculous. She'd give away what she already had. The bureau drawers were still full of unused gifts her mother had received. Undoubtedly something there for Susan, Grace, Mr. Kemmer—maybe even Phyllis and Bob. Matthew, Mark, Mary, and Betsy, *not* Jonathan Simms.

She thought of Maurice. One of those warm cashmere scarves. She wondered if he would respond to Grace's letter. At least she could get his Bloomington address and send a package that would be forwarded. For the children she had some things from her childhood, practically antiques: well-preserved stuffed animals, several rag dolls. Time to get rid of all that junk. Then she could go anywhere, travel light with no encumbrances—peacefully, quietly, privately.

Willamae's retreat on the ridge rose inevitably in her mind's eye. She wondered if she could live that simply. Maybe she could even live on that very ridge.

But the stupid, vicious Klan had to somehow be stopped from ruining decent people's lives. First Maurice—fine, talented—and now that poor Michelle. Probably nothing could be done. Probably, contrary to what Momma had believed, some people were evil, and society in general wouldn't ever change. By far the wisest solution was to separate from society, rather than to waste one's life in futile efforts to change people, singly or in groups.

Grace Kemmer, now, led a useful life; but she'd learned—from Willamae and from Ora—the secret of separating mentally from stupid society, of getting in touch with her true self. Maybe Maggie could learn a thing or two from Grace, even though the logger's daughter wasn't much more than an adolescent herself.

* * *

"The young people of this church, the 'Tween Group," Phyllis Stockton told Susan, "have always prepared everything themselves for the Christmas Eve party for the little ones. Betsy—Mrs. Simms—had such original ideas for this year. She makes wonderful plans, but she can't carry them through by herself and still take care of her own babies. Of course, we had expected you to be baby-sitting."

Susan felt hot and guilty. Mrs. Simms really needed her, had been so nice to her, and now... Mrs. Stockton patted her, must've noticed that she was upset.

"Well, never mind, you've too much else to get used to this vacation. Anyway, Betsy did collect gifts for the Primary children—thirty presents, I think she said—but there's no way she can wrap them all *and* decorate the tree *and* have everything ready for her own family.

"There, see, the lights are on in the sanctuary. Let's just see what's happening with the tree Bob—Mr. Stockton— brought over last night."

Mrs. Stockton parked in front of the church and hurried Susan through the icy air into the entrance hall. They hesitated a moment at the closed office door on the left, then went through the open double doors into the brightly lighted sanctuary.

Jerry Haskins was down by the chancel rail, unstacking large cardboard boxes. Strings of popcorn and cranberries and red and green paper chains were heaped on the front pews.

"Jerry!"

He looked up. "Mrs. Stockton! Susan! Right on! I'm official tree-decorator, and I sure need more hands. Dad and Reverend Simms are pow-wowing in the office because they decided I could do this all by myself, but just look at all the stuff Mrs. Simms and her kids fixed and sent over. And none of it can go on the tree till these strings of lights are up."

Susan had stopped near the back of the sanctuary, but Mrs. Stockton advanced and circled the enormous tree positioned in front of the pulpit. She nodded approvingly.

"It's an unusually beautiful tree, very symmetrical. You'll need more help than just a ladder to decorate it, though. How about if I leave Susan here? I'll go on over to the parsonage and be a gift-wrapper for Betsy."

"Hey, yeah, Mrs. Stockton, that'd be great! Susan, will you please give a hand with this thing?"

Susan shrugged and nodded, but couldn't quite look Jerry in the eye, even though she did want to help.

"All right. I'll be back when we're through. Or if you finish first, Jerry, will you walk Susan over to the parsonage?"

"Sure thing, Mrs. Stockton."

Susan shyly approached the chancel rail. "What should I do first?"

"Come look in this box," Jerry said. "There's the manger scene we always put on the Communion table. How about setting it up while I go looking for an extension cord? I'm pretty sure there's one upstairs in the kitchen with the electric coffee urn. Be right back."

"OK," she responded softly.

With great care she unwound tissue paper from the crèche figurines—a blonde angel in white with golden wings, a bearded shepherd holding a removable wire crook, another with a fluffy lamb braced over his shoulders, a Baby Jesus lifting His plump arms, a heavenly beautiful Mary in royal blue.

"His mother," Susan whispered. To her surprise, a sudden tear moistened her cheek.

* * *

Hiram had scarcely entered his empty house Monday night when the slick young guy arrived to serve him with the restraining order. Right after that the woman from the Community Mental Health Center or the school office or somewhere, he wasn't clear about that part, called to set up an appointment with him for Tuesday after work at the C.M.H.C. place.

He raged around cursing for a while, then called up Greg Haskins and told him the story. Hiram had hoped Greg would come over to help him drown his troubles, or would at least meet him at Hoosier Hollow to bend elbows, but Greg sounded odd and insisted he had to get to bed early. Having the police chief for a brother and being fairly smart himself, he knew more about matters of law than Hiram. Greg's advice was to stay sober and rest up till after the next day's appointment.

Hiram took his friend's advice and managed to get through the night and the next day at work. After his interview at the Community Mental Health Center, though, something snapped. He went straight home, downed a pint of whiskey, and convinced himself that Jonathan Simms had maliciously forced Susan to betray her own father.

The more he thought about it, the more certain he was that even though he couldn't see his own daughter, he could sure as hell tell that self-righteous preacher how to mind his own business.

Too angry and drunk to drive, Hiram lurched the few blocks to Sardisvale's First United Methodist Church. Intending to enter the office, he was first attracted to the brightly lighted sanctuary and rushed down its center aisle toward the figure kneeling beside the huge green fir.

"Simms! Simms! I'm gonna tell you a thing or two!"

But instead of confronting Jonathan, Hiram came to an abrupt halt before the last person he expected to find there— his daughter Susan.

* * *

Sometimes Sunday afternoon with Jonathan was relaxing for Timothy Haskins, and sometimes, like this week, it was stimulating. Timothy had lain awake for a long time Sunday night, his brain teeming with an overabundance of ideas. One scheme after another for educating the community and ending its racial prejudice had popped into his head. Finally, he arose and began jotting them down.

First, the white people of Sardisvale had to become acquainted with some blacks. Blacks would have to live here, work here, play here. That meant homes, jobs, games.

Sounded hopeless, but Timothy believed in starting with himself. He would take in somebody black. How much safer could one be than living with the police chief?

Next, jobs. What were safe jobs? Maybe working in the forestry with old Ora Kemmer? Teaching in a public school? Working in a hospital to make people well? Those might be the safest places.

And play. Now there was a subject dear to the heart of this community! The importance of winning high school football and basketball teams in Sardisvale could hardly be overstated. A search for superior black athletes and maybe a black coach or assistant coach was called for.

Superior black teachers, medical personnel. Or maybe not superior. Maybe only very, very good. That was the ticket: better than average, but still believably human. It was the humanity, the common denominators, that must be stressed. Acceptance of his own humanity was something Jonathan had helped him with: one didn't have to be perfectly adjusted, perfectly in control; plenty of other people know deep despair and truly empathize. Yes, perceiving what humans have in common would definitely be a key.

Timothy made extensive notes far into the night. Jonathan would be pleased, could take the ball from here and run with it.

Before the police chief went to sleep, his enthusiasm had obscured his concern for his brother Greg's Klan activities; but nightmares plagued his rest. He had slept late Monday morning and struggled groggily to the phone when Jerry called him from the Stocktons' about the young encyclopedia saleswoman.

The nightmares didn't stop because Timothy was awake. They continued as he arrived at Hoosier Hollow to find the woman dead. He himself was stuck with the initial interrogations because Dwight Mitchell had to be sent home; the rookie was soaked with blood, head to toe. Hell of an experience for a new patrolman—for anyone.

By the time Mitchell returned to the station, Timothy had questioned the Hoosier Hollow bartender, who claimed total ignorance, and the rest of the sales crew, two very shaken white men and the grief-stricken, frightened best friend of the victim.

An ugly day. And then, of all things, he had to take a deposition from his own son, since Jerry was thus far the last person known to have seen Michelle Riddick alive.

Bad day, bad night, but nothing compared to Tuesday, when the fingerprint checks were performed. First, Timothy got reports on Hoosier Hollow's window: no good prints on the inside; on the outside nothing, either.

Then, after lunch, reports on the Andersen house: many fresh, clear prints on the forced back window, on the whiskey bottle and drinking glass in the living room, and even on the inside of the curtained front window. *That* was the *good* news. The bad news, the terrible news that drove Timothy to leave the station early, to pace the floor of his apartment, and finally to rush Jerry to the Burger King for carryout and then to the church for Jonathan's confidential advice: the terrible news was that the Andersen house prints belonged to Greg Haskins, his own brother.

* * *

Jerry Haskins, also, had had a really bad two days. Monday, the murder. That beautiful girl. And *he* was the one who had left her alone. He felt almost responsible, even though his dad had told him about a million times that he'd done the right thing. He could have stayed with her, though. Then maybe he'd be dead, too. Or he could have taken her with him back to Miss Maggie's, and then maybe they'd all be dead. No, no use thinking about what might have been.

He'd told them at the police station—told his father, that is, but Dwight Mitchell had been standing there all the time, listening, and Hattie Winthrop had been taking everything down like crazy in shorthand—everything just exactly the way he remembered it. He'd gone over it a bunch of times; and Dwight, the rookie, who'd gotten all covered with her blood just finding her, kept asking, "Didn't you see anyone? Any cars?" till his dad had used that shut-up-now stare that Jerry had gotten once in a while all his life and hadn't realized it was sometimes given to policemen, too.

Anyway, that was yesterday. Today his dad had come home from the station early looking like the world was coming to an end. He'd made a phone call and announced to Jerry that they were picking up hamburgers on the way to the church and Jerry would have to eat his by himself and not disturb him and Reverend Simms while they ate theirs in the church office.

Totally bewildered, Jerry had eaten alone, worrying that his dad was starting another depression. In the sanctuary Jerry had sadly begun dragging strings of Christmas lights up a side aisle, untangling them, grumbling a lot, when who should come along but Mrs. Stockton, bringing him Susan on a silver platter.

Well, not really, of course, because Susan still wasn't exactly talking to Jerry; but he had high hopes that before the night was over...

The extension cord was in the church kitchen, attached to the coffee urn, just as Jerry had supposed. He detached it, started for the stairs, returned to the kitchen, took two cold Cokes from the refrigerator, opened them with the wall opener, and took them and the cord down to the sanctuary.

As he entered through the double doors, he saw Hiram Marshall clutching Susan's right shoulder with his left hand and swinging his right fist into her left cheek.

"Hey!" Jerry yelled.

Susan gave only the thinnest of moans. Hiram didn't look around.

Jerry whirled and rushed to the minister's office. Dropping the cord, he burst in, shouting, "Come quick! Hiram Marshall's beating up Susan."

The startled men ran at once into the sanctuary and down the aisle. They grabbed Hiram and had no trouble overpowering him, although he continued to struggle. Resisting arrest—that was such shocking behavior that Jerry had thought it happened only on TV.

"Hold his arms back," his dad said to Reverend Simms, "while I put handcuffs on him."

Meanwhile, Jerry put his arm around Susan and supported her weight as he led her to a pew. She collapsed, whimpering, face buried in her hands.

Hiram was yelling at everyone; Jerry couldn't make sense of most of the words.

"He's drunk, totally smashed."

"Let's get him into my office."

The two men virtually dragged Hiram up the aisle.

Jerry, feeling helpless, kept his arm around Susan, kept patting her. She didn't look up; but she didn't move away, either.

His dad came back in only a few minutes and sat down on the pew beside Jerry and Susan.

"Susan, I'm Chief Haskins, Jerry's father. Let me look at your face, please. I won't touch it. That's the way. I know it hurts, but I don't really think anything's broken. Jerry would you fix an icepack in the kitchen? Some ice cubes in a dish towel to keep the swelling down.

"Listen, honey, there's a court order to keep your dad from seeing you, so I'm going to take him to jail now. He's awfully drunk. We'll hold him at least till he's sober and then get him some help."

Susan was nodding when Jerry bolted for the kitchen. He was proud of how gentle his dad's voice could be.

When Jerry returned with the improvised ice pack, his dad was still speaking slowly, reassuringly. "I've called a patrol car to come get him. When it arrives, I'll take you to Miss Maggie's and explain what happened. OK?"

Susan nodded again.

"Thanks, son. That was fast. Now, Susan, just hold this against your cheek. Good girl! Jerry will stay here with you while I go see about your dad."

Susan kept her head bowed until she and Jerry were alone, then slowly raised it and looked directly at him. A first!

"Thanks," she said.

As a reflex, Jerry stretched his hand toward her discolored cheek.

"That's what you did to that girl," she breathed, "to Michelle. That's nice."

Jerry felt himself blushing—darn' redhead complexion—with pleasure, with confusion. "I know it hurts."

Loud footsteps resounded from the entrance hall. Susan and Jerry turned, startled, toward the back of the sanctuary, where Patrolman Dwight Mitchell appeared.

Susan screamed, then sobbed hysterically, "No! No! Get away! Get away! Don't touch me! Get away!"

As Mitchell started down the aisle, Susan wailed louder. Jerry jumped up and gestured toward Jonathan's office. "In there. In the office." He quickly turned back to Susan with comforting words.

Nothing changed, however. The girl trembled, sobbed, and shouted "Get away!" over and over, so loudly that Reverend Simms came running to her as soon as the opened office door allowed her to be heard.

The minister shook Susan in an effort to calm her, but the police chief joined them at the altar and finally succeeded in quieting her by holding her close while she cried.

Speaking to Jerry over her shoulder, his dad said, "I'm going to take Susan by the emergency room, let Dr. Cobb check her face to be sure nothing's broken. Maybe he'll give her something to help her sleep.

"Jonathan, give Miss McGilvray a call."

"She doesn't have a phone, Dad."

"Well, Jerry, run over to her house, please, and tell her what's been going on. Wait there till I bring Susan home. I'll pick you up then."

"OK, Dad. Will do."

Jerry took off running, around the corner, past the parsonage, another corner, down Chicago Street, a turn onto Foliage Street that would take him past Hoosier Hollow. There he slowed, almost tiptoed, along the sidewalk where he had last seen Michelle Riddick alive. At the alleyway, the "scene of the crime," he stopped and forced himself to stare.

The dusty, broken pavement of the recess had been covered with fresh, white gravel. No bloodstains were visible by street light. None at all.

Jerry noticed the Hoosier Hollow window, for it shone surprisingly clean amid the aged bricks.

Also for the first time, he noticed a rusty old gate dripping with tangled brown vines and in the gate, a barred opening.

He hurried back along the front of the bar, broke into a run at the corner, and circled the building. Half a dozen cars were in the parking lot, but Jerry was the only person outside.

Behind the gate he bent his knees a little to look through the peephole.

That was how Susan knew he had reached out to Michelle! Of course! She had watched him with Michelle. Then maybe she had also seen Michelle come out of the Andersen place, and maybe she saw the guy who hit Michelle. If she had kept watching, she must have seen... maybe...yes, she must have been watching when Dwight Mitchell arrived. So that was why...!

* * *

Maggie had finished her Christmas lists and then dozed a little, her head dropping several times against the worn wing of the overstuffed chair. She jerked awake, however, at the pounding of feet up her front porch steps. She jumped again at the doorbell's ring. Had she forgotten to give Susan the key? Tomorrow morning she'd have the hardware store make Susan one of her own, definitely.

Maggie opened the front door, realizing as she did so that first she should have asked who was there, or at least looked out the window.

"Jerry!"

"Miss Maggie, I got to talk to you."

"Come in. What's the matter?"

"Miss Maggie, you and me, we've got a job to do." He looked behind him nervously.

Maggie pulled her robe tighter and motioned him along the hallway toward the kitchen.

Jerry slammed the door behind him and hurried after her.

"Miss Maggie!"

At the insistence in his voice she turned and faced him, frowning.

"You and I, Miss Maggie, we've got to catch the murderer quick , before he gets Susan!"

The blast of cold air that had entered with Jerry and followed him and Maggie down the hall weakened to caressing fingers of chill.

CHAPTER XIV

BROTHERS

Every time Timothy Haskins went to his brother Greg's, he went "home." Jonathan had pointed out that fact in one of the counseling sessions, and Timothy had immediately recognized the truth: staying with Greg in the house where they had both grown up was healing because it was home, a good home they had shared as children, a good home still.

Timothy had some idea of his importance to his older brother because of the way Greg miraculously had sobered up and helped out while Timothy and Jerry lived in the old Haskins place after Lisa had died.

Recently, since Timothy and Jerry were doing well in their own apartment, Timothy had wondered if he should manufacture some sort of family crisis to allow Greg to be needed again. Greg was drinking more lately, spending more time with Hiram Marshall and Andy Smythe.

Greg's Klan membership had seemed almost a logical consequence of his deteriorating self-image, but murder—not a thought Timothy could take hold of directly. Instead, he invented several elaborate explanations. Perhaps some drinking buddy had been living in the old Andersen house and invited Greg in for a drink. In that case, Greg could tell

Timothy who had molested the girl. Or maybe Greg had been in the house after the girl had left and had no idea there had been any trouble.

Too many unanswered questions. Timothy had shut off his conscious mind, but his anxiety escalated. He had slept only fitfully after he and Jerry returned from taking Susan to Miss Maggie's Tuesday night. Wednesday morning he felt actually queasy by the time he entered the gate of "home," passed beneath the huge sycamore where the tire swing had been, and climbed the well-worn limestone steps to ring Greg's doorbell.

The inside and screen doors opened, however, before Tim reached them. Taller even than Timothy and much heavier, Greg grabbed the police chief in a powerful hug that made him wince. "ESP, Little Brother. I guess I was expecting you."

"How come? Why are you dressed already? I figured with school out you wouldn't have to be at work this week."

"You figured right. Coffee's hot, and I'm sober and scared. Shit, I've hardly ever been this scared. Or ashamed. Oh, Timothy, I promise you... Tim, you don't look so good. Tim? Tim, what is it? Is something wrong with Jerry? Tim?"

Timothy couldn't answer. Greg's words were like a punch in the stomach. Timothy sank onto the worn black leather couch, tried to disperse the dark edges of his field of vision, tried to resume breathing normally. His unconscious fears had shape at last: Greg had killed that girl. In a drunken stupor his beloved brother had murdered another human being, and now, sober and scared, was promising like a child to never do it again. Greg was expecting Timothy, the big chief, to make everything right. The big chief—helpless to bring back Jerry's mother, and now helpless to save Greg. Helpless, always, with those he loved most. The wave of despair he had struggled with for months after Lisa's death now threatened to engulf him again.

"Tim, listen to me." Greg was shaking his shoulder.

"Timothy, get hold of yourself and tell me why you're here. Are you sick? I'll help, but you have to tell me what's wrong."

"What's wrong!" Timothy heard his own voice echoing down a tunnel to consciousness. "What do you mean? You know what's wrong!"

"I don't, Timothy. Now you sit right here. Put your head down if you feel faint again. I'm going to bring us coffee, and then you're going to tell me why you're here."

"No! Wait! No more coffee. Come back here." Timothy pulled up his head until he sat very tall. He closed his eyes for a few moments. Better.

Greg had hurried to his brother's side, eased onto the other end of the couch, facing Timothy. "All right, what's wrong?"

"You know already. You said you're ashamed and scared." Timothy raked his hand over his face and then covered his eyes, rested his forehead on his open palm. "You *know*, Greg. Your fingerprints were found all over the Andersen house—doorknobs, glass, whiskey bottle, window panes—everywhere." Timothy was beginning to feel professional again.

"OK, sure, I was there. I was drunk and angry—she led me on, I swear she must've—and when she tried to kick me in the balls, I hit her. I'm ashamed, and I'm scared of how I act when I drink, and I swear I'll never do it again. I called AA Monday night, and I went to a meeting last night, and I was waiting for Friday to tell you, for a Christmas surprise. I swear I'll never drink again, and you'll be proud."

"Wait a minute. You hit that girl—"

"I thought she'd kiss me. I thought she wanted to screw, but she kicked. It was just a reflex to hit her back. Then she ran out the door, and—"

Timothy was losing control again; he fought to keep from shouting. "And you followed. Didn't you see Jerry? Your own nephew? He's crazy about you."

145

"Hold it! I didn't follow her. How could I have seen Jerry? I felt like such an old fool, I ran out the back door, didn't even lock it, and went over to Andy's."

"Andy Smythe's? Can you prove that?" OK....he was OK now. He believed his brother, but he must investigate as carefully as if Greg were a stranger.

"What do you mean? I told him I was through drinking forever, and he said he thought I'd better call AA, so—"

"Greg, did you watch that girl out the window?"

"Sure I did. That's how I knew she was at the door. The doorbell doesn't work."

"No, I mean after you hit her. Did you watch her run out?"

"No, man, I told you: I ran out the back and went to Smythe's."

"Back up a minute, Greg. You've left out something important. What were you doing at the Andersens' in the first place?" Good, he was conducting the investigation properly. Keep working slowly. Think of everything.

"That's what I was telling you I'm so ashamed of. I was waiting for her."

"Her?"

"The black girl. Michelle Something-or-other."

"How could you be waiting for her?"

"Well, I just busted the flimsy little hook on the back door and went in. Nothing to it. Nobody cares. I think some school kids have used the upstairs bedrooms. Sometimes when I've come out of the Hollow, I've seen—"

"Stop with the busting-in nonsense," Timothy's voice rose, "and tell me why, why you'd go anywhere to wait for that girl!"

Greg's color deepened; but instead of shouting, he ducked his head and lowered his voice. "Timothy, kid, you know I love you and I'll always be straight with you, but I've

146

got some friends whose trust I can't betray. Please don't ask me how I knew about her."

"Knew? You knew she'd be there? On Foliage Street, on Monday morning? What the fuck kind of insanity is this? And what did you care, anyway? Who cared? Who, Greg?"

"Timothy, I warned you not to ask."

"*You* warned *me*? Now you listen: *you* are a murder suspect, and—"

"Murder suspect? No way, man! I told you I went out the back and to Smythe's. Ask him. Ask Jerry. God, our Jerry! *He* knows she was still alive. You can be sure I wasn't the only one waiting for her!"

"All right, Greg, pay attention. Your prints are all over the Andersen house. You admit you were waiting for some encyclopedia salesperson who wasn't even supposed to be working in Sardisvale at all this week."

"Not *some* salesperson, Timothy. A black girl. A lot of us don't want blacks in town."

"Who are 'a lot of us'? An organization, Greg? Is that how you knew?" Timothy buried his face in his hands for a long pause. "God Almighty, this makes no sense, does it? How the hell did anybody know she was here? It was an accident; the car broke down; the guy at the gas station gave them a ride...that's it! That's it, isn't it? The gas station?"

"See, Tim, some things you can figure out so I don't have to betray my buddies."

"Betray! Listen, Greg, you start with when you got up Monday morning, and you tell me everything that happened, or we'll have to call you a lawyer and take you in for questioning and maybe book you for murder." The last word came out in a croak, but Timothy sat erect and felt reasonably calm.

Greg began quietly, "I woke up about four-thirty and couldn't get back to sleep, so I fixed myself some ham and eggs and had a couple of beers. It was still dark, so I had a few more beers."

Timothy shook his head sorrowfully.

"I know, but I can quit drinking any time I want to. I'm not like Hiram; he's a genuine alcoholic. Anyhow, I promise you, I'm never drinking again.

"OK, so then I got in my car and started driving down the highway. I was thinking about bumming around Bloomington for the day, but before I even got out of town, I saw the signal."

"What signal? From whom?"

"Now, listen, Timothy, I'll tell you the most I can."

"Everything!"

"The most I can. This group...club..."

"The Klan?"

"I can't say because it's secret. Let me tell it. This group has a signal for when there's news. And the person I go to when I see the signal works at the Full Stop, so I went in there and got the news."

"Which was...?"

"That this black girl was going to be working door to door down Foliage Street, and I've heard that the main reason a black girl knocks on a white man's door is 'cause she wants a white man. Some of the...club want to get rid of blacks, but I—"

"You just wanted to fuck her! God, Greg, how can you be so great in some ways and so... Never mind. Go ahead with the story."

"I was pretty sure some of the guys would go to Hoosier Hollow to wait for her. I thought if I hurried, I could get to her first. Then I remembered the Andersens' house, and I went in."

"Where'd you get the whiskey?"

"I always keep a fifth under the car seat. Used to, that is. I had way too much waiting time alone with that bottle, I tell you."

* * *

By the next day, Thursday, Christmas Eve, Timothy felt as though he had been rolled through a wringer. During two days of questioning, Greg stuck to virtually the same version of his meeting with Michelle that Jerry had reported Michelle told him. Andy Smythe had further corroborated the story. The realtor looking after the Andersen place was a buddy who didn't want to press charges for breaking and entering, so Greg was a free man, a man with a lot of buddies.

The police chief was certain the murder was Klan-instigated, but the likelihood of identifying the killer by evidence that would convict seemed...well, there was loyalty among bigots. Those who depended on the Full Stop gas station for enlightenment were not going to weasel to the cops. Klan brothers were, for the time being, familially tight.

* * *

Ora Kemmer had his old-fashioned ways, and avoiding the telephone was one of them, even on Christmas Eve. The phone rang thirteen times, but Ora kept polishing his axe blades until Grace ran in from the yard to answer. She didn't mind; it was just his way, and she always humored him about it.

"Yes?" she panted. "Hello."

"Ms. Kemmer, Merry Christmas!"

"Oh, Maurice, it's you! Are you all right? Were you hurt? We've been so worried."

"I'm fine. No sweat. Thanks for the note."

"I have a lot more to tell you now than I did Monday when I mailed it. Your landlady was very protective... wouldn't give me your address. Insisted that would be an invasion of privacy...something she'd never do to any of her tenants."

"She's cool. But I'm sorry I worried you. I shouldn't have left without explaining. I never expected you to find out from somebody else. And it *was* Susan's daddy waving that gun around! I might've figured that out one of these days if I'd tried."

"Maurice, so many things have happened this week!"

"I know about the murder. My old roommate called me up and read me the story from the Bloomington paper."

"It was horrible! And, Maurice, the strangest thing... Maggie McGilvray thinks Susan was a witness and knows who the murderer is. It can't be Hiram Marshall because he was at work. Susan hasn't admitted to seeing anything, but she confessed that Hiram beats her—you said that all along—so Maggie's become her foster parent, and—"

"Slow down, Ms. Kemmer. You're losing me. If Susan was a witness, why hasn't she told the police?"

"Well, I don't think anybody but us suspects that she was. Maggie didn't want to press Susan to tell. We think Susan's right on the edge of a breakdown."

"But if she was a witness, then she may be in danger from the murderer."

"With the murderer walking around free, a lot of people may be in danger!"

"Danger is kind of what I called about, not just to say Season's Greetings."

"What do you mean?"

"Even before I knew about the murder, I was feeling bad that the guy who threatened me got away with it. I chickened out, you might say, by running away and quitting school. I've spent time with my uncle and my mom and some home folks who used to be pretty proud of me for going down to I.U. We chewed over some heavy stuff, like what's justice and who're my brothers. Remember the first time I met you— how you gave me some ginseng tea and said people can make a lot more things happen than they realize? Well, my folks and I've been talking about what kind of life I can make for myself, how I'd better realize my brothers aren't only black people: they're people like you, and Mr. Kemmer, and Miss Maggie, and my landlady, and Susan. I wasn't alone down there; I know that now. I have to go back. Face the music, so to speak. Ha!"

"You mean back to Sardisvale? Or just back to school in Bloomington?"

"I want to finish the job for Miss Maggie, if Mr. Kemmer isn't scared to have me around."

Grace had to smile. "Daddy's too old to be scared for himself. Anyway, I don't believe he's ever been scared the way you mean."

"I talked to the dean. I can be reinstated. In fact, I'm coming back day after tomorrow, after I spend Christmas here in Detroit with my family."

"I know they're proud of you again. And proud you're brave."

"They are, and I'm going to pretend I am, too. I'll be flying into Indy on Saturday."

"I'll meet your plane and bring you here for the weekend. Tell me when."

"Eleven-thirty Saturday morning. United Airlines. Ms. Kemmer?"

"Yes, Maurice?"

"I want to see to Susan. Can you arrange it?"

"I'm pretty sure I can, though I haven't talked to her or Maggie since Monday, when I took them to Susan's new foster home. I'll go in to Maggie's tomorrow and make arrangements for Susan to visit us while you're here."

"Right on. Thanks, Ms. Kemmer. You're my brother, too."

"Well, Maurice, I'm beginning to think that you're probably one of my sisters!"

CHAPTER XV

CHRISTMAS EVE AND CHRISTMAS MORNING

After Maurice's call Grace had a clearer idea of the problem and of what would lead to its solution. She relived her conversation with Maurice about ginseng the day they first met, back in the home ec kitchen. His courage and optimism, always evident, were impelling him to reach out to Susan, to save her and solve the murder. Grace decided it was her immediate mission to connect those two strong young people.

She awoke Christmas Eve morning eager to ask the Universe how to direct her mounting excitement. A temperature drop accompanied the lowering sky and rising wind, so Grace didn't even consider going all the way to the magic circle. Instead, she climbed only to the same fallen log on which Maggie had dozed on her first visit to the forestry.

Grace sat comfortably on the log, feet apart, shoulders slightly hunched. The backs of her hands rested on her knees. She tilted her face skyward, closed her eyes, and concentrated on what she wanted to happen: Maurice would tell Susan why he had left and why he was back, Susan would tell Maurice what she had seen, the killer would be convicted, and the community would unite to heal itself. Grace was vague about how the happy ending would be effected, but she did imagine rather vividly the scene between Maurice and Susan.

At last she let her mind "go blank" in an attempt to notify Susan about a meeting with Maurice. After half an hour of blankness, Grace rose invigorated and started back to the house. She decided to drive to Maggie's that afternoon to announce that she'd take Maurice there on their way back from the airport Saturday. No time to waste with a killer on the loose and Susan perhaps in danger.

Possibly Susan had already told Maggie about the murder, but Grace thought that highly unlikely. Maggie was herself so reticent and so respectful of other people's privacy that she surely would not press Susan.

Grace was becoming impatient with the way Maggie drew back from involvement with others, but realized that might explain why Maggie seemed to be avoiding making any plans to squelch the Klan. Of course, the murder had postponed their strategy meeting, yet rendered decisive action all the more necessary.

Grace was ready and eager to do her share. That Maggie was drawn to her seemed a sign, one of those logical consequences she was always trying to bring about by visualization and then "going blank." Grace, would help Maggie relate to the human community somewhat the way Willamae had directed Grace toward work with the elderly and then with young people.

Although Maggie apparently had become Susan's foster parent by chance, Grace considered that actually a logical consequence.

But the older woman needed help. She was probably still bewildered by her mother's death, had not yet diverted the love and energy previously expended toward her mother. Ironically, Maggie believed Grace was aiding her to escape from human associations instead of facilitating those very relationships. Maggie would soon understand; Grace was not yet sure how, but it would happen.

Back in the house for lunch, Grace poured tawny liquid into her father's blue and white pottery mug.

"Good thing," Ora commented with a twinkle, "I didn't sell all the ginseng to that shyster from Hong Kong. With Maurice comin' back to help, I'm gonna need all the extry energy I kin git."

"Why, Daddy, you said he saved you lots of work."

"I ain't really talkin' 'bout the work load. I figger with a black man livin' and workin' here, there's gonna be plenty of call for energy jest to keep us all alive."

"Are you serious?"

"Oh, I don't rightly know anymore, Hon, what folks might do—not that I ever did understand. That's why I like keepin' to myself and mindin' my own business."

"But you do want to help Maurice, don't you? You were so wonderful about taking him on in the first place. Please don't back out now. We need you."

"I'm not backin' out. Not at all. But you're even more taken with this whole mess than I s'posed. Sounds to me like you think somehow it's your job to reform every last dangerous fool in the county."

"Not by myself. I don't believe that. I believe in a ginseng cure."

"There you go again—pullin' my leg. I know you think this sang's no 'count 'cept for tastin' mighty warmin' on a cold day."

"No, no, you've misunderstood. I think ginseng really helps people who believe it will help. I see it over and over—for me, for you, for my Meal Dealer shut-ins, for my students."

"The tea?"

"Daddy, not the tea, not literally. I'm speaking metaphorically."

"Grace, Honey, you know I ain't educated like you."

"Listen, Daddy, I don't mean everybody drinks ginseng. I mean everybody can do much more in life if he believes he can. I mean...well, never mind. What I really think is that if everybody around here who wants justice gets together and is convinced we can make a difference, we surely *will* make a difference. Positive thinking can bring that about. We just have to get together. Come on, Daddy, say you believe."

* * *

Susan slept most of Wednesday and all morning on Thursday. Police Chief Haskins had predicted she would. In fact, that's exactly what the doctor wanted her to do and why he'd prescribed medicine to knock her out, although Maggie wasn't sure she approved.

Maggie had been horrified at the girl's appearance, face swollen and purple, eyes slits already glazed from the drug and, also, undoubtedly, from the shock. What irony—to be beaten up in a sanctuary. Well, it wasn't ironic to Maggie, was only what she expected from a hypocritical institution. Not even ironic that Phyllis's and Bob's attempts to protect Susan had resulted in the worst physical abuse the child had ever had. So much for taking over other people's lives!

Maybe that was unfair to Phyllis. The woman did know a great deal about adolescents, had reared a lovely daughter of her own who had produced, to hear Phyllis tell it, the world's most wonderful granddaughter. No one could have been more distressed about Susan Tuesday night than Phyllis.

"I never should have left her in the sanctuary. I should have taken her to Betsy's with me," she had lamented.

"Shhh, Phyllis, she's asleep and needs to stay that way."

"I never should have left Jerry in charge."

"Nobody expected Hiram to show up at church. Now get hold of yourself and go on to Marianne's for the weekend. The best thing you can do for Susan now is to leave her alone."

"Maggie, you always say the wrong thing. Actually, though, your idea may be somewhat sensible. Susan is going to need some time to process everything that's happened to her this week. I just want her to start being around some people her own age."

"Not this weekend. Good-night, Phyllis. You have a Merry Christmas with your granddaughter."

"And you...this first Christmas without your momma will be so hard..."

"I have other things to think about. Good-night, Phyllis." Maggie softly slammed her front door in Phyllis's tear-streaked face.

* * *

Lingering over breakfast while Susan slept late on Christmas Eve morning, Maggie did, however, think about what she had hoped to accomplish after her mother's death: the trees down, the house empty and ready to be put on the market, and herself ensconced in peace, quiet, and solitude, maybe at Willamae's.

Instead, though, Maurice had been threatened, the Klan had met and killed that poor Michelle, and Susan... Like Jerry, Maggie was sure that Susan had been a witness to the murder. Maggie had almost told, had certainly hinted at her suspicions to both Betsy and Phyllis. Betsy, who might tell Jonathan Simms, and Phyllis, who would surely tell Bob Stockton; and the men, in turn, might blab to the world. As long as the killer remained free and unidentified, adequate protection for Susan in Sardisvale was impossible.

Maggie rose to wash dishes, satisfied with her own clear, logical problem-solving. There were two things to do immediately: take Susan to safety, and find out from her who the killer was. Maybe Susan shouldn't be pressed to remember just yet, but Maggie did know a *real* sanctuary, and she could prepare for the journey while Susan slept.

* * *

"Miss Maggie, I'm awake."

"Susan! Come have some breakfast...lunch...whatever... and see what I'm doing." Maggie succeeded in making her voice cheerful and tried not to stare too closely at Susan's swollen, purple face.

"I didn't mean to sleep all day again. Is it really noon?"

"Half past, actually. Here's some french toast all ready to drop into the skillet. Can you do it yourself? How about some Tylenol with your orange juice?"

"My face does hurt some."

"Take these, then. I've an idea for a holiday surprise where you can get a natural ice pack for that eye. Guess what I'm doing."

"Looks like you're packing for a picnic. But isn't it awfully cold?"

"Not only cold; they're predicting snow. That's why I'd like to get started, to get where we're going before the roads are bad."

"Where are we going?"

"That's the surprise. I'll show you, not tell you; but we're going to need provisions. I'd like to take enough for a week, but I've never done this before."

"I've packed for Daddy's...my dad's...Daddy's fishing trips with his friends. Will we really be cooking outside? In the winter?"

"We will be. What do you suggest we take?"

* * *

In a way Maggie couldn't believe she was making the expedition: taking Susan and food and clothes for cold weather and trudging behind Grace up to Willamae's again. In another way, though, this seemed the easiest, most reasonable action possible.

Susan might be traumatized psychologically, but physically she was strong. Maggie was convinced that the peace and quiet of the ridge would provide healing for Susan more effectively than drugs could.

In addition, Susan would be away from the killer, who might suspect he had a witness and try to shut her up permanently. Too many suspicious people: she, Jerry, Betsy, maybe Jonathan, Phyllis, certainly Bob, and on and on. No, she couldn't have let Susan stay in town, where rumors would be flying.

Then there was the consideration Jerry had brought to her attention, the reason he hadn't gone to his father instead of to her. He insisted that the murder was Ku Klux Klan-instigated. If so, many people would be covering for the killer. The most frightening thing was that non-Klan people didn't always know who the Klan members and sympathizers were.

Jerry was sure his father was not a Klan member, but he did have strong suspicions about his uncle, Greg Haskins, and didn't trust his father to be completely impartial about Greg.

"My dad thinks Uncle Greg is great, even though he drinks too much and goes along with the crowd just to have friends. Dad would do 'most anything for him 'cause Uncle Greg's done an awful lot for us."

"How about you?" Maggie had asked Jerry, "Would you do almost anything for your uncle?"

"No, Miss Maggie. I love him, but I want to do what's right for society. We have to think about the future of our community."

Easy for the young—and even for the older folks who managed not to have intimate relationships that could interfere with What's Right! Maggie had managed that self-righteous detachment for the two months since her mother had died; now here she was feeling so fiercely protective that she knew she would toss away the Good of the Community in an instant to save the one mixed-up teenager who was now her foster child.

"Miss Maggie, just listen to our feet! It sounds like a dog scratching when we step on these deep pine needles. They must have been here for years and years. Listen. It's ever so soft, but listen!"

Susan was following Grace on an irregular zig-zagging through the pines of the upper ridge. Maggie was ten yards behind them, though having an easier climb than her first trip up to the ridge. It had been only last weekend, but light-years of strange events away.

Grace hardly raised her eyebrows when she had opened the door to Maggie and Susan Christmas Eve afternoon... seemed almost to be expecting them. She had insisted, though, that the refugees from town spend the night in the Kemmer house and so reach Willamae's Christmas morning with plenty of daylight to settle in.

Although Maggie hadn't probed too deeply, she was pretty sure Grace thought Maggie had been "led" by some mystical power to bring Susan to the Kemmers', especially since Maurice was coming there, too, on Saturday, and wanted to talk to Susan.

Grace had told Maggie about Maurice's call after Susan had gone to sleep. Maggie had been delighted, of course, that he was all right and thinking of them; but the whole business of risking his life to come back—she couldn't immediately agree to the sense of that.

She also hadn't decided how she felt about urging Susan to reveal who the killer was. If Susan knew, would it push her over the edge of sanity to remember and to testify? Whom should she tell? Was there any possibility her testimony would be believed? Who would have to know? Would the Klan let her live? Who was the killer, anyway? Some ignorant redneck, or someone they all knew and maybe some of them loved?

Maggie sighed. This was the kind of situation Thomas Merton would have prayed about. Jesus, too. But first—

Maggie almost laughed out loud—first they would have gone off by themselves to the silence of the woods. Here she was taking people with her, people who were listening to noises that proved there was no real silence, even in the woods.

She could see that Grace and Susan had entered the magic circle. Susan actually jumped up and down like a child and clapped her hands.

"It's gorgeous! Oh, Miss Maggie, what a wonderful Christmas present. It feels so peaceful here. And Ms. Kemmer says she'll teach me how to meditate, and how to use herbs."

"Wait till you see the home of her old friend Willamae. It made me want to live there forever, even though I don't know the first thing about living out in the wild."

"You know a great deal about survival, Maggie; and I can teach you and Susan the rest," Grace said.

Maybe Grace thought it was too dangerous for Susan to go back down to Sardisvale. That morning, while Ora was showing Susan his Chevy engine-powered saws, Maggie and Grace had had only a few minutes' privacy to discuss the girl's safety. Grace believed that something would happen when Maurice talked to Susan, but Maggie had insisted Susan shouldn't be told Maurice was coming back because he could still change his mind.

Their plan was for Grace to help Maggie and Susan settle in at Willamae's Friday morning, Christmas. Then, on Saturday, Grace would meet Maurice at the Indianapolis Airport and bring him up to the ridge.

Ora had concocted a plan to slow down the Klan, maybe even stop it for good; but Susan had joined the women before Grace had told Maggie exactly what he had in mind. Maybe they'd be able to talk tomorrow while Maurice and Susan were visiting.

"Susan," Grace was saying, "I'm sorry, but I don't think we should stay here in the magic circle right now. I want to help you and Miss Maggie build a fire for cooking before I leave you, and I need to get back home before dark."

"That's OK, Ms. Kemmer. Do we need to gather sticks for the fire?"

"See, you do know something about getting along up here. But no, the last time I was here I left plenty of kindling right beside the regular logs. It's always best to leave the place ready for the next time."

Predictably, Susan was enchanted by the waterfall and by Willamae's limestone boulder house. She was competent at sweeping out the dark interior and arranging the bedding. An old hand at planning and preparing meals for Hiram, she anticipated much of Grace's instruction about cooking over a campfire.

"Remember," Grace warned Maggie in a whisper while Susan was off exploring, "if you even think you hear the Klan convening—surely they won't on Christmas weekend—douse the outside fire, go into the house, and stay there till morning. No use risking their attention."

"Don't worry. I don't want them to know we even exist."

"But Maggie, they'll have to know when we expose the murderer. It's just that we don't want them to give any thought to us till their conviction's a sure thing."

"Sure thing? What are you talking about, Grace? We have to choose what's safest—"

"Look, Miss Maggie! Quick, Ms. Kemmer, a bunch of birds sitting all around the waterfall, almost like they're tame. Can I give them some bread? Please, can I?"

Maggie sighed with relief. Enough of a Christmas Day discussion of what to do about the killer!

CHAPTER XVI

SECRETS

When Grace had waved a last good-by and disappeared down the ridge, Maggie experienced an uncomfortable emptiness and returned quickly to the fire and moved as close to it as she could.

"I'm so glad you brought me up here." Susan voiced the polar opposite of Maggie's sentiments at that moment.

"Why exactly, Susan?"

Susan sat cross-legged on a flat stone and stretched her bare hands toward the flames. "This week has been so crazy, I'd forgotten there was Nature. This reminds me that there's a whole big world apart from Sardisvale, where it seems like nothing happens except people hurting other people." Susan clapped a hand over her mouth after looking at Maggie's face. "Oh, Miss Maggie, I didn't mean that. I do appreciate everybody who's helped me—you, Mrs. Stockton, the Simmses, Ms. Kemmer, Jerry's daddy, but..." Susan's voice was edging toward hysteria.

"Susan, be quiet and listen. Of course I know what you mean. You've had some horrible things happen to you. If I was looking upset, it was only because I was thinking how senselessly we give each other pain."

"I give my daddy pain."

"How on earth?"

"It happens a lot. Really. Sometimes I remind him of my mother, and she hurt him real bad."

"But that's not your fault. You can't blame yourself. Of course, maybe you look like her or act like her sometimes, but that's natural."

"I know that. I know Daddy gets mad at me sometimes because he still loves her. I understand why he behaves the way he does."

"That's no excuse for you...for us...to let him hit you, though, Susan. No one has a right to beat up on someone else."

"I realized that from thinking about the black girl. She was so beautiful, and she hadn't done anything at all, but all those men... They hadn't any right. I could see they had no right, and in a flash I knew I didn't want to let Daddy beat me any more. That girl wouldn't have let somebody keep beating her. If she could have stopped that man... I couldn't have stopped him, either, could I? Do you think I could have? It happened so fast, Miss Maggie...so fast..."

"There, dear. There. Cry all you like." Maggie had produced a small pack of tissues from her coat pocket. She sat awkwardly on the ground next to the girl, patting her shoulder.

"What could I have done? What should I do now?"

"Susan, I'm sure you couldn't have done anything. The other side of that gate was a block away. You—"

"You know where I was? I haven't told anyone! How?"

"You were in such a state of shock, it didn't even register with you that I saw your eyes looking through the bars. I went around the building, and there you were, still staring, frozen to the spot."

"I saw her die, Miss Maggie! I saw him kill her!"

"I thought you said 'them.' I'm sure you said 'those men' hurt her."

"Yes, well, first her mouth was cut from the man in the Andersen house. She told Jerry—"

"So you saw Jerry through the fence?"

"And then the boys came out of the Hollow's window and gagged her and held her down. Gary Scheider watched the street while Brad Abel tried to get her to...well, I think he was going to rape her. Then Gary said the cops were coming, and they climbed back in the window."

"She was still alive?"

"Brad banged her head on the cement...knocked her out, but she hadn't been stabbed yet."

"The policemen were almost there, though?"

"The cop was by himself. Nobody saw but me."

"The policemen—"

"Just one, the young one who came to the church to get Daddy. He stabbed her. He's pretending she was already dead when he got there, but he stabbed her. The policeman did it!"

Susan immediately began to yawn and shiver. Maggie led the girl into the stone house and tucked her in for the night. Unburdened of her secret, Susan was asleep before Maggie had unzipped her own sleeping bag.

Imagining the girl's relief reminded Maggie of her childhood "heart-to-hearts," naughtiness confessed at bedtime by Maggie, accepted and forgiven by her mother. The "naughtiness" changed over the years from childhood pranks to the thoughtless or perverse acts of an insensitive and/or egocentric adult. Still, her mother never berated her, instead only gently scolded, pointing out the other person's humanity and serving up an extra dollop of love.

Her mother's wise guidance had always allowed Maggie self-esteem and independence, so she had never been in awe of authority: not of school authorities—after all, her own mother was one—or church authorities—they were all quite human and usually foolish—or law enforcers, who were responsible to the citizens. She had always recognized policemen as possessing the same foibles as everyone else.

She had even several years ago made a public statement—well, public at the Thursday Study Group—when some empty-head had expressed doubt that Timothy Haskins could ever again function adequately as police chief after his depression. "If we wait for a perfect police chief, we'll have none at all," Maggie had announced.

No special effort was required for Maggie to believe that a policeman was the murderer. Her immediate intuition was that it was true...horrible, regrettable, but true. As clear to her as the truth of Susan's story was the certainty that Susan's testimony, in the absence of any other evidence, would never hold up in court. No jury could vote against the young policeman and in favor of the child who, the very day of the murder, had at last admitted her fear of her family authority figure. Surely even an incompetent defense attorney would point out that Susan was at last rebelling against authority on that Monday of Christmas week, and psychologists bickering about cause-effect would be ignored by the jury.

What consequences *would* Susan's testimony in court bring? Public announcement that Hiram battered her. Would that impede his progress in stopping drinking and trying to be a good father? Probably. Impede Susan's acceptance by her peers? Certainly; weren't adolescents' peers always more critical than supportive?

Maggie had no faith that the community would rally together to oppose a Klan whose membership included even local policemen. How much power could Timothy Haskins have over his men if they condoned a murdering bigot?

What about the police chief himself? Jerry trusted his father implicitly, but seemed to have no delusions about his beloved, but renegade, Uncle Greg. Things were indeed complicated, though Jerry's surprise visit Tuesday night to enlist Maggie's aid made more sense in the light of Susan's story: Jerry suspected the truth but had no proof, couldn't even admit to himself that a policeman might be the murderer. That would explain why he was so afraid, why he didn't go to his father, and why he was so concerned about Susan's safety. He knew intuitively that Susan wouldn't be believed and that her public protectors, the police, had the best opportunity to harm her.

Now Maggie, as Susan's private protector, had to decide the future of their dreadful shared secret. She must make some hard decisions, some concrete plans, that very night, before Maurice returned.

She was the only human awake in the forestry on Christmas night. She fumbled her way to the door. The campfire was almost out, its glowing coals hissing when large, lacy snowflakes made contact. The sky was very white, but Maggie was skeptical that there'd be much accumulation— too unseasonable in this part of Indiana.

She scooped up a soupcan of dirt and doused the glow, then made her way back to her sleeping bag. Maybe she could think better in a horizontal position. Fat chance she'd be able to sleep any time soon, though, and that in itself was worth thinking about: she actually felt stimulated, excited, eager, not what she would have predicted as an aftermath of the week's events.

Hadn't she been longing for solitude, peace, the life of a recluse? To be honest, she had not had that longing lately. Her dream of going away had been at its most cogent while her mother was alive. Had she really wanted only to leave responsibility behind? Phyllis would say so; Jonathan Simms, too; but now that she had the responsibility of keeping Susan safe, she felt much more alive, the way she had expected to feel as a hermit.

Was she seriously confused? Had she no idea what she really wanted? What had been so attractive about the life of a recluse, anyway? Well, she might have an answer for that. Yes, she'd try it on: what she had longed for was control. She had not been tired of the daily effort of caring for her mother, but, rather, of having no control. Her mother's dreadful, progressive, debilitating illness had been in charge of Maggie. The nature of the illness and her love for her mother had usurped her autonomy: all she could have done was what she did do.

Caring for Susan was nothing like that. Maggie could say no. She wasn't going to, but she could. Since Susan was able to make some choices of her own, there was room for alternatives. Maggie, for the first time in her adult life, was aware of alternatives, possibilities. She could fly in any direction...no anchor to hold her, nothing to set her course, no one to guide or restrain, all had become her own choice— where to go, how to live, whom to love. She hadn't chosen her mother, hadn't chosen to love her, that had been a given. Now the gift was gone.

The darkness of the cave house descended heavily onto her chest. Maggie pressed her hands against her eyelids and felt great rivers of tears flow between her fingers. She cried copiously, silently—cried herself to sleep and began to dream.

In the dream, the house within which she and Momma lived was huge, three stories high, but bare within its walls. Maggie walked into each room and decided what should be where: the reading lamp near the fireplace—she pointed, it appeared; the piano on the inside wall—she pointed, it appeared; heavy blue draperies on the porch window— she pointed, they appeared. She progressed, decorating painstakingly in great detail throughout every room. Finally, her mother's room. She pointed to the space the hospital bed should occupy, but no bed appeared. Instead, Momma was suddenly there, sitting in a wheelchair, looking well and strong, smiling her beautiful, loving smile.

Maggie pointed again, but Momma shook her head. Nothing appeared. Then Momma began zipping her wheelchair down the hall, out the front door, down the steps, rapidly away. Maggie, frantic that she could not fill the back room, ran after the wheelchair, mouthing unintelligible words; but her mother began to vanish, swallowed by mist, till all Maggie could see was her mother's hand waving good-by.

The Dream-Maggie's head was seized in a Herculean grip, as though it were being tightened in a vise. The crushing pain increased, became unendurable. Then suddenly stopped.

Maggie woke up. No pain...no pressure...in fact, she felt wonderful. It was the middle of the night, but she felt steady, logical, clearheaded, energetic...ready to accept all responsibilities that might come her way...ready to make decisions.

What should be first? What to do about Susan the witness, of course. Maurice, who by then knew Hiram had threatened him, wanted to talk to Susan—undoubtedly something about prejudice. That would be OK; that was up to them. But if Susan's witnessing of the murder became generally known, she would be in danger, even though her testimony surely would never stand up in court. For years she had been the abused child who had insisted her father never touched her. A defense attorney might, indeed, be the instrument for driving her over the edge. But it would never come to that. Out of all those Klan members, someone would surely accept the risk of silencing Susan before the case ever came to trial. She and Susan *must* keep the secret—from everyone.

That would require giving the outward appearance of normality, and camping out up on the ridge in a driving snowstorm was definitely not an ordinary thing to do. No, home was where they needed to be, where Susan could participate in the sort of routine that healthy youngsters ought to have. Neither Maggie nor Susan had had any experience of such a routine, but together they could learn.

* * *

"I never thought I'd have a breakfast of scrambled eggs and bacon outdoors in snow," Susan said as she blew over her mug of hot chocolate.

"We slept so late I think we'll have to call this brunch, not breakfast. Look what else we have." Maggie pulled a box of donuts out of her backpack.

"I wish I'd known they were there, or at least been able to find some matches. Then you'd probably still be sleeping," Susan said.

"You may be right. It's certainly dark inside the cave, especially during a snowstorm."

"The woods are so beautiful I could stay here forever."

"Susan, we have to have a talk about that; I think we should go home tomorrow."

"But I don't have school till a week from Monday. Is it because of what I saw?"

"Yes, mostly, but not the way you're probably thinking."

"You want me to go tell Jerry's father?"

"No, I definitely don't, and I want to explain why. There's no real evidence, so it would be only your word against that policeman's; and he's got lots of friends and maybe the Klan on his side, and you—"

"I know, they'll say I'm too young and I need a counselor."

"And you do. You *are* getting professional help."

"Yes, but I also saw a murder. I'm the only witness, and that man ought to be in jail."

"I believe the best thing is for you and me to keep this secret. It's the best advice I can give you."

Susan frowned, staring off down the hill of snow-laden branches for several minutes.

Maggie, too, remained silent. She hoped fervently that Susan would trust her foster parent to know best.

"All right, Miss Maggie, it's our secret. I can keep it easier now that you know, too."

"Well, that's settled. Now we need to clean up this tenderfoot-looking campsite because you're going to have a surprise visitor this afternoon."

"Who?"

"Ms. Kemmer's gone to Indy to meet Maurice."

"Maurice! Is he all right? I thought—"

"He's fine. He's coming back to help Mr. Kemmer finish cutting down my trees. I think he's even going to live out here with the Kemmers."

"He's not afraid?"

"Since the murder, you mean? You can ask him yourself. He and Grace are going to climb up here when they get back."

"I have something to tell Maurice." In response to Maggie's raised eyebrow, Susan added, "Not about the murder, though."

Maggie believed her.

* * *

The storm continued, but altered; by mid-afternoon the large, lacy flakes had given way to tiny sparkles of ice that beat thickly on the remains of the campfire until it mounded silver in the gray light. Maggie and Susan watched from pillow seats in the house doorway.

"Maybe Maurice's plane couldn't even take off," Susan said.

"No, it's more likely that beltway traffic is slow because of icy roads. Or the plane was late because of holiday crowds. It is Christmas weekend."

"I haven't forgotten. It's a real white Christmas. Usually all it does is rain, and I—Look down there! I saw something moving. I'm sure I did. Something red right through there."

Maggie followed Susan to the edge of the clearing and spotted movement among the silver-glazed branches.

"Hellooo!" Susan called through cupped hands.

"Su-san!" came back in a rich baritone.

"It's Maurice, for sure!"

"You go meet him, then, while I put on water for some cocoa."

After Maggie had built up the fire in the large room of the cave house and was emptying packets of instant cocoa into Willamae's mugs, Grace entered with a big canteen of water.

"We were beginning to speculate on how icy the roads are and whether the flight was on time," Maggie told her. "Did you have any trouble?"

"The flight was on time, but I probably would have had trouble driving back if Maurice hadn't insisted on taking the wheel...says Michigan winters prepare a person for anything."

"The roads are bad, then?"

"They're not good and getting worse. I'm glad we're here and don't need to go anywhere. You and Susan, too."

"I'm planning, though, to take her home tomorrow afternoon."

"You're not going to hide out here for a while? I thought—"

"No. No, we had a talk."

"Did she tell you what she saw?"

"We've decided to go back home and try to live as normal a life as possible."

"What do you mean? Was she a witness to the murder or wasn't she?"

"She has nothing to tell anybody else."

"So she did tell you! You know who did it! Maggie, there's a murderer on the loose. It's your duty to society to bring him to justice."

"And what is my duty to my foster child? To get her killed, or to see that she at last has a normal life, free of violence?"

171

"Maggie, I just can't believe you're willing to let a murderer walk the streets."

"Hey, what's going on in here?" Maurice and Susan rushed into the cave room and straight to the fire.

"Hello, Maurice. We've missed you. I hope your family's well."

"They're fine, Miss Maggie, but I owe you an apology for the way I just disappeared."

"Please, don't waste words on me. I understand. No cause for you to apologize. Drink your hot chocolate and I'll be happy. There's a mug for everyone. Grace, will you help?"

The four warmed themselves with the fire and cocoa in a silence that was awkward with what remained unsaid.

Finally, Maurice set down his empty mug and took a deep breath. "Susan, if you'd put on another sweater or two, we could take a walk."

"OK!" Susan jumped up and pulled a hoodie and plaid jacket out of a pile in the corner.

"I pointed out the Magic Circle to Maurice on our way up. Now you can really show it to him," Grace suggested.

Maggie picked up her own scarf and wound it around Susan's head and neck. The process allowed Maggie to meet Susan's eyes in what she hoped was a reminder of their agreement to keep their secret.

"We'll be back before we turn into icicles."

* * *

To Maurice the frosted Magic Circle had a special shine. The woods around it became mere background, while the circle of stumps seemed to attract the day's dull white light and turn it into crisp glitter. Just the right setting for him to help Susan see the truth.

She had picked up a loose pine branch on the way to the Magic Circle and used it as a broom on two of the stumps so that she and Maurice could sit down. He could feel the wet, cold wood through the seat of his jeans, but he'd just have to suffer. Their talk shouldn't be rushed. They were quiet for a few moments, then both began to speak at once.

"Susan, I—"

"I thought you were—"

"Go ahead."

"No, you...please."

"OK, Susan, you're one of the reasons I came back."

"I thought somebody...my daddy..."

"I know it was your daddy who pulled a gun on me."

"I thought he might have shot you. I was afraid you'd think it was my fault; but, honest, I didn't—"

"I know you had nothing to do with him coming after me. If he hadn't done it, somebody else would have."

"He wasn't drunk."

"I know that. I also know he beat you...used to beat you... when he was drunk. I'm really glad you told some people who could help you. That's not something somebody ought to keep to themselves. People ought not to be allowed to hurt other people."

"Like Daddy tried to hurt you. *Did* he hurt you?"

"He didn't hurt me physically, just scared the shit out of me."

"You think I should have told about that, too?"

Poor kid. She was desperate for approval, but felt so guilty. She was tough, though, tougher than the ladies knew. He could level with her, he was sure. "I don't know, Susan.

I don't blame you. You were probably too scared for yourself, then. But if it were to happen now, maybe you'd be able to think about other people, too."

Susan flushed, her hands fidgeting in and out of her mittens; when she spoke, her voice trembled. "I think you're wanting me to tell another secret. You think I ought to tell because of other people. Right?"

173

"There are a couple of reasons I came up here to talk to you. Of course, I'm glad to see you and Miss Maggie; but that's not why I'm here. First, I wanted to tell you I know about your daddy—that I know he's the one who threatened me and that I'm OK and don't blame you. But more important, I want to try to make you understand why I came back."

Susan sat very still, leaning forward as though afraid of missing a word.

"I've never been so scared as when your daddy held that gun to my head. I left without explaining to anybody except my best buddy at I.U.; he's black, too, so I was pretty sure he'd keep his mouth shut.

"My family was freaked out, you better believe, when they heard I didn't ever plan to set foot in Indiana again. My mother cried and carried on and called my uncle to come over and give me whatfor. He didn't exactly do that, though. He just went on for a long time about what a beautiful voice I had and how nobody in my family had had a chance to go to college till me. Made me feel awful.

"Then he talked some really serious shit about prejudice and civil rights and black folks holding their heads up— pride..." Maurice stopped mid-sentence and buried his face in his hands. It was hard, really hard, to admit how cowardly he had been.

Susan prompted him softly, "So you decided to come back to school."

"No," came the muffled reply. When Maurice raised his head, he knew his tears were obvious, even through the steady sleet. "No, Susan, I told my uncle and," his voice broke, "my mother that I didn't want to die, didn't want to risk my life because of some honky fools way down in Indiana."

"Were they mad?"

"Disappointed. Sad. My family's neat, though; they stayed off my case. Just let me lie around feeling sorry for myself for days. Then, last Monday night, my buddy in Bloomington called and told me about the murder."

"Did you know her...Michelle?" Susan's eyes were wide, her head held tensely.

"I never saw her. My buddy didn't know her, and neither did anyone else we know. But I felt like it was my fault. I felt like if I'd gone to the police about your daddy and the gun—"

"Daddy didn't kill her! He was at work. It was...it had to be somebody else."

Maurice had been listening to and watching Susan attentively, but was determined to let her tell things her way. He didn't respond to her directly. "I called my buddy Wednesday night, and he read the Bloomington and Indy newspaper accounts to me. Everybody seems to think it was a Klan killing."

"I couldn't sleep very well. What happened to me in Sardisvale kept going 'round and 'round in my head."

"You mean what Daddy did to you?"

"No, I mean the good stuff. Mr. Kemmer showing me how he loves trees. Miss Maggie bringing me hot chocolate. You wanting to hear all about I.U. And, of course, Ms. Kemmer, when she first called me up about the job with her dad. All she really knew about me then was from the time she made me some ginseng tea."

"Ginseng tea?"

"Yeah, see, that's the most important part because then's when she told me about this idea she has of a 'ginseng cure.'"

"I've heard ginseng will keep you young...and...and sexy."

"But Ms. Kemmer doesn't believe that. She believes that when people think ginseng will keep them young and sexy, they themselves do things that keep them young and sexy and think the tea did it when it was really them."

"I'm confused."

"Listen, it's simple. If people work hard as they can to make their good dreams come true, most of the time they get pretty much what they want. So, I got to thinking about fairness, justice, and how I had quit trying because of only one person when a whole bunch of people were already going out of their way to help me."

"I'm still confused."

"I ran away because I was scared of your daddy, even though I knew the Kemmers and Miss Maggie and her friend and you and my landlady and my buddies and my professors were all on my side. But I've done a lot of thinking; I've decided to stick around and demand justice, help myself, and drag along all the other people I possibly can. I've got to believe we can make a difference. I *do* believe it. I've got to be true to myself and my family, to Michelle and other black strangers, to my white friends, and even to white strangers who're willing to be on my side. I can't run away, and I can't keep quiet."

"Oh, Maurice, you think I'm being a coward by keeping quiet. You think I'm guilty, too!"

"What do *you* think?"

"I think nobody would believe me. A dumb kid who lets her daddy beat on her—"

"You don't let him any more."

"I lied about it for a long time. I lied to the Guidance counselor and the social worker and the police lady."

"But now you've told the truth."

"They'd never believe me about the murder, though. There's no evidence. It'd be just my word against the cop's, and maybe he'd kill me, too."

Maurice sprang to his feet. "A cop!"

Susan clapped her hand over her mouth. "Oh, God! Why can't I keep a secret?" She began to cry.

Maurice knelt on the deepening ice and put an arm around her shoulders. "You have to tell, Susan. That man has to be stopped. All of us who believe he's wrong have to stick together and believe we can make a difference. We need your help...I need your help. Please, Susan."

Maurice continued to hold Susan until she finally stopped crying. Then the sleet sounded loud, like rocks being hurled at a frozen world from an angry white heaven, he thought.

Very soon both young people began to shiver. Maurice stood up and stamped his feet.

"Miss Maggie thinks telling the police will be too dangerous for me; I'm afraid of him, Maurice. I don't want to die."

"Of course you don't. There's got to be a safe way. Let me think about it and try to figure it out. Trust me?"

"I do...really I do, but I promised—"

"Go on and keep your secret for now; but I need for you to tell the truth soon. Lots of people's lives may depend on it. Now let's go; we've got to get back before we freeze to death. Don't tell anyone yet, but you and I are going to bring on a ginseng cure. That can be our secret, yours and mine, till I get the details worked out."

CHAPTER XVII

DOWN FROM THE RIDGE

U nlike the trip up, when the utter silence of snowfall had prevailed, the descent from the ridge was a noisy procession that heightened the nervous anticipation Grace already felt. Every step she and Maurice took was a cracking and crunching through icy crust.

Grace led the way. About two hundred feet below the Magic Circle, she stopped and beckoned Maurice to sit beside her on a dry limestone slab under an overhang of tangled brown vines. "All right, Maurice, I can't stand waiting any longer. Did Susan tell you what she saw?"

"I'm afraid the answer is yes and no. She didn't actually tell me what she saw, but she let slip a very important, very serious fact about the murderer."

"What's that?"

"He's a cop."

"A policeman? My God!"

"Now we know why she can't just go walking into the station house and point her finger at the murderer."

Grace shook her head slowly. More complications. "Is she willing to tell anyone?"

"She's scared. Miss Maggie thinks it's too dangerous and has advised Susan to keep quiet."

"Maggie knows, then? Of course, she must."

"I think so. Yes, I'm sure Susan's told her everything, and she's trying real hard to keep Susan safe, but that's not fair."

"Of course not! Did you explain why?"

"Yes, and Susan's almost convinced. I did say she should keep the secret for a few more days, till I think this whole thing through. Miss Maggie doesn't expect people—a jury, I guess she means—to believe Susan. Do you agree?"

"That's something we've got to get an expert opinion on. You're right; this is going to take some thought and maybe some research. I don't know where to begin. Let's head on home and sound Daddy out. He can come up with some amazing insights."

Shivering with emotions as much as with cold, the two continued their walk through the icy woods, down to the Kemmer house.

A picnic ham in the oven was sending clouds of fragrance throughout the house. Ora met them in the hall with a worried frown. "That phone's been ringin' every half hour since y'all left."

"It's probably Maurice's folks wanting to know that the plane made it. Think you should call them, Maurice?"

"They wouldn't call today. I promised to call them on New Year's Day."

Before Grace could tell Ora the latest developments, the mystery caller reached her.

"This is Jerry Haskins, Ms. Kemmer."

"Hi, Jerry. I hope you had a Merry Christmas."

"No, not really. Something bad's happened—I mean, might happen. My family has a terrible problem, and I need to talk to Miss Maggie and Susan right away. I've been trying to find them for two days, but their house is empty. Nobody's at Mrs. Stockton's, either, so maybe they all went away together. Finally today I decided you might know where they are. If you do, please tell me. I'm desperate, Ms. Kemmer. Please!"

"Why?"

"It's...it's a serious family problem. Do you know where they are?"

"I want to help you, Jerry, but you'll have to tell me what's going on."

"I don't know if I should. I'd like to, but..."

"Maggie was here Thursday and told me you thought Susan had seen something that might put her in danger if other people found out."

"That was before my dad told me my uncle was in trouble."

"Your uncle!"

"Susan may be the only person who can keep my uncle from going to jail. I've got to find her. Maybe something awful's happened to her. I told my dad—"

"Oh, no! Jerry, what did you tell your dad? I thought you and Maggie agreed to keep a secret."

"Well, she told you! I just told my dad we had to find Susan and he mustn't let anybody—and I mean anybody— else know we were looking for her."

"Where's your dad now?"

"He went down to the station for the afternoon, but he should be back by six."

"Do you think you could get your dad to come out here tonight without anybody else knowing where he is?"

"Sure. No problem. Is Susan out there? Is she all right?"

"She's fine. When you get here, we'll explain what's going on. Wait. Jerry, does your dad always use a police car?"

"No. He never uses it for personal stuff."

"Good. Don't use it tonight. Just come for a personal visit."

"OK. Thanks."

Grace's report of the police chief's prospective visit pleased Maurice. "Now's my chance to report Hiram

Marshall's threat to me as well as Susan's story. You do think we should tell him what Susan saw, don't you?"

"I think he's got to know before she goes back into town. No other way to protect her from a policeman."

"What's this about a police?" Ora asked. When the logger had been brought up-to-date, he voiced some opinions of his own. "Seems like Klan fools is ever'where. Might near anybody could be one. Long's those stupid fools is organized, there's bound to be trouble. If some of them's police, some more of them's prob'ly lawyers and judges and preachers and doctors and teachers and—"

"Surely you're exaggerating!" Grace interrupted. "I guess you're basically right, though; an organized Klan can be dangerously powerful."

"I got a plan for fixin' their wagons—at least for a while, and maybe for good."

"You started to tell me the other day. Go ahead. What is it?"

"This here forestry's state property, right?"

"Right."

"So if someone's trespassin', then the police chief could call in the state troopers to pertect it, right?"

"I guess so. Right. But who'd be trespassing? Surely not Maggie and Susan?"

"'Course not. Use your head, Grace. The Klan's trespassin' ever' time they hold a meetin' up here at night. Big sign at the entrance says the forestry closes at dark. If they was to meet out here now, they'd have to have a fire to keep warm, and I know that'd be a serious enough offense to bring in the law. S'pose their meetin' was surrounded by troopers 'n' those fools was all arrested 'n' fingerprinted 'n' had their names in the Bloomington 'n' Indy papers..."

"Daddy, that's a great plan! Not only would it embarrass a lot of people, but I bet some key citizens of this community would decide to drop their Klan membership. The murder has probably turned away some of the Klanners anyhow, and there weren't very many at that meeting we saw."

"It takes just one," Maurice commented grimly.

"Yes, but it takes a lot more than one to carry out justice. That's the part we need to concentrate on. Daddy, how do you expect the troopers to know when there's a Klan meeting?"

"I'll tell 'em. This fella who's the chief, he can have a battle plan all ready for whenever he gets a call. Troopers might not oughta be told till the last minute, 'case some of them's Klan sympathizers. When I see the guys comin' to set up them loud speakers, I'll just call the chief."

"But you don't use the phone."

"I can use it, and that'll be a 'mergency. I'll use it if you ain't here. I gotta do my share, too."

Grace grasped her father's tough, stained, mutilated old hands in gratitude. She had known he would come through with more than moral support. Surely they could see justice done before anyone else got hurt.

* * *

Timothy Haskins' car alerted the group inside the kitchen when it shattered through the ice glazing Ora's yard. Grace held the door open in welcome as Timothy and Jerry held each other's arms on the slippery path to the porch.

"Not much fit for man nor beast tonight," the police chief said as he stomped snow from his shoes on the Kemmer porch. "Good evening, Ms. Kemmer, Mr. Kemmer."

Grace had forgotten what a large man Jerry's father was. He completely filled the door. His redhead's complexion was, like Jerry's, rosy from the cold; and his smile, like his son's, was vulnerably sweet. Permanent worry lines, though, had begun between his eyes; and the eyes themselves had a guarded look still absent from the boy's. Timothy Haskins had suffered and learned to be careful. Grace liked that.

"Hello. Hi, Jerry. This is Maurice Saunders."

"You're the guy who was working for Mr. Kemmer before I was," Jerry said. "You're the one who just took off..."

"Yeah, I ran out on my job and my friends."

"We'll explain it all," Grace said hurriedly. "Sit down and have some soakberry tea."

"My daughter, here, she thinks hot tea cures 'bout ever'thin' that ails one. Me, I'm not so sure what ails this place can be figgered out, much less cured."

"I hope you're wrong, Mr. Kemmer. In fact, I'd resign my job tomorrow if I believed nothing would get better. I may be asked to resign next week as it is."

"Dad, would they really make you resign if Uncle Greg—?"

"Officer Haskins!" Grace interposed firmly, teapot in hand, with her calling-a-class-to-order look.

The four men immediately sat more erect. "Yes, Ms. Kemmer?"

She was flustered at the reflex responses. She must remember she was on vacation. More softly she said, "Well... let's not be so formal. Please call me Grace."

"And call me Timothy. I have a feeling we're going to be saying things meant only for the ears of friends."

Maurice had been fidgeting during Grace's and Timothy's preliminaries. He spoke at last. "Chief...Timothy, I think maybe I brought on this whole mess by coming to work for Mr. Kemmer."

"You ain't to blame, son."

"Well, anyway, I think I ought to start this discussion by telling what I did."

"And what was did to you," Ora put in vigorously.

So Maurice related his Sardisvale history: his meeting Grace at school, his work at Maggie's, Hiram's threat, the Christmas call to the Kemmers, and their insisting that he live with them and work part-time for Ora.

"I don't know," Timothy said, "what difference it would have made to have charged Hiram at the time he threatened you. I do think it might have kept him from seeming such a hero to the Klan, but you never know. I have an informer who reported to me about the meeting. Since then Jonathan Simms and I have been trying to cook up some community action to educate those ignorant bigots.

"One thing I thought of was that my household ought to be the safest in town. I'd like for you to come live with Jerry and me instead of way out here."

"Yeah, Dad, that'd be neat."

Maurice was obviously pleased. "I don't suppose it'd be any more dangerous than being out here. I have to get a car to commute from Bloomington anyhow. Thank you very much, sir. I'll do it if the Kemmers think it's OK."

Grace realized that the arrangement would undoubtedly be more fun for the young man than their accommodations out by the forestry. She and Ora exchanged glances and simultaneously nodded approval.

Timothy shook Maurice's hand. "Welcome, then. I hope you'll be willing to let me know if anybody doesn't treat you right."

"Now that that's settled," Grace said, "we need to talk about the murder."

Everyone silently shook his head.

"I guess it's up to me," Jerry finally began, "to say why I think Susan can save Uncle Greg."

When Jerry's narration had reached the part about his Tuesday night visit to Maggie's, Maurice interrupted. "Susan told me this afternoon who the murderer is."

"She did? I wasn't even sure she remembered exactly, she was so spaced-out afterward," Jerry said.

"I think Miss Maggie knows, too. She'd convinced Susan to keep it secret, but Susan sort of let it slip...I mean, some of it."

"Who was it?" Jerry asked.

"To tell the truth, I'm not sure that now's the time or that I'm the one who should tell."

Timothy's voice had an urgent tone. "Maurice, my brother will be charged with murder—the circumstantial evidence is damning—unless Susan comes forward with the truth. If you'll tell us what she told you, we can get an investigation going that will save him. He did not kill that girl, but right now he can't prove it."

"The trouble, sir, is the *we*.

"What?"

"You said 'we' can investigate, and I guess you mean the police. The whole situation is so dangerous for us all, though, because the murderer is a cop."

"A cop! A policeman?" Timothy looked stunned.

"Dwight! Of course!" Jerry had jumped up from his chair and grabbed his father's arm. "That's why Susan went crazy when he came into the sanctuary looking for her father. She doesn't know him, but she recognized the murderer."

Timothy seemed to be coming out of his daze. "Then Michelle wasn't dead when Dwight found her. But how come he was carrying a knife? Could he have known she would be there? Of course, Greg implied the Klan has some kind of communication network..."

Ora leaned forward. "That's why I say the Klan's gotta be split up. Old rotten wood, they is. I say get the troopers to axe 'em down so's they can't get up."

Timothy looked quizzically at Grace.

"Daddy has an idea for arresting the Klan the next time they meet here in the forestry. I think it might work if he helps. There are quite a few of us, you see, who want to help stop the Klan, educate our community, and catch the murderer. I just know we can do it if we work together!"

Her impassioned speech over, Grace was suddenly aware that Timothy was staring at her. Did he disagree? Think she had impossible dreams? Think she should mind her own business? He seemed to be staring at her hair. She smoothed it nervously.

At last, to her great relief, he smiled—hugely. "That's wonderful news! Maybe we *can* do what you say if we work together."

* * *

It was obvious to Maggie that Susan didn't want to talk about the conversation with Maurice. All she would offer was "he's very brave" and "he doesn't blame me for Daddy going after him with a gun."

"Well, of course he doesn't; you weren't the one who told your dad about Maurice's working in town. Bob Stockton took care of that gossip-mongering."

Susan gasped. "Mr. Stockton? But how did he—? I remember! Mrs. Stockton came to your house with cookies one day."

"Phyllis Stockton tells everything she knows."

"And she was with you Monday morning, so she knows I was watching."

"How could she know? I didn't tell her."

"She saw how upset I was when you took me to the Simmses'. I can't believe how dumb I acted."

"You had had a terrible experience."

"And they all know it—Reverend Simms, Mrs. Simms, Mrs. Stockton, Mr. Stockton, probably my daddy by now."

"Bob Stockton certainly wouldn't tell your daddy."

"Why not? You said he told him about Maurice. Then there's Ms. Kemmer and Mr. Kemmer and all the rest of the world. No way is it even a secret. It's just something everybody knows except the ones who can arrest the murderer. I don't see how anybody's safe the way things are now."

Clearly, Maurice had given Susan ideas. "So Maurice thinks you ought to go to the police? He agrees with Grace?"

"He's got enough guts to come back and stand up to the crazies. Seems like I've been a coward all my life, and now I finally have a chance to maybe make up for it."

"Susan, this isn't a contest to see who's bravest. We're trying to stay *alive*. You're my responsibility now, and I can't be looking after everybody else—just you. You're too young to have had so much go wrong. It's time somebody thought of you first. That's what I'm going to do."

* * *

Both Maggie and Susan used the task of cleaning the limestone house as an excuse for ending the conversation. After that there was supper to prepare—a can of chili combined with Minute Rice and scooped up with saltine cracker spoons.

The sleet stopped, and the frozen world of the ridge glistened invitingly. Maggie and Susan set out on a walk. After Maggie slipped several times on patches of ice, they decided not to venture farther.

"Anyway, Miss Maggie, I have a surprise for you in my backpack. Come on into the cave house and I'll show you."

Maggie was, indeed, surprised that Susan produced a portable radio. They tuned it in to the I.U. station and settled back to enjoy some classical music and the weather report: "Clear and cold tonight with a low of twenty-two. Increasing cloudiness tomorrow morning with snow beginning by noon and continuing into Monday. Possible accumulation of four to six inches. High tomorrow, thirty degrees; low tomorrow night, eighteen degrees."

"We'll be snowed in!"

"Maybe not actually, but I see nothing wrong with staying here till this Alberta Clipper passes through. Listen, Susan, we have a serious problem without an easy solution.

I know we disagree about what you should do, but can't we agree not to discuss it again until we get home? We'll let our ideas incubate till then, and we'll reach our final decisions about what to do after we're down from the ridge. OK?"

Susan showed her assent and relief with a big grin—rare for Susan, precious to Maggie.

* * *

Sunday morning on the ridge was whiteness: sky white with the impending storm, trees and ground white with ice.

Susan was first up, eagerness apparent in her movements.

"You seem to have some plans for the day," Maggie commented as she unzipped her sleeping bag enough to struggle to a sitting position.

"I do, Miss Maggie. I'm going to the Magic Circle to try to meditate the way Ms. Kemmer told me about. She says we have the solutions to our problems right inside ourselves, but we have to release our thoughts to let what's hidden come up into our consciousness. I woke up this morning remembering all she told me on our way up here. Do you ever meditate?"

"No, I've never been interested in spiritual or mystical things. Maybe you'll be a good apprentice for Grace, but I have years of training working against me."

"How? Training in what?" Susan poked up the somnolent fire and settled the teakettle into the coals.

"I've always been skeptical of some of the things Grace swears by, like arranging for your subconscious to take over and direct your life."

"It seems sorta like praying to yourself instead of to God. But then Mrs. Simms says the Lord helps those who help themselves."

"Betsy *would* say that. Yes, that's the way she lives. She's very sensible, and caring, much more concerned about other people than I am."

"I wish I could be like her. Reverend Simms is a little scary, though. How long do I have to go to him for counseling?"

"If your father can stay sober and get some professional help himself, maybe not very long. He's going to want to make a home for you again as soon as possible."

"I'm supposed to have a session on Tuesday with Reverend Simms, remember, at two o'clock. He said that after the holidays he'll change my appointment time to right after school."

"We should plan to leave here Tuesday morning. If the roads are too bad, we can stay overnight down at the Kemmers."

"Mr. Kemmer'll probably be ready to work on your trees again. I guess he won't need Jerry with Maurice back."

"He might have both of them work with him, since he's behind schedule."

"Do you like Jerry, Miss Maggie?"

"Yes, indeed. I think he's an unusually sensitive young man. His mother died a few years ago, you know, and he's had a difficult time. Do you like him?"

"I do. I wish...he's very friendly to me, but I feel like... paralyzed...when he's around."

"You probably need some practice being with other young people...boys."

"Did you ever have a boyfriend?"

Maggie was startled by Susan's candor. The child's prying questions had an innocence Phyllis's lacked. Maggie wanted to answer as honestly as possible, so she paused to get her bearings. "No, actually I never did."

"Didn't you like boys...or men?" she asked with shy hesitation.

"No, I don't think so. I don't remember my father, and men I was acquainted with seemed like dumb clods." Maggie heard herself as unexpectedly bitter.

"But you do think Jerry is sensitive."

"Yes..."

"And his father seems like him...sensitive and...and gentle."

"He was very kind the night you were hurt."

"And you said Maurice is 'a fine young man.'"

"He certainly is."

"And don't you like Mr. Kemmer?"

"Ora Kemmer saved my life when I was a little girl. I'm giving him the walnut trees because of that. Momma greatly admired him. He's been a wonderful father to Grace."

"Well, there you are, then." Susan smiled happily. "The men you know best are extra nice. Even Daddy might be nice again if he can stay sober."

Maggie sat in stunned silence while Susan dressed in many layers of sweaters, grabbed a granola bar, and, waving cheerfully, stepped out into the icy day.

Was it possible the poor, mousy child, abandoned by her mother, abused by her father, was more astute than Maggie herself? Her observations were frighteningly accurate: Maggie knew a number of men she trusted and admired. Why hadn't she ever been interested? Or had she? She and Phyllis had talked intimately long ago about their potential relationships with men. Maggie had blocked all that out. Only Phyllis had remembered and persisted in trying to "fix up" Maggie with a series of eligible men.

The fact was, Maggie was no more practiced in peer relationships than Susan—and less honest about it, she saw that now. Surely it was too late for much improvement. Unkempt, clad in ridiculous clothes, she couldn't expect to attract any males. Yet, as Susan had pointed out, Maggie had some good male friends. Ora helped her; Jerry wanted her for a partner in a dangerous enterprise; Chief Haskins respected her as a foster parent.

If she was to be a good foster parent, she needed to live up to her own standards and set an example, a good one, for Susan. This whole parenting business was much more complicated and involving than she had envisioned it. Phyllis, of course, had tried to tell her the joys of motherhood, but no one could really communicate the awesome revelations about self that went with it.

Maybe Susan, though, was a special case. Their conversation that morning had presented Maggie with a clue to Susan's optimism in the face of the terrible experiences of last week: Hiram had once been "nice." It seemed incredible. Still, what else could begin to explain this child of changes?

Was it possible that Susan could precipitate some changes in Maggie herself? Grace, of course, insisted that everyone could change; but Grace, like Susan, was young and optimistic.

Ora, now, was much more cynical and worldly-wise. Maggie needed to have more worldly-wise friends, to talk to and listen to. Yes, if she were one to make New Year's Resolutions, having more friends would be on her list.

* * *

Surprisingly, the weather man had predicted with accuracy the severity and duration of the year's last Alberta Clipper. The sky emptied its white to become blue again, and the chill Canadian air had left Indiana behind by Tuesday morning. Melted snow poured down soggy trunks and added to the mush underfoot.

Maggie and Susan were only five minutes past the Magic Circle on their trip down from the ridge when Grace's shouted greeting promised them extra arms to carry their loads. They had left their pots and pans in the cave house in anticipation of future visits, but they held more clothing than they wore because of the warmer temperatures.

True to their agreement, they had abstained from discussion of the murder and the problems it caused its witness. Instead, they had sung, told jokes, entertained each other with stories of childhood escapades, including incidents Maggie had had buried in her memory for forty years. Finally, they made lists of New Year's Resolutions: private ones, public ones, and ones to confide only to each other.

Maggie's list of private resolutions was the heaviest thing she bore on her descent from the ridge to home and the new year.

CHAPTER XVIII

PREPARATIONS

On Sunday morning, before the snow had begun, Grace had driven Maurice down to Bloomington for the last week of school vacation.

"Chief...Timothy...said you could move in with him and Jerry right away if you want to."

Maurice smiled. "I know, but it's probably going to take a few days to find that used car driven only to church by a little old lady. Also, I need to see the dean and a few professors, and hang out and party some, too."

"It's good to see you a bit more cheerful."

"I trust Timothy to get Susan's statement without putting her in danger. He has too much at stake himself not to, what with his brother being a suspect, and maybe his own job on the line."

"Maurice, don't you believe he's a fair person? Don't you think he wants to see justice done?"

"I may seem optimistic, Ms. Kemmer, but the truth is I'm expecting other folks to look out for number one, same as I'm doing."

"Ha! You don't fool me. You've put Susan way up on your own list of people to look after."

"Well, 'cause she has a history of not being able to look after herself, like me. I guess I lump her and me together as weak minorities. My kind, though, are getting stronger; and I think more people are feeling obligated to protect her kind."

"We have in-service training at my school on how to recognize abused children, but it's true none of my education courses at college ever even mentioned the issue. Communities are still too often impotent when it comes to children abused by their parents."

"And when it comes to former slaves abused by former masters." Maurice's smile had become grim. "But now we're finally getting uppity. What could be more uppity than moving in with a police chief whose brother is suspected of committing a Klan murder?"

"By the time you move in next week, next year, that is, the murderer should be safely in jail, and maybe the Klan will be broken up. While you were dressing this morning, Daddy asked me to call Timothy after I get home today and see if they can't work with the state troopers this week. He's decided the Klan might schedule a meeting for New Year's weekend, maybe New Year's Eve during Sardisvale's annual bonfire."

"What kind of bonfire?"

"Believe it or not, old Christmas trees. High school kids collect everybody's dried-up trees and pile them in a vacant lot a couple of blocks from the gymnasium. All the Sardisvale churches' young people's groups get together and have a worship service at the gym that starts at eleven and ends at exactly midnight. Then the fire station sirens go off, everybody from the gym runs down to the vacant lot, and the mayor lights the bonfire."

"Lord, the government stuff black kids miss out on!"

"Of course, only kids and a few preachers and other church advisors are at the gym; but almost the whole town comes to the bonfire. Fire trucks are there, and community groups have free coffee and cookies, and people sing informally. A few fireworks go off, just harmless fun."

"And your dad thinks the Klan will be there?"

"On the contrary, he thinks that would be a perfect time for them to meet in the forestry and not be noticed. He wants the troopers to be ready, just in case."

"I think I can do without New Year's Eve fires, except to cook up some black-eyed peas. Eating them on the first day of the new year is supposed to bring good luck, according to my granny from Down South. We sure could use some good luck around this place!"

"As somebody else from Down South said, 'You ain't just whistlin' Dixie!' Really, though, it's not luck that'll get us through, but actions we ourselves can control. You'll see, Maurice. You'll see."

* * *

Timothy Haskins missed church again that Sunday morning because he was arresting his brother for the murder of Michelle Riddick.

"Fuck the circumstantial evidence! I didn't do it, and you know damn' good and well I didn't."

"Greg, I believe you. Everybody else will, too, before this is over."

"Then how come you're arresting me? What the fuck's going on? When you and Jerry left here Christmas afternoon, you didn't say a goddamn' word about arrest!"

Calmness had descended on Timothy while Jerry was explaining what Susan must have witnessed, and optimism had set in during his meeting with Maurice and the Kemmers. He knew he was not alone, and he was confident he could do what he must about his brother.

"Greg, sit down and listen. I've come by myself so I can explain some things that have to stay strictly confidential. But I do have to take you in this morning."

"This is insane. You are insane. Or maybe *I'm* insane and imagining all this!"

"Nobody's insane, except maybe the killer and the rest of his Klan brotherhood."

Greg abruptly stopped his pacing to sink into an armchair opposite his brother.

"The district attorney—" Tim began patiently.

"Ken LaRue, right?"

"Yes. Ken LaRue called me at home yesterday morning and insisted he had to see me at the station right away, even though it was Saturday and Christmas weekend.

"I went straight in, and he was really upset...didn't want anyone but me to hear what he had to say.

"Somebody—he wouldn't say who, but it had to be somebody from the station—told him your fingerprints were all over the Andersen house; and he and everybody else in Indiana has read in the paper about Jerry's deposition. Anyway, he wanted to hear the findings officially, from me."

"Didn't you tell him my story? Good God!"

"Hear me out, Greg. Ken said the circumstantial evidence is strong enough to take you to trial."

"Holy shit! My own brother!"

"Ken said *because* you're my brother, if I don't arrest you by Monday, tomorrow , I'll no longer be police chief. I didn't respond, and he left my office.

"Now here's the part you've got to keep quiet about."

Greg had leaned back in the chair and closed his eyes. Perhaps, Timothy thought, his own calm had gotten through to his brother.

"There's an eyewitness to the murder, but only a few people who really care about her know she saw anything. She told one of them who killed the girl, and that person told me. I can't arrest the murderer till the girl makes her statement. She's out of town right now; but once she makes her statement, I have to put her in protective custody. Trust me, Greg. Because of who she is and who the killer is, things have to move slowly and surely. I may as well tell you, too, that the Klan connections are complicating things in a very messy way.

"I think justice will be served soonest and best if I stay police chief and if you are the temporary scapegoat. With you in jail, the murderer will feel secure, the witness will be safe—"

"And I'll be paying my dues for what I did to that colored girl."

"That's one way of looking at it."

"I hope you'll look at me and know I'm sorry about her." Greg rose and held out his hands for the handcuffs.

"I will. I do," Timothy said in a husky voice as he snapped the bracelets shut.

* * *

Phyllis and Bob Stockton sat in their daughter's living room Monday noon eating cold turkey sandwiches and discussing the weather.

Bob speculated: "If we start home tonight as planned, I'll bet the roads will be bad and the trip will be slow. I dread it already."

"Bob, please let's wait another day. Can't you call somebody and arrange to stay out till Wednesday?"

"Well, I guess so. The only thing not taken care of is the trucks for the Christmas trees. I promised the kids they could use two for hauling trees to the bonfire pile. If I tell Hiram to give them the trucks, there's no problem."

"Yes, call him now. He might know if the murderer's been arrested. He'll surely know if Susan has said she's a witness."

"I dislike mentioning Susan to Hiram. He's having a hard time, and he's embarrassed about his own arrest. Anyway, Maggie was just guessing."

"Don't mention Susan to him, then. Just give him a chance to bring you up to date on things."

So Bob called Hiram, who sounded sober and capable. "I'll see that the boys get the trucks, Mr. Stockton. Anything else?"

"Are you OK, Hiram?"

"I'm a little down, sir, since Greg Haskins was arrested."

"Arrested! For what?"

"For stabbing that colored girl. I don't believe he did it, though. No way. Not Greg."

"There was a witness, then?"

"No. No witness, just circumstantial stuff. They'll never convict him; he didn't do it. I guess I'll be going to see him in jail after you get back on Wednesday, but I sure hate that place!"

* * *

When Maggie tried to start her car Tuesday afternoon in the Kemmers' yard, the battery was dead. Ora failed in his efforts to charge it and finally gave up.

"Miss Maggie, old age and the weather done your battery in. If you'll stay here tonight, I'll dig my car out first thing in the mornin' and go get you a new battery."

"That suits me fine. Susan won't mind a bit missing her counseling session with Reverend Simms. I guess I'd better go call him and postpone her appointment."

* * *

Jonathan Simms had been decidedly unsettled ever since the murder. He liked to know everything going on among his congregation; but he depended heavily for that knowledge on Betsy, and she had been too busy to keep abreast of the news.

First, the murder had somehow prompted Susan to identify herself as a battered child. That resulted in too much upheaval for her to babysit and give Betsy extra help during the holidays.

Then the church's parents had, because of the murder, been afraid to have the 'Tween Group Christmas Party. That had piled even more work on Betsy, just when many of the older women in the church went off to visit children and grandchildren. Even the Stocktons went off to visit instead of celebrating at home.

Of course, the general fear had died down after a couple of days because people were convinced the murder had been racially motivated. That meant lily-white Sardisvale was safe. He and Timothy were going to change all that, though, by bringing in some blacks to be members of the community. It wouldn't be long till the town joined the twenty-first century.

In addition, the murder had occupied the police chief so that he'd canceled his Sunday time with Jonathan, and the minister missed him. When Timothy had called to cancel, he had refused to discuss the case with his friend and had requested to be present at Susan's Tuesday afternoon counseling session without explaining to Jonathan why. If Susan had been a witness—and Jonathan had all along attributed that idea to female imaginations—then her pastoral counselor should be the first, not the last, to find out. Time he and Timothy had a talk!

Just before Susan's scheduled session Tuesday afternoon, Timothy knocked on the door of Jonathan's office.

"Come in, Timothy, but you're out of luck."

"No Susan?"

"Miss McGilvray called from out of town and said they were still visiting and wouldn't return to Sardisvale until tomorrow. I rescheduled the appointment for three tomorrow afternoon. Maybe you'd better let me in on what's happening so I can adjust my therapy accordingly."

"I can't do that yet, Jonathan. I wish I could. And I need another favor from you."

"Anything."

"I need to have Susan evaluated by a psychiatrist."

"I think I understand: she's told you what she saw."

"No. No, she hasn't. I haven't even talked to her, and I want you to forget any possibility that she saw anything."

"Oh, no! Timothy, can she testify against your brother?"

"Stop. You're way off base, Jonathan. I want to end this conversation now. Please, though, I beg of you; no more about Susan, not even to Betsy."

"But Betsy was here when Susan came in after the murder."

"Not even to Betsy. If you are my friend, Jonathan—"

"You know I am. Of course you're upset. What can I do? Do you want me to go see Greg in jail?"

"No. You must *not* talk about the murder till I give you the go-ahead. What you can do for me right now is call a psychiatrist and get him to come here to examine Susan tomorrow afternoon. I'll wait while you call." Timothy abruptly sat down.

"It's such short notice in a holiday week," Jonathan protested. After looking at Timothy, he turned to his address book and the telephone.

As he had predicted, though, two psychiatrists in Bloomington were unavailable until late in the following week. Finally he scheduled one from Indianapolis to see Susan in Sardisvale on Tuesday of the first week of the new year.

Timothy exploded sarcastically, "Not for a week! Great... just great!" Then, immediately contrite, he apologized to Jonathan, thanked him, and left.

Jonathan stood unhappily at the door for a few minutes. Timothy wasn't behaving normally, and the worst part of his secret plan was that he was excluding his best friend. Jonathan was hurt.

* * *

Feet dragging with reluctance, Hiram climbed the steps of the jail Wednesday afternoon to visit his friend Greg Haskins.

"What the hell you doin' in my least favorite place, good buddy?" Hiram growled.

"Hiram! My God! I didn't expect anybody to come to see me!"

"Well, I ain't stayin' long. You didn't kill that nigra, though. I know you too well to believe that. I'm sorry to see you here. It's a place I never want to be shut up in again. They kept me till I was sober and let me out in time for the holiday, but I couldn't even see my own little girl on Christmas."

"How come?"

"Her foster parent took her away somewhere, and they still ain't back. Nothin' about it seems fair. I hadn't even touched her for days when she told the preacher."

"Just went out of a clear blue sky and told him, did she?"

"Well, she was supposed to babysit his kids the same mornin' as the murder. After she and a bunch of biddies stood around the body bein' upset, they all went to the preacher's. She musta went off the wall hysterical and up and told him I knocked her around sometimes, so then the authorities wouldn't let her come home. Said she was about to have a breakdown, but she looked all right two nights later in church. Well, I think she did...I don't really remember much, I was so pie-eyed. She wasn't hysterical, though. And after that she left town."

"Hiram, shut up a minute and let me think. Something crazy's going through my mind."

"Sure, Greg, this place'll do it to you for real."

"No, I mean I think I got some things figured out. I got a notion your Susan's out of town because it's dangerous for her to be here."

"Why?"

"Please don't ask me or anybody else. Trust me, Hiram. Keep an eye on your daughter."

"They won't even let me see her 'less a social worker's present."

"That's in private. Nobody can keep you from being around her in public."

"She's not in town, I told you."

"But if she comes back, she'll probably go to the bonfire party at the gym. I was supposed to be cleaning up for it this week; all the kids go."

"I ain't never let Susan go. I us'ly end up at the bonfire, myself, but not sober. I'd rather stay home alone than go there sober."

"Well, you'd better go anyway, and sober, if Susan's going to be there. Just keep her in your sight if you want her not to get hurt."

"Ha! That's a switch. Everybody else thinks *I'm* the one going to hurt her."

"Not if you're sober. Neither one of us is going to hurt innocent girls if we're sober, and that's how we're both going to be from now on."

"Benny down at work says there may be a Klan meeting Thursday night."

"When I get out of here, I'm through with the Klan. I'll give you my arguments when we got a more leisurely situation. In the meantime, though, you gotta stay outta trouble to get Susan back, and—trust me on this—you gotta watch her as much as possible. Thanks for coming, Hiram, but you got more important things to do. Watch Susan!"

* * *

When Maggie and Susan had arrived home late Wednesday morning, Jerry was sitting on their front steps.

"Well, Jerry, my goodness, you're just in time for lunch," Maggie greeted him.

As Susan opened the front screen, an envelope fell to the floor. "Miss Maggie, here's a letter for you with no stamp."

Maggie promptly ripped it open. "Susan, Reverend Simms has had to postpone your appointment with him till after school on Tuesday. Think you can wait?"

"Forever!" Susan replied.

"Hey, then, you've got lots of holiday time," Jerry said. "I was hoping you'd go collecting Christmas trees this afternoon with a bunch of us. Mr. Stockton's letting us use his trucks again this year."

"Trees for the bonfire?"

"Yep. All I have to do is go over to Stockton Construction and borrow a truck."

"Thanks, but I think I'll stay here today and help Miss Maggie unpack."

Maggie realized at once that Susan didn't want to see her father at the construction company. "It's true we have lots of dirty clothes. Susan, will you please take these to the basement while I warm up some hot dogs for us?"

"Here, let me." Jerry picked up one of the backpacks and followed Susan down the basement stairs.

While Maggie was alone, she re-read the note from Jonathan Simms and frowned. Why call in a psychiatrist? No need to mention that part to Susan till she had more information. Another of Reverend Simms's self-righteous schemes, she supposed. She'd have to go over there to find out. Sometimes—not often, but sometimes—lack of a telephone was an inconvenience.

Jerry and Susan seemed more at ease with each other when they re-entered the kitchen.

"One load of clean clothes coming up, Miss Maggie. We managed to put soap in and everything," Jerry announced.

"Miss Maggie, Jerry's asked me to go to the Watch Party and bonfire with him tomorrow night. May I, please? I've never been before."

"What, may I ask, is a Watch Party?"

"It's neat. I go every year," Jerry replied. "All the church youth groups get together in the gym and have a worship service starting at eleven."

"Eleven! That's so late!"

"Not on New Year's Eve. It's to watch the New Year come in. At midnight everybody runs down the hill to watch the mayor light the bonfire of old Christmas trees."

"Yes, I've heard of the bonfire. Well, I guess you can go, Susan, if you try to nap tomorrow afternoon. You, too, Jerry."

"Yes, ma'am!" Jerry bit into his hot dog and continued with a full mouth, so that Maggie could barely understand him. "You sound just like my mother used to sound."

"Not like mine," Susan added softly.

CHAPTER XIX

SETTING FIRES

G race, Ora, and Timothy had agreed that if the Kemmers needed to contact the police chief, they would avoid going through the police station switchboard.

Jerry promised to stay home on Thursday until time for the Watch Party, so he would be in the house when Ora's call came.

"Is this the police chief's boy?" Ora quavered.

Jerry instantly recognized the old logger, the unsteady voice reminding him how leery Ora was of "new-fangled" telephones.

"It's me all right, Mr. Kemmer. Jerry. Will there be a meeting tonight?"

"They's up at the clearin' now, gatherin' dry sticks into a pile and sweepin' around it. They's plannin' a fire, for sure. They prob'ly ain't 'spectin' much of a crowd, 'cause they's no sign of loud speakers or chairs, so far just one car with two idiots."

"Thanks, Mr. Kemmer. I'll see Dad gets the message."

"And tell 'im, son...tell 'im take care."

"I will, sir. Happy New Year."

"Sure, well, we might..." Ora's voice faded and the receiver clicked down.

"Way to go!" Jerry exclaimed and dashed to his bedroom to lace on his sneakers. Elated as he was that the Klan's power might be broken that night, he regretted playing such a small part in the round-up. Still, he was happy to be accompanied to the Watch Party and bonfire by Susan. That would have to be excitement enough.

* * *

For five minutes or so after Jerry had delivered Ora's message, Timothy sat alone behind the closed door of his office and mentally reviewed his plans to arrest the Klan.

Earlier in the week, two state troopers had driven by a back route into the forestry from Bloomington to meet with him and Ora Kemmer at the clearing where the Klan always convened.

Surrounding the clearing, the four men chose trees suitable for posting spotlights, hammered boards up each trunk, and mounted lights connected by brown outdoor electric cords to a central switch behind the fallen log from which the Kemmers and Maggie had watched the previous Klan meeting.

The men mapped the terrain, figured where the troopers could park, and assigned a position to each of half a dozen troopers.

Battle plans called for the troopers to take their places before dark, something much more safely accomplished if the Klan officials weren't there.

Timothy looked at his watch. Two o'clock. Earlier than expected. He hoped that meant the Klansmen would leave their equipment and head home for supper. There were contingency plans, though, if a Klan guard remained.

Ora was supposed to stay in his house out of sight till Timothy got there, at which time the logger could be an invaluable guide.

Surely Timothy had thought of everything. He was particularly proud of the casual, routine way he had taken care of his Klan informer-policeman, Eben Hazlitt.

Impressed with Ora's certainty that there would be a New Year's Eve meeting, the chief had said to his inside man the previous evening, "Eben, since Dwight's off tomorrow— bachelor's night out, you know—I've got you down for gym and bonfire duty. Give you a chance to relive the Good Old Days."

Yes, a clever move: Eben couldn't go to the Klan meeting and so wouldn't be caught in the round-up. Dwight, however, would be free to attend the meeting. His arrest would give him a taste of the other side of the law at the police station and establish in writing his Klan connection. As Jerry would say, very cool move.

Now to hurry home, call the state troopers, and go "civilian" in dress and transportation so his trip to Ora's wouldn't be noticed.

* * *

Eben Hazlitt groaned out loud when he saw the empty Coca Cola carton on the hood of the pickup near the gas station. Klan meeting tonight! And he had the gym and bonfire assignment. A New Year's Eve meeting definitely needed an informer; the chief would surely want to rearrange things.

But when he phoned in, Timothy had already left for the weekend. These bachelors! That reminded him of Dwight Mitchell, who had been moping around lately because he'd broken up with his girl or something.

Eben called Dwight's house and caught the rookie at home. "Tonight? No, got no plans, Eben. You go on to the meeting. I get impatient with you old geezers sometimes. Anyhow, maybe some of those high school chicks'll be snowed by the sight of my uniform."

Mitchell sounded unhappy, bitter even, to Eben. Bigot kids needed to see more of the world, meet more people, live different places. Those ten years in Chicago had sure changed Eben's perspective, and he didn't think Dwight Mitchell was a hopeless case. At least this trade-off of assignments for the night would keep the rookie away from the Klan meeting.

* * *

Grace shopped with unusual pleasure New Year's Eve afternoon. Foremost in her mind was the possibility that Timothy Haskins would join her and her daddy to eat the food she was buying.

Her culinary skills easily compensated for Sardisvale's lack of a health food store. She had learned many tricks, and she passed them on to her foods classes whenever possible.

Hard to believe winter break was nearing its end. So much had happened that concentration on a mundane school day would surely be difficult. As if Susan's testimony—well, testimony-to-be—and Maurice's return were not enough, this surprising man, Timothy Haskins—she whispered his name aloud to enjoy its fullness, its importance—lodged in her thoughts most of the time.

She had admired his strong public comeback from grief and depression, and she was fond of his son, but Timothy's trust of and candor with her motley group of Daddy and Maurice along with his determination to protect Susan and Maggie and to fight injustice, his gentleness... Well, she was running on at the mind, but Timothy Haskins had indeed impressed her as a very special man.

Her trunk loaded with bags of groceries, Grace stopped at the highway traffic light, ready to ease her car onto the road in the direction of the forestry entrance and home. Glancing into the rear view mirror, she was not surprised to see Timothy Haskins grinning and waving from the car behind.

Of course he would appear while she was thinking of him. Such phenomena occurred all the time; she was used to them by now, expected them. They resulted, she was sure, from all her efforts to be psychically attuned to herself and others.

Timothy followed Grace at a discreet distance as they proceeded along the highway, swung into the next road after the forestry entrance road, then bumped over the final stretch and into the wooded lane that opened into the Kemmers' yard.

Grace was daydreaming happily, but jolted back to the wider world when she realized Timothy had driven around the logging shed, thus hiding his car on the far side of the ramshackle barn that housed the pickup truck and log trailers. Hiding! Then the Klan would convene on New Year's Eve. Her daddy had been right. She leaped from the car, leaving the door open, and ran toward the barn.

Timothy was even quicker. He grabbed her arms to stop her fall as the two collided at the front corner of the building.

For a long moment, panting, trembling, she looked at Timothy, then stepped back as he dropped his hands. "I didn't mean to knock us both to the ground," she said softly.

They both blushed.

"No...well...I seem to have rescued us."

"Did Daddy call you?"

"He did. That is, he called Jerry. Let me carry those bags. Looks like enough for an army."

"It's enough for you to join us for supper."

Ora met them at the door, eager to report more fully the Klan's preparations. Talk from then on was about the coming raid.

When it was too dark to distinguish the woods' edge from the clearing, Ora and Timothy donned jackets, hats, and gloves and waved to Grace. As soon as the men disappeared into the blackness, Grace put on her own outer clothing and slipped out the back door.

She had been ostensibly an obedient child, chiefly because what adults expected of her usually coincided with her own desires. She was accustomed to doing what she pleased with no argument from Ora. When Grace had made a move to go out with Timothy and Ora and Timothy said, "Oh, no, you stay here," Ora had locked eyes with her momentarily. He expected her to follow.

Timothy was off-duty and an employee of the city rather than of the state, so he didn't want anyone but the troopers to know he was involved in this raid. He thought it safer for Ora and Grace if nothing was known about their part in the plans. Safety, though, was relative. There was no such thing as long as people with Klan mentality were bound together for action. No, she might as well be where her men were.

Her men? OK, she admitted she was thinking of Timothy that way. He wasn't invulnerable; he needed the Kemmer lore tonight, so she'd be nearby just in case.

The night was unusually dark but only moderately cold. Faint light from the living room window guided her to the edge of the clearing. From there on, she was going to need all her wits about her. She felt in the pocket of her quilted car coat for the flashlight. It was ready for an emergency, but using it was sure to attract attention. She stretched out her gloved hands and walked cautiously in darkness along the beaten path.

After a slow ten minutes, Grace swung off to her right onto one of the many alternate routes she used to reach Willamae's. She had decided to go above the clearing and come down only close enough to be sure the Klan got arrested. Another half-mile sideways, and she had but a short climb to the forestry road that would bring in the troopers' vehicles.

Pausing to get her breath and her bearings, she watched the first of the state trucks pass only ten feet from her and continue to approach the clearing from the side opposite the road the Klansmen would take. Quickly she ascended the hill above the road. No use alarming the troopers unnecessarily.

Another half hour or so found her comfortably settled on a limestone promontory far above the downed log where she assumed Ora and Timothy to be. She had not heard anything else that might be troopers, but she could see several pairs of headlights moving along the road from the highway.

Grace sat crosslegged—palms up, eyes closed—and chanted her mantra, gave herself up to psychic possibilities, lost realistic perception of the passage of time.

Much later, she suddenly felt unpleasantly chilly. She stood up, stomped her feet, clapped her hands, and performed a few knee bends before huddling down again, somewhat warmer.

She became aware of a slow drumbeat, then a flare of light, a cross burning brightly. Her daddy had observed the two Klansmen planting it in a bucket of sand that afternoon. It illuminated a clot of hooded men, but Grace was much too far away to hear anything they might be saying.

The drumbeats ceased. She heard intermittent strains of song. "Onward, Christian Soldiers," she guessed.

The area where the cross had cast shadows burst into blinding white. The troopers' floodlights. Men's voices, shouts. Grace's heart pounded as she began her descent to the fallen log.

The closer she got, the more evident it was that the raid was successful. The Klansmen were being herded down the road to the waiting state trucks. The cross continued to burn, but the bonfire laid around it remained unlighted; not a gun had gone off.

Grace whistled softly to Ora their signal. He bent toward Timothy. Both men were grinning when she crawled the last ten feet to their sides.

"You're a very determined lady," Timothy whispered.

"Very," Grace replied.

211

* * *

"Miss Maggie, I can't decide. What do you think?" Susan stood at the hall door to the kitchen holding up navy pants and a green and gold plaid skirt. "The pants are warmer, but the skirt looks a lot better with my quilted jacket."

Maggie the fashion consultant! Susan looked so serious, though, that Maggie assumed her new role gravely. "No contest. Wear the warmest things you have. So many people go to the bonfire, you may not get close enough to feel it. Your hair looks nice...different."

"I tried to have spikes just on the very top. I don't want anything extreme. I could fix yours this way sometime. It's supposed to make you seem taller and your face longer."

"No, thanks."

"I guess I will wear the pants tonight and save the skirt for Monday."

"You seem to be looking forward to going back to school."

"I always do. I've been so busy bathing and dressing for tonight that I forgot to tell you I saw a girl from my class this afternoon having her hair cut at the same time I was. She just started talking to me like we were friends. She said she heard I had problems with my daddy. Said I wasn't the only one, that there was a lot of stuff like that going on. Said she was sorry and hoped I'd be at the Watch Party tonight."

The doorbell rang.

"Oh, no! It's Jerry, and I'm not ready."

"It's too early...only a little after nine."

"He's coming early. Before the Watch Party he has to meet Reverend Simms at the church to rehearse. He's reading the scripture on the program," Susan called from the back bedroom.

Maggie opened the door to Jerry.

"Hi, Miss Maggie. Is Susan ready?"

212

"She'll be right here. It surely is late to be starting a date. What time do you think the bonfire will be over?"

"I'm pretty sure we'll be back here by one-thirty."

"One-thirty! I thought the mayor lit the bonfire at midnight."

"Pretty near. But nobody leaves while it's still burning. And the church ladies have all kinds of junk to eat. You wouldn't want us to come home hungry."

"No, certainly not," Maggie smiled, catching some of Jerry's humor and enthusiasm, "not if you could be filling up on junk."

Maggie glanced toward the back of the house, then continued. "You seem not to be worried about Susan the way you were last week."

"No, ma'am. I think by morning everything will be cleared up. My dad—"

"Ah," said Maggie quickly, "here she is."

"Hi, Susan. Miss Maggie just OK'd a one-thirty curfew."

"I did?"

"So we'll have plenty of time to 'crash and burn,' as the saying goes."

"You don't alarm me one bit, Jerry Haskins. You two have fun."

As Susan started out the front door, she turned back impulsively to give Maggie a quick hug. "See you next year!"

The door's slam echoed, and Maggie felt suddenly as hollow as the empty house. She was not about to stay home alone all evening. That morning it had hit her that during the Watch Party would be the perfect time for a visit to the parsonage to find out why Reverend Simms wanted Susan to be seen by a psychiatrist on Tuesday. Jerry had said the minister would be at the Watch Party rehearsal; but Maggie preferred to obtain information from his wife. She hadn't seen Betsy since the day of the murder, the fateful day Maggie had become a foster parent.

The usually cheerful young woman, however, looked anything but eager to greet the new year when she opened her door to the late-night caller. She wore a soiled apron, her black hair bristled untidily, and dark smudges underscored her eyes.

"Maggie! Heavens, what brings you here? Oh, come in. How can I make you stand out there in the cold? I'm a little rattled tonight, and you're the absolutely last person I was expecting to see."

"I figured you'd be home with the children."

"A baby-sitter wasn't even a consideration. The fireworks and sirens and uproar at midnight are sure to wake the baby, who'll probably wake the boys. I think I ought to be here. Where's Susan?"

"Jerry Haskins picked her up, and by now they're over at the church rehearsing for the Watch Party."

"Oh, Maggie, do you think it's wise for her to be out in public?"

"She's doing fine. Her face isn't swollen anymore; it's still a little yellowish, but she's hidden that with makeup."

"No, I mean is she safe?"

"Hiram's supposedly sober and can see her next week if—"

"No, Maggie, I mean what about the murderer? You said you thought Susan was a witness."

"Betsy, please don't mention that again. Susan has made no statement to the police. You have no reason to think she's seen anything."

"But I do! I know Gregory Haskins has been arrested, but—"

"What? Greg Haskins? Are you sure? Jerry said nothing about it. It doesn't seem possible!"

"I agree. Nevertheless, he is in jail; and something very strange is going on. Timothy came by to see Jonathan but avoided me, and Jonathan wouldn't tell me why...says he can't discuss it with me till after next Tuesday."

"Why Tuesday?"

"I have no idea. He won't tell me...says it's very dangerous, but he won't say for whom. Oh, Maggie, he's always confided in me before. It isn't like him not to trust me. I'm so upset!"

"Listen, Betsy, I came over here to ask you something about Susan. She had an appointment with Reverend Simms yesterday, but he sent me a note postponing their session till a psychiatrist from Indy could see her with him next Tuesday."

"That's it! Something to do with Timothy and Susan and the psychiatrist. It has to be that! I'll bet you were right, Maggie. Susan knows who the murderer is, but for some reason they have to get a psychiatrist's OK before they take her official statement. She's...Maggie, are you all right? You're awfully pale."

"Betsy, please, please don't tell all this to anyone else."

"I won't, but I'm right, aren't I? Gregory isn't the one, and Susan can straighten all that out. Why hasn't she said anything? And she's out with Jerry while his uncle's in jail."

"We didn't know about the arrest. Since Jerry didn't tell us, he must not want Susan—"

"Maggie! Think what this means! The killer's out there somewhere, and Susan can recognize him."

"I think I should go to the bonfire tonight to keep an eye on Susan."

"I'm sure Jonathan and Timothy will be doing that, too. I have an idea, though. Why don't you help at the church's refreshment booth? Phyllis should be here by ten to pack all the donuts and drinks into our car. You can ride in our car with her. Then she'll go home afterward with Bob while Jonathan drives you home."

"This is much too complicated for me. Why is Phyllis taking your car?"

"Because the refreshments are here, and Jonathan has to go to the Watch Party with the youth group, and—"

"And it all sounds confusing...and dangerous."

215

* * *

In front of the Stockton home, Bob boosted Phyllis into the high passenger side of a Stockton Construction Company pickup truck. He was proud to drive his firm's vehicles, although they certainly weren't classy enough for his wife.

"I'm glad," Phyllis said as Bob turned on the ignition, "I have to ride in this smelly cab only once a year. You should enclose bottles of deodorant with your Christmas bonus checks."

Bob gave his wife's knee a playful pat. "I know it disappoints you, Honey, that body odor has very little to do with building contracts. Try to stick it out for the six or eight blocks to the parsonage. Time the bonfire's over, you'll be too tired to notice."

"Especially since you and I'll be the only ones in the booth. I thought for sure Betsy would arrange for a sitter, but she's afraid the children will be frightened by all the racket at midnight. Also, she hasn't wanted to replace Susan since their baby-sitting arrangement was ruined by the murder."

Phyllis was given to overstatement and overreaction, but her responses were a source of endless amusement and excitement for Bob. He enjoyed being gently more rational than his wife. "Not really by the murder, Phyllis—by Susan admitting Hiram abused her."

"I'm convinced that's only part of it. Susan saw something. *I* say she can identify the killer, and Gregory Haskins is way down my list of possibilities, much as he drinks sometimes."

His wife could be stubborn in her intuitions! "Then why has he been arrested, and why hasn't Susan come forward?"

"It's obvious to me that Maggie has stopped her. You know quite well, Bob, that Maggie has always focused only on her own tiny little world. Now she's influencing Susan to shut herself off from the community and her obligations to it."

"And I'll bet you're going to try to change all that."

"Of course I am. But I think this time, instead of beating my head against a brick wall by talking to Maggie, I'll talk to Susan. After all, Hiram works for you."

"Yes, and he's apparently been sober for a whole week. He seemed a little edgy today, but I guess that figures; New Year's Eve has always been his big night to tie one on. I wished him luck when he left work today, and he said he'd need it."

"Well, if he's really home sober tonight, and if Maggie's stupid enough to let Susan go to the bonfire, maybe *you* ought to keep an eye on that poor child. I can't help thinking something else awful is going to happen."

Feminine intuition again. Sometimes, though, it was accurate, maybe more often than not.

At the parsonage Bob went to the door with Phyllis. Betsy greeted him gratefully. "We do so appreciate your offer to load, Mr. Stockton; but Susan's going to the Watch Party with Jerry Haskins, so Maggie's here to help put stuff into the car, and then she'll work the booth with you two."

"Maggie? Maggie McGilvray?" Phyllis looked from Betsy to Bob with wonder. "I can't believe it!"

"Believe it, Hon." Bob gave Phyllis a brief kiss. "I'll get on to the bonfire site and set up the booth so it'll be all ready for the goodies. See you later."

* * *

At the usually vacant lot two blocks down the hill from the high school, the air hummed with activity and expectancy. Along the field's periphery, several church groups had already erected booths with signs announcing fresh popcorn, roasted peanuts, corn dogs, and fruit punch.

Bob backed his truck up to the curb and unloaded booth struts and awning and a big red and green sign: "Donuts and

Dunkin' Drinks—hot chocolate, coffee, and tea—and warm New Year's Greetings."

In the field's center, Christmas trees, mostly brown and shedding, were piled at least eight feet high in a circle some twenty feet in diameter.

A young policeman rounded the pile and stood watching Bob construct the booth. Dwight Mitchell, the basketball star, classmate of the Stocktons' daughter. He looked a lot older, tired.

"That's a fine-looking sign you got there, Mr. Stockton."

"Hello, Dwight. I didn't recognize you at first. Haven't quite gotten used to seeing you in a uniform that isn't for playing basketball. You got the duty here tonight?"

"Yes, sir, and I'm a little early. But I remember one year when I was in high school some clown lighted the fire before the mayor had a chance to, so I'm keeping a kind of lookout to prevent something like that."

"There's something else you might keep a lookout for, Dwight, and that's a dangerous killer."

"What the hell are you talking about, man?"

"Well, I know this sounds a little crazy; but there's a kid going to be here tonight who may really need a police guard."

"Mr. Stockton, I think you're pulling my leg. Police business is not a joke, you know; I take my job very seriously."

"Hey, don't get me wrong, son. I know you do, especially since you found that murdered girl last week."

"Yeah, and Gregory Haskins is in jail for that."

"Quite a few folks don't believe he did it. *I* don't. He's worked all these years at the high school...always been above reproach. He says he didn't kill her, and he's honest as the day is long. Circumstantial evidence won't be enough. Anyway, some of us think Hiram Marshall's daughter may have seen something that will help catch the real killer, but she hasn't talked yet—at least, I don't believe she's told anything officially. She's here tonight with Jerry Haskins, and I think she ought to be watched. If I see Timothy, I'll tell him, but you'll probably see him before I do."

"I think he may be out of town for the weekend. I'll take care of her, Mr. Stockton, right away." Dwight turned toward the hill to the gym.

"You sure you know which one she is? Kinda ordinary-looking."

"Yes, sir, I'll recognize her. You say she's with Jerry?"

"Hiram never let her go out with boys. I've warned him not to rein her in too tight—just leads to trouble—but he hasn't any say-so now that Maggie McGilvray is her foster parent. He's not even supposed to be anywhere near her—been abusing her."

"I know. I took him in last week when he beat her up at church." The policeman had begun backing away from Bob.

"Well, then, I'll count on you tonight. Thanks, Dwight."

"Sure, Mr. Stockton. I'll just go on up to the gym, then, and check out the Watch Party. Don't worry anymore about Susan. I'll take care of her."

Dwight rushed off before Bob could caution him to be a bit circumspect. Bob felt a moment of *deja vu* before identifying the situation as similar to the one from which Hiram had hurried off to threaten that black boy. Surely this was different, but still...

* * *

From the log above the clearing, Timothy was not able to identify any of the hooded Klansmen being herded quickly down the back trail toward the troopers' trucks.

"I don't intend to wait till morning to find out who's been caught. Listen, Grace, if you'll be my 'date,' I'll have an excuse to go to the bonfire. We'll just happen to see the troopers at the police station on our way. Then I'll stop there long enough to find out whether or not we've caught the killer in our net."

"Well, I guess satisfying our curiosity is a good enough reason to accept your invitation. Let's go."

"Hold on," said Ora. "I don't fancy bein' seen by that last bunch o' idiots."

"Your dad's right. Let's wait till they've gone. We'll get there in plenty of time." Timothy recognized in himself an unprofessional interest in being alone with Grace, soon. "We may even have time to go to the Watch Party."

"No, thanks. I don't want to monitor students again till Monday."

* * *

An hour later, Grace and Timothy walked into a police station teeming with grumbling Klansmen, triumphant troopers, and a few very rattled city policemen.

"What's going on here?" Timothy asked, feigning ignorance.

"Chief!" said the clerk, "I thought you were out of town."

"I was, but Ms. Kemmer and I came in for the bonfire and saw that caravan of state trucks outside..."

The clerk explained the round-up of Ku Klux Klansmen. He ended with bad news: "You'll never guess who was arrested— Eben Hazlitt!"

"Son of a bitch!" Timothy exclaimed. "You've got to be kidding!"

"No, sir. He's one of 'em, all right."

"Where is he now?"

The police chief's voice rose with emotion that the clerk must have interpreted as anger. He winced as he replied, "He's downstairs being fingerprinted."

"Bring him up to my office, please, Matt. Wait! Any other bad news?"

"No, sir, thank God!"

Why Hazlitt and not Mitchell? The smooth operation had developed a hitch. "Grace, you just wait here at Thompson's desk. I won't be long, I'm afraid." Timothy grimly entered his office.

He paced from desk to window and back half a dozen times before the clerk tapped at the partially open door and announced, "Hazlitt, sir," then disappeared as Eben Hazlitt entered the office, closing the door behind him.

"Good Lord, Eben, what in hell happened? Why the fuck aren't you on duty at the gym?"

Eben's mouth dropped open. "You mean...I get it! You knew this raid was going down! Why didn't you—?"

"No, I'm asking the questions around here. Why aren't you on duty at the gym?"

Eben licked his lips, then swallowed hard before he spoke. "When I found out there was a meeting tonight, I thought sure you'd want me there. You wasn't here or at home, so I asked Dwight Mitchell if he'd be willing to take my post."

"Who?"

"Dwight Mitchell. Remember, he had the night off, so—"

"What did he say?"

"He said he'd be glad to take—"

"Do you mean to tell me Dwight's at the gym?"

"Yes, sir, I—"

"You go to hell!"

Timothy stormed from his office, grabbed Grace's hand, and pulled her out of the station so fast she stumbled. Eben Hazlitt would have to go back to the basement's fingerprint line unofficially, on his own recognizance.

CHAPTER XX

WATCHNIGHT

During the noisy ride from the church to the Watch Party, Susan said not a word. Everyone else was babbling too much to notice, and she could hardly breathe anyway, squashed as she was between Jerry and a girl she'd seen before but never spoken to. Jerry's smiling profile was visible by streetlight and reassured her, at least until they arrived at the gym.

Dozens of high school students were milling around the gymnasium yard when the two cars from First United Methodist discharged the 'Tween Group and Jonathan Simms.

"Greetings, Brother Simms," called another pastor. "I suppose it's wishful thinking on my part that you have a key to this edifice."

"Yes, Jim, I have no key."

"Well, we better call somebody. Greg Haskins is always the one to let us in, but with him in jail...oops, sorry, Jerry... didn't see you standing there. This just shows you how this whole community depends on your Uncle Greg."

Reverend Simms took the other minister's elbow and ushered him toward the phone booth down the hill on the corner.

Frowning, Susan turned to Jerry. "Your uncle's in jail? What for?"

Jerry took a deep breath. "Yeah...well...he's been arrested for murdering that girl."

"Not the colored girl! But...oh, no!" Susan held both hands to her cheeks. It was all her fault. She would have to do something, tell someone right away. She couldn't wait to hear from Maurice.

"Listen, try not to worry. We know he didn't do it. My dad has everything all worked out. It'll be OK."

"But, I—"

"Don't talk about it now. Don't mention it anymore tonight. Hear? No more tonight. Everything's under control."

Someone had arrived with a key at last, and someone else ran to the phone booth to tell the ministers. The crowd swirled through the gymnasium doors and across the polished yellow wood.

Fumes from fresh floor wax mingled with stale sneaker scent, but no one complained. The atmosphere was festive, friendly.

In front of the backboard at the far end of the court a small stage had been erected and festooned with pastel streamers. A large silver arrow affixed to the basket pointed straight up, toward the large clock on the red brick wall. The clock itself shone like a clown face amid ruffles of pastel crepe paper.

Feet thundered on the hollow wooden bleachers as the young people climbed around searching for ideal seats. The top rows were occupied first, decisively, by groups of males a little younger, a lot more boisterous, than most of the audience.

Susan and Jerry moved with their church group till they were almost even with the stage. Many boys and girls spoke to Jerry, then, as though surprised, to Susan.

"I'll have to be up on the stage to read the scripture, but when the 'Tween Group comes up in front of the stage to sing, I'll join you and come back here with you to sit."

Susan couldn't think straight. She had to get out of there—so many people, so many strangers. "Jerry, I don't really know all of that song; I never sang it before tonight."

"Don't worry. Stand on the back row and just hum. See ya!" He squeezed her arm and joined four other students on the stage.

Susan thought she might be going to cry. She had to trust Jerry, distract herself somehow from panic. She tried to concentrate on the busyness of the crowd of which she no longer felt a part.

Several ministers walked around the gym floor urging people to be seated and ineffectually waving their arms for quiet. It took three episodes of lights-off to effect relative silence.

A giant of an athletic-looking boy stood behind the stage microphone. "Welcome to the nineteenth annual Watchnight Party sponsored by the Sardisvale Ministerial Association. Please stand for the opening prayer."

Feet thumped bleachers as the crowd rose to bow their heads for the invocation, excerpted from *Psalm* 90: "Lord, you have been our dwelling place in all generations. Before you created the mountains or even the earth or the universe, you were God, from forever to forever. A thousand years in your sight are no more than a yesterday, no more than a watch in the night. So teach us to number our days that we may apply our hearts to wisdom. Amen."

A subdued mood, a serious one, seemed to have settled over the audience as they sat down. Susan felt calmer.

Music from the piano beside the stage alerted one of the church youth groups. A dozen boys and girls filed to the floor in front of the stage and sang "The Lord's Prayer," which reverberated meaningfully around the rafters.

When the choir had returned to the bleachers, Jerry advanced to the microphone and read the scripture chosen by the speaker as appropriate for the evening's sermonette.

He looked small but sincere. His voice squeaked and wavered as he began, but quickly strengthened. "And I saw a new heaven and a new earth: for the first heaven and the first earth were passed away; and there was no more sea.

"And I...saw the holy city, new Jerusalem, coming down from God...

"And I heard a great voice out of heaven saying, Behold, the temple of God is with men...

"Behold, I make all things new."

* * *

Dwight Mitchell feinted, temporarily delayed rushing up the hill to the gym, and took another turn around the Christmas tree pile while he tried to slow his pounding heart and think what must be done. He told himself Bob Stockton's theory that the Marshall girl was a witness might be wrong, but intuitively he knew better. The recognition in her face when she'd started to yell that night at church...even then he'd had a pang of fear. She had seen something, but would anyone believe her?

A problem, as Dwight figured it, was that too many people believed Gregory Haskins. Even though he drank a lot, even though he admitted to making moves on that nigra and hitting her, his buddies didn't believe he had killed her. Those same people just might think crazy, mixed-up Susan Marshall was telling the truth.

But what, exactly, could she tell? Dwight needed to know *before* she told it. In fact, there was a missing piece Dwight longed to find, but till now had thought it unwise to search for, or even to spend time wondering about.

Now, though, he had to give it serious consideration. The thing was, that nigra had been unconscious when he'd gotten to her...been out cold from a smashed head. She'd even had a handkerchief stuffed in her mouth—something he'd forgotten till he'd found it, blood-spattered, in his uniform pocket—something he'd left out of his official report. He'd have to make like a detective, like a TV private investigator. Surely he could do that.

OK, here goes, he thought. Maybe she stumbled and hit her head. Possible, but that could never explain the handkerchief. And how likely, anyway, that a nigra lying on a pavement in Sardisvale had had an accident? Zip!

Then maybe Gregory Haskins followed her across the street and knocked her down after Jerry had left. Or...hey... or before Jerry left, so Jerry was lying to protect his uncle, and maybe Susan was in on the whole thing. Then why had she started yelling when Dwight had just walked a little way into the back of the church? At the time, of course, Dwight had thought her weird way of looking at him was because he had come to arrest her father. That weird look, though, sure stuck in his mind.

So what if she did see the stabbing? Did she also see whoever KO'd the nigra first? Was there somebody else besides him and Gregory? There might just be, since quite a few of the Klan brothers had known she was door-to-dooring on Foliage Street that morning.

But Dwight had lost faith in the Klan's protection. That's why he'd been so willing to miss the last meeting of the year. Ever since the murder, the old geezer Klansmen—like Eben Hazlitt, for instance—had been claiming that murder was going too far. Hypocrites! They'd shouted loudest of all about keeping niggers out before, but now that somebody, Dwight, had been brave enough to do it, they'd all chickened out.

Somebody, though, must have at least tried. Somebody had bashed her on the head, somebody had gagged her, and Dwight had to find out who, then decide what to do about it. His best bet right now seemed to be Susan Marshall— getting her to talk to him and not to anyone else. That was going to be very tricky. He'd have to play it cool.

Dwight suddenly realized that he'd been circling the tree pile slowly for quite a while, for no telling how long. That was too weird, and he definitely didn't want to look weird.

His watch said after eleven. He was late for checking out the Watch Party. No more fucking around. Got to get his ass in gear. Go up there, spot Susan, and figure out how to arrange a talk.

He waved at Mr. Stockton and walked briskly up the hill toward the high school. His swift movement dried the sweat dripping from his hairline and made him shiver in spite of his long underwear and heavy sweater under his uniform coat. No real breeze, perfect weather for the bonfire. He'd have to stop sweating and acting like someone was after *him*. *He* was the one on a hunt, for Susan, for Jerry, for whoever'd got to the nigra before him.

What then? Did he want to catch whoever got away? Was it somebody easier to pin a murder on than Gregory Haskins? What did Dwight actually think ought to happen? Well, that was one question he used to have the answer to. He wanted for nobody, ever, to be convicted, and for everybody who knew anything about the murder to keep quiet forever because they believed in the same principles the murderer did.

OK, now he was onto something. He needed to find out whether or not Susan, and probably Jerry, believed that Sardisvale should stay white. He already knew about Susan's daddy. After all, Hiram had run that nigger boy out of town, so Susan's immature ideas were probably colored— hah, funny word—by the way Hiram had been treating her. Pretty complicated. Dwight began to wish he'd learned more about psychology than just enough to get by at the Law Enforcement Academy up at Plainfield. Too late now; he had to do *something* this very night.

His mulling over the situation was interrupted by his arrival at the gym. No one was outside; that meant the program was well under way. Dwight looked at his watch by the porch light: eleven-forty. The sermon had probably begun by now.

He pulled open the outer door and surprised a couple of high school boys lighting cigarettes in the passageway to the boys' locker room.

"Hey, guys, fire hazard! Save the match for the bonfire."

Brad Abel and Gary Scheider jumped guiltily and put away their cigarettes.

"We were gonna take them right outside, Dwight. Just wanted to light them outta the wind," said Brad.

"Yeah? What wind? How about sneaking quietly back in for the rest of the program? It couldn't hurt." Dwight grinned.

The boys started quickly for the swinging double doors to the basketball court. Gary went immediately through; but Brad stopped short, then took a few steps backward and leaned toward Dwight.

The boy whispered, though there was no one to hear but the young policeman, "What you did last week was great. You're really something, you know. Thanks!"

Dwight's hand raised in a reflex gesture of protest that Brad misinterpreted, turning it into a high five before reentering the court.

Dwight stared in disbelief. What the fuck? Could Brad possibly mean stabbing the colored girl? What else could he mean? Did he *know*, or was he guessing? What about other people? How could Dwight find out?

He hurried back out into the cold air and unbuttoned his jacket to ease his breathing.

The gymnasium had a colonial front with white columns holding up the roof of the porch, which had entrances at each end. Without thinking, Dwight strode the full length of the porch to the other front door and entered. No one was in the passageway at that end. He pushed one of the swinging double doors open slightly.

228

Part of the temporary stage was visible, blocking a clear view of the bleachers where the participating students sat. Dwight couldn't see Jerry Haskins, couldn't see anything with perspiration trickling steadily into his eyes.

The preacher's words penetrated Dwight's consciousness. "…because *you* are in charge of your life in the year that will arrive in only a few minutes. You must not expect others to make your difficult moral decisions for you, and you must not expect others to protect you from the consequences of those decisions."

Dwight released the door as though it were hot, left the building, and trudged blindly down the hill toward the bonfire site.

Sardisvale Senior High School reared its three ugly red brick storeys at the corner of Sycamore and General Wayne Streets; its gymnasium and playing fields stretched along Sycamore Street.

Across from the playing fields, occupying an entire block, was the Marsden mansion, a Victorian monstrosity vacant for at least ten years and soon to be rejuvenated as an old folks' home for county welfare recipients. No one would be happier to see that structural facelift than the school administration and the police department, for the Marsden ruins were ideally located to attract kids hooking school. Dwight Mitchell had already routed several groups from mischief-making in and about the old house, and spring weather would greatly increase the number of police calls to check on trespassers there.

Dwight crossed Sycamore from the playing fields and proceeded along the mansion's six-foot iron fence until he reached the corner. He turned onto Wayne Street, able to see, even from the corner, floodlights set up around the booths at the bonfire site.

Along Wayne Street the mansion's fencing was in very bad condition. Entire six-foot iron spikes were gone in some places and curled back in several others so that access to the ill-kept grounds was easy. To make trespassing even more enticing, the intact portions of the fence were so entangled with clematis that even in winter they supported an impenetrable mass of brown vines.

As Dwight descended the hill, he became aware of the fence and its potential for concealment. He needed a place to smoke a cigarette, something no policeman on duty was supposed to do, and a place to watch for Susan. He slowed down, found a break in the fencing, and stepped into the black, deserted, overgrown mansion grounds.

* * *

Hiram Marshall had no plan of action. If he hadn't trusted Gregory Haskins' intelligence, he wouldn't be wandering around sober on New Year's Eve. Of course, it was more interesting than sitting home alone in front of the TV; and he might be able to get a look at Susan this way.

He had begun to miss her, to appreciate her, really. He knew now that with Susan at home, his house had been a lot neater than his friends', and certainly the food had been better. But, more surprisingly, he missed being able to look at his daughter and listen to her. That was something the therapist was helping him with—to know how she was like his wife, but different. He had been too hard on her. All that was going to change. He was going to have to let her be with other kids, invite them to the house.

The police chief's son! Well, that was something to make Hiram secretly proud. A fine boy, Jerry Haskins. Everybody said so and would think more of Susan if she was seen with Jerry. Yes, things were going to be different; and he'd tell Susan so when he had the meeting with her and the social worker the next week.

In the meantime, the crazy stuff about Susan being in danger had him a little antsy. He'd always worried about letting her go places; in fact, the therapist had him about convinced she needed more freedom. Now Greg Haskins, who was smart about all sorts of things, was sure Susan had to be protected, but wouldn't tell him why, and Greg had always given him good advice before. That's why Hiram had decided to hide out at the Marsden place and just keep an eye on Susan if he could.

He slouched quietly along the bottom of the bonfire field and crossed to the Marsden fence. At the break opposite the pile of Christmas trees, he ducked in, satisfied himself that his lookout post had a good view of where the mayor would light the bonfire, leaned against a bent iron spike, and, before he fished out a cigarette, patted the pocket that held his revolver.

* * *

Maggie had known Bob Stockton was wrong. He had assumed that Phyllis, Betsy, and Maggie could load Jonathan's car in short order; but it actually took considerable time. There were three large coffee urns, cups, napkins, plastic spoons, coffee, sugar, milk, cocoa, tea, dozens of boxes of donuts, towels, folding chairs, and a few miscellaneous items, like a first aid kit.

At last Phyllis and Maggie wished Betsy a happy New Year and set off for the bonfire site, leaving the young woman wistfully waving from the parsonage steps.

"Maggie, I can't believe you're doing this. Everybody else in the church was suddenly unavailable. They know what a madhouse it always is—kids all clamoring at once for service. They consume every last drop and crumb, even though we increase the amounts we take every year. It's such good publicity for the church, and I'm sure it keeps some kids from getting into trouble drinking. Which reminds me, does Susan actually have a date tonight? Poor child, it must be her first one."

Phyllis's non-stop monologue seemed to have run out. Maggie briefly treasured the silence, then sighed and answered, "I guess you could call it a date. She's gone to the Watch Party with Jerry Haskins."

"A nice boy...and they can talk about the murder."

"Phyllis!"

"Well, Maggie, it seems to me Susan needs to do some talking, but not to the Haskins son, to the father!"

"If you want my help tonight, you're going to have to stay off the subject of the murder."

"But Maggie, I just think... Maggie! Close that door! The car wasn't even stopped!"

"I'll get out while it's moving if you don't change the subject."

Phyllis clamped her lips tightly, gripped the steering wheel, and drove the two remaining blocks to the bonfire site without saying a word. Maggie relaxed and tried not to look victorious.

While Phyllis backed up to the First Methodist booth, Bob hurried to the trunk to unload. Maggie joined him as his wife huffily emptied the front seat and began on the rear one.

"Well, Maggie," said Bob, "an unexpected pleasure. And I have good news: you can really enjoy the festivities tonight knowing Susan has the best possible protection."

"What on earth do you mean?"

"We've all been worried about Susan, that the wrong person will find out she saw something, you know, so I just told Dwight Mitchell, confidentially of course, why he should keep an eye on her."

"You what? Dwight Mitchell!" Maggie raised the coffee urn with an overwhelming urge to hit Bob.

He retreated a few feet in shock. "He said he'd take care of her. He's gone up to the gym."

"You fool!" Maggie slammed the coffee urn to the ground and began running up the hill.

She didn't get very far at a run. Heart galloping, she had to stop for air. That people in the booths were staring bothered her not at all. Nothing mattered but reaching Susan before Dwight did. Maybe she was already too late.

Laboring mightily, she climbed the hill. When she reached Sycamore Street, a flat stretch, she ran again until she was even with the first front door of the gymnasium. Crossing the playing fields to the gym porch was no easy task. The ground was muddy, and Maggie was severely winded. Halfway up, she had to rest again.

In the stillness, she suddenly heard music, hundreds of young voices singing "Are Ye Able?", a rousing evangelical hymn of commitment.

By the time Maggie resumed her ascent to the gym, silence reigned again. Just as she reached the door, a roar of voices burst from the building along with a stampede of teenagers shouting "Happy New Year!" over the shrill background of the firehouse siren accompanied by rat-a-tats and booms of fireworks.

She tried to mount the porch steps, but bucking traffic was impossible. She was jostled left, then right; then, jolted by a strong male shoulder, she stumbled and fell backward to the ground.

Maggie didn't hit her head; but her buttocks were numb, and the sharp pain in her left shoulder made her curl in agony on the cold mud while the excited herd of young people made their way to the bonfire.

She lay without thinking for a moment, then struggled to a sitting position as she remembered the reason for her desperate haste. The noisy teens hurrying past her had the porch lights behind them; Maggie couldn't distinguish one face from another. She despaired of finding Susan in the boisterous mob. Hopeless.

Soon the crowd was reduced to a few stragglers. By then Maggie had been accidentally kicked a few times. At last she was alone and turned to a crawling position in an effort to rise without bearing weight on her left shoulder.

"Maggie! Is it you? My God, what's happened?" Grace was suddenly squatting beside her, Timothy bending to give her a hand.

"Ouch! My shoulder! Please, not that side."

Timothy and Grace together lifted Maggie to her feet. Grace produced several tissues and attempted to clean off the mud smeared over Maggie's face, hands, and clothes.

"Do you think your shoulder is broken?" asked Timothy.

"Oh, surely it's only bruised. I fell backward off the porch just as everybody came running out. But Susan...we've got to find Susan before Dwight Mitchell does!"

"We know. That's why we're here, too," Grace answered. "How did you know Dwight was here? He wasn't supposed to be. Timothy assigned—"

"Grace, not now," urged Timothy. "We've got to get down the hill. Quick. Maybe, though, you and Maggie should stay here."

"No, I'm all right," insisted Maggie. "Let's go."

The three set out across the playing field toward the pile of Christmas trees awaiting the mayor's match.

CHAPTER XXI

BEGINNING A NEW YEAR

Susan loved the Watch Party. At first, of course, she had been very anxious, especially at being left alone while Jerry was on the stage. As his date, though, she received immediate attention from several girls who asked her to sit with them and acted like her best friends. It was a new experience, one she enjoyed.

Jerry came to stand beside her while the 'Tween Group sang in front of the stage. He even gave her hand a squeeze before they filed back to their seats on the bleachers.

The minister on the program, a favorite speaker at high school assemblies, particularly inspired Susan. In fact, everything on the program seemed to be addressed just to her, from the scripture heralding a new Jerusalem to the final hymn urging active involvement.

For the first time in her life, she wanted to shout "Yes, I *am* able. I *am* ready for a new year, a new life, a new attitude about Daddy and myself."

She didn't actually shout, or whisper, but her head was full of resolutions and the certainty she could keep them. Her heart swelled with confidence and joy. A New Year! She couldn't wait.

The very last thing on the program was three minutes of silent prayer. The packed gymnasium was unbelievably quiet. Susan folded her hands in her lap and closed her eyes. She jumped when Jerry reached over to touch her hand. He withdrew his own hand at her startled response.

Susan squeezed her eyes tightly shut again, but an afterimage persisted: Jerry's hand reaching out—toward her hand in the gym, toward her face in the sanctuary, toward Michelle Riddick's bleeding mouth. The blood, Brad smashing Michelle's head against the pavement, Hiram's fist smashing into Susan's cheek, the policeman stabbing the unconscious girl—all those pictures jumbled in her head. Tears rolled from under her eyelids, and she began to tremble. Nothing could be right with Michelle dead and her killer unpunished.

The firehouse siren split the silence. Fireworks exploded outside, and cries of "Happy New Year!" resounded in the gymnasium.

Susan's tear-streaked face stopped short Jerry's greeting to her. He produced a handkerchief. "Just stay in here till things clear out. Let's talk some. We don't have to go to the bonfire at all if you'd rather not."

Susan shrugged helplessly.

"Stick with me, kid." Jerry nodded and greeted friends pushing past them. He took Susan's hand and pulled her slowly and gently down the bleachers to the basketball court.

Most people were hurrying to the exit nearer the corner, but Jerry went toward the door at the opposite end. Instead of crossing the floor to exit, he pulled Susan down a dank ramp.

"This is the way to the girls' locker room!"

"Not tonight, silly. I'm sure it's all locked up. There's a bench, I think...sure, here it is. We can have privacy here for a few minutes."

They sat on the cold wooden bench in near darkness.

"Now, please tell me why you're crying."

Susan blew her nose again. "Jerry, I know who killed Michelle. I was watching through that old gate. Miss Maggie thinks I'll be in danger if I tell, that it will do more harm than good; but I can't just let that man go around like he's a hero when he's really evil. I want to tell your daddy what I saw."

"Daddy knows you saw something."

"He does? How did he find out?"

"Never mind that...he knows, and he's trying to fix things so you'll be absolutely safe when you make an official statement. He wants you to wait till next Tuesday."

"Tuesday! That's days away. I can't—"

"Uh oh...they're starting to turn out the gym lights. We better leave before they lock us in." He grabbed her hand and ran toward the exit as the rest of the lights went out.

"Let's go on down to the bonfire the way we planned. Nothing bad's going to happen tonight."

Susan shrugged again. Might as well go.

* * *

Daggers of pain sliced from Maggie's shoulder up her neck, down her upper arm. She gasped and massaged the bruised area with her other hand.

"Maggie," Grace cried, "you're really hurt. Don't try to rush so."

They had reached the corner of Sycamore and Wayne Streets and could see the crowd filling Wayne Street in front of the bonfire site.

Timothy studied Maggie's face by the street light.

"Grace's right, Maggie. We'll go on down and find Susan and Jerry. Please stay here and rest."

He looked more closely at the Marsden mansion. "Here's a perfect place for you to wait." He led her by the elbow to the entrance gate and indicated a rectangular stone planter full of dirt but no plants. "You can see the street from here but not be in anyone's way."

Maggie, clutching her shoulder, sat down on the dirt. "I'll wait right here till you bring Susan safely to me."

* * *

Susan and Jerry were running hand in hand down the sidewalk and looking toward the bonfire site when they passed within a yard of Maggie.

She leaped to her feet. "Susan! Jerry! Wait!"

No response.

Again she called, much louder, "Susan, stop!" and hurried down the hill.

Susan and Jerry stopped, turned, and saw Maggie.

"Oh, wait, Susan!"

The spotlights surrounding the bonfire field were suddenly extinguished, plunging General Wayne Street into darkness. A gasp rose from the crowd. Maggie tripped on an uneven sidewalk block, pitched forward. Just in time to save herself from falling, she grabbed an iron fence spike. She moaned aloud at the intensified pain in her shoulder. Tears sprang to her eyes, overflowed onto her dirt-streaked cheeks.

Sparks, then flames, ascended from the bonfire..."Auld Lang Syne" from the crowd. Lengthening tongues of fire lapped the air above the pile of dried trees and smeared their light across the street. Even before the chorus ended, firecrackers popped and Roman candles streaked skyward.

Maggie, however, in the increasing light, experienced a desolating mental darkness; Susan and Jerry had disappeared.

* * *

Before Hiram could light his own cigarette, he perceived a match's flare farther down the hill in the Marsden yard. Someone else was there, also next to the fence, but exactly even with the bonfire site. He could see the shadowy figure, tall, male. Hiram decided not to smoke. He stood motionless.

The other man at last extinguished his cigarette. Maybe he would come out of hiding, cross the street, and join the others, leaving the best lookout spot for Hiram.

The crowd around the pile of trees was getting noisier. He could hear running footsteps of several latecomers, then his daughter's name: "Susan, stop!" and "Oh, wait, Susan!" The words faint, but unmistakable.

Hiram stepped back a little into the break in the fencing through which he had entered. Susan and Jerry stood on the walk down near the place where the stranger had smoked. They couldn't see him and looked beyond him up the hill. Susan's eyes were wide, beautiful, like her mother's; but her mouth was curved in a gentleness all her own.

The lights went out. Hiram retreated into the yard and waited. With "Auld Lang Syne" as background, he heard moans from the woman who had been calling Susan; but, more insistently, he heard his daughter's distressed cry, "No! Let go of me!"

Hiram pulled his revolver from his jacket pocket and crept swiftly down the yard side of the Marsden fence.

* * *

Maggie groped blindly along the fence, unable to raise her left arm because of her shoulder pain. A hiatus in the iron bars brought her up short. Of course! Susan and Jerry must have gone through a break in the fence.

She wiped her eyes and ran again in the increasing light from the bonfire. At the bottom of the hill, sure enough, there was an opening. Maggie stepped through it, bumping into Jerry.

He was holding one of Susan's arms, Dwight Mitchell the other.

A man's voice grated harshly above the singing. "Let go of my girl!"

The group turned as one toward the mansion yard's darkness, from which Hiram Marshall emerged.

"Daddy! Thank God!" came Susan's happy cry.

* * *

Timothy regretted having to leave Maggie at the corner, but she was obviously in no shape to run. Grace, in contrast, was agile and quick, exhilarating to have at his side.

First, they circled the tree pile separately with no success. Next, together they asked several young people where Jerry and Susan might be, but received replies no more helpful than "They were at the gym" and "They're here somewhere."

The crowd grew denser, so Grace and Timothy stood close to each other, embracing, actually, while they scanned the myriad faces. Through a path from the curb, Lewis Storch, mayor of Sardisvale, stepped up to the pile of crisp Christmas trees and struck a long match, the kind stored in decorative boxes on living room hearths. He touched its flaming end to crumpled newspapers concealed strategically along the ground under the front of the massed trees. Someone turned off the spotlights.

Timothy put a hand under Grace's chin, turned her face up just enough to place a short but loving kiss on her welcoming lips. "Happy New Year!" they whispered in unison.

The dry fir and pine branches crackled and sparked as the fire spread up the mound of trees. Timothy pushed Grace through the singing, laughing crowd. Almost to the street, he suddenly squeezed past her and ran, propelled by the certainty that at least two of the loud explosions were not fireworks, but gunshots.

CHAPTER XXII

SPRING

Maggie cut the car's engine and coasted down the small slope of the Kemmer yard to the very edge of the woods. She got out, shutting the car door quietly. Although Grace's car was gone, she thought Ora might still be sleeping at seven-fifteen on Saturday morning of a holiday weekend.

An April thunderstorm had cooled the night, and Maggie zipped her down ski vest to her chin. She didn't even glance behind her before beginning to climb to Willamae's house above the ridge.

The trees were still bare of green, but redbuds smudged the brown hills with blush, and pink and white dogwoods were at the peak of their Oriental mystery. The distant ones reminded her of Susan's exclamations about the Magic Circle; perhaps invisible fairies suspended the blossoms among the dark trees.

While green-tinged dogwood blooms arched daintily over her path, twigs snapped underfoot, not yet putting forth softer vegetation. She didn't try to walk silently, but it did occur to her that the entire forestry was much noisier than it had been on her last visit, Christmas weekend, four long, eventful months before.

Then, early snow had hushed the occasional rustles of wildlife in the undergrowth. Now, birdsong was constant. There were even intermittent whirrings of cicadas, avant-garde of the seventeen-year phalanxes predicted to surface in May and June.

Maggie didn't herself notice that she never had to stop to catch her breath. With a more active lifestyle, her general fitness had improved so that the unaccustomed climb wasn't a physical drain.

At the Magic Circle she removed her small backpack for long enough to shrug off the vest and roll and stuff it into the pack.

Glancing around the circle, she realized that although Grace was busy socially as well as professionally, she had still managed to keep the stumps free of debris. On the central, table-like one, a fresh arrangement of pussy willow rose stiffly from a red clay pot, and white dogwood stretched horizontally around the pot's lip.

Maggie smiled at the persistence of Grace's optimism. To think that Maggie had actually tried to follow Grace's instructions for meditation! Of course, nothing mystical had happened. Grace was the inveterate believer in that sort of thing; Maggie definitely was not, and so perhaps couldn't adequately test the hypothesis or ever believe. Who could?

How could Grace? Sure, she was young, in love. Yet how could that outweigh the horrible injustice rampant in Sardisvale? Grace deluded herself by preserving dangerous blind spots.

Maggie shrugged and resumed climbing.

Spring had touched Willamae's house, too. Dandelions yellowed patches of "lawn" beside the limestone. The waterfall was spectacular—violets nestling among the stones, a brilliant cardinal lingering next to the fall even after he became aware of Maggie's presence.

Maggie dumped her pack in the entranceway of the house and seated herself by the waterfall with a thermos of iced tea. The cascade calmed somewhat her angry thoughts. She dozed a little, rearranged herself so that her back was against a smooth limestone boulder. The waterfall gurgled. Maggie slept.

When the sun was directly overhead, she awoke slowly, pleasantly. Only gradually did she become aware of the stimulus drawing her back to consciousness—a whistled "whip-poor-will" piercing the clear spring air.

Maggie attempted a whistled reply; her effort was breathy, too thin. A second try resulted in a shriller version of the original and provoked an immediate response. The interchange continued until Maggie discerned Ora's wiry figure approaching from the direction of the Magic Circle. She picked her way down to meet the logger.

Ora held out a small paper bag. "Lunch, Miss Maggie. Wanna share?"

Maggie nodded thanks. "Give me a minute."

While Ora splashed his face and hands from the waterfall, Maggie readied a meal on the smooth flat rock on which Willamae had ministered to little Grace's rabbit many years before. Paper napkins, mugs of iced tea, dill pickles, potato chips, and chicken salad from her knapsack. Ham and cheese on rye from Ora's bag.

Ora sat down on one of the chair boulders without being asked.

Maggie pulled out the last item Ora had brought, homemade raisin spice cookies, and shook her head. "How does she find the time, what with wedding preparations and work on the house?"

"Weddin's gonna be plain, very plain, you know, just that preacher friend of Timothy's in the parsonage parlor. And Timothy's brother's kept the house in pretty fair repair, so there ain't much has to be done 'fore they move in. Gregory and Timothy and the boy's paintin' a few rooms, and Grace's makin' new curtains at school. That's all."

"Susan says that there's plenty of room for you, that they could make an apartment for you as big as the one they're partitioning off for Greg."

"Forget that! Long's I can still drag around my equipment, I'll be out here in the forestry. Miss Maggie, I ain't one to be real civilized, and I've allus knowed it."

"Ora, you and Grace have been together so many years; she'll miss you, and you—"

"She'll be busy with her new family, and I'll be busy with mine."

"What do you mean?"

"I mean just like Susan occupies you, Maurice'll occupy me. A young student in the house's bound to liven things up a bit."

"Maurice! Then he's not moving to the Haskins place with Timothy and Jerry?"

"Nope. They's all got along real good, but Maurice and I had a talk. He feels like he's proved somethin' by stayin' alive in Sardisvale, but he 'spects he'll be pushin' his luck when that Mitchell devil's trial gets goin'."

"Oh, Ora, what jury around here's going to convict him of murdering Hiram? Hiram had his own gun ready to fire. The people who believe Susan's and Jerry's and Greg's stories won't be the ones who can bring about justice."

The two ate for a while in companionable silence. Then Ora spread an abundance of bread crumbs along the rim of the waterfall. Soon a pair of robins came to feast. A mourning dove. Three song sparrows.

After the birds had completed their clean-up, Ora and Maggie continued to sit for a long period without speaking.

"Miss Maggie," Ora almost whispered, "do you want I should leave you alone now?"

"No...well...I did come up here to try to get away from all the mess of 'civilization,' as you call it."

"The forestry's allus suited me, but I wouldn'ta wanted not to raise up Grace."

"No, of course not. You've done a wonderful job."

"Me, and her mother, and Willamae, and even some ladies at the church, like Miz Stockton. Miss Maggie, Grace said the Stocktons would of taken in Susan after Mitchell killed her daddy."

Maggie sighed. "Do you think I should have let them?"

Ora frowned at his opening and closing fists before he responded with a question. "You think I oughta tell Maurice to stay in Bloomin'ton?"

Maggie's only reply was a small smile.

"Miss Maggie, my Grace thinks there's been one o' her 'ginseng cures.'"

"What? Love has surely been 'messin' with her head,' as Susan would say!"

"Yes'm, she'd agree."

Ora sounded serious, so Maggie looked at him more carefully.

"Grace says—we had a long talk just the other night— she says this cure's happened because people got together."

"She doesn't really believe this community is cured of anything, surely."

"Oh, yes, she does. That preacher fella has got a activist group goin' at the church. And the Klan's not meetin'."

"Just wait till the trial gets started. There'll be more trouble then."

"Yes, but some thin's, she says, 've changed for good."

"Like what?"

"Like Maurice'll be bringin' some o' the bigger world to me ever' night. Like you've got Susan now, so you won't be movin' up here to Willamae's."

"But I'm here right now. I left home the minute I saw Susan off on the 'Tween Group's Easter trip to Cincinnati," Maggie answered defensively.

"It ain't the same. Grace says—and I agree with her this time—you ain't the same, I ain't the same, and the whole community's got bound up with the outside world."

"Come on, Ora, that's really going too far. The jury won't convict Dwight Mitchell just on Susan's testimony. Those boys claim they were nowhere near Hoosier Hollow, and the bartender says they're telling the truth. Mitchell's a Klan hero; and the Klan surely isn't dead, only laying low. A few do-gooders are hardly the whole community."

"No'm, but those few has changed. *I*'ve changed: I squealed on the Klan, I'm takin' in Maurice, and I feel different. You ain't the same, neither." Ora's tone was gentle but firm. "You're here now, but you'll be back down in civilization by Monday."

Maggie sat staring at the waterfall. A lone hummingbird hovered in the mist above the cascade, even though the honeysuckle gave no evidence yet of greening.

After a while she realized Ora had gone. At last—peaceful solitude.

Maggie put away the lunch remains. She gave the boulder house a thorough cleaning. Following Grace's example, she gathered spring blossoms—redbud for the slab table, dogwood for the limestone-walled bedroom. She laid wood for a dinner fire and made a woodpile sufficient for that weekend and several more.

An hour and a half before dusk, she descended to the Magic Circle to perform the minimal tidying it required.

Sheepishly she glanced around the circle's perimeter. Of course no one was watching! She sat cross-legged with only a little difficulty, leaned against a stump, and placed her hands, palm up and open, on her knees. Eyes closed, she intoned the syllables Grace had instructed her to use. At first, she felt silly. Later, she felt relaxed, empty.

When katydids and tree frogs became more insistent, Maggie scrambled to her feet and headed back up to the house in the gathering dusk. Chilly, eager to start the dinner fire, she looked forward to darkness.

Her mind remained vacant for most of the evening. Along about her usual bedtime, it occurred to her that by dark the next night, she would be home from the woods, listening to Susan's account of her trip.

Maggie looked forward to that, too.